Halloween
Miracles

by

Chrys Fey

Halloween Miracles

Contact Information: info@thewildrosepress.com

Cover Art by *Teddi Black*

The Wild Rose Press, Inc.
PO Box 708
Adams Basin, NY 14410-0708
Visit us at www.thewildrosepress.com

Publishing History
First Edition, 2025
Trade Paperback Print ISBN 978-1-5092-6343-1
Digital ISBN 978-1-5092-6344-8

Published in the United States of America

Dedication

To everyone who has ever thought there's too many Christmas rom-coms and not enough Halloween rom-coms.

Chapter One

Silk autumn leaves scattered over Kellen Collins's coffee table where a witch's cauldron held her secret stash of candy. Black, creepy cloth draped over her couch, making it appear decaying. In one corner of the couch lounged a plastic skeleton named Fred that wore a purple bow tie. As a joke, Kellen called him her boyfriend. Except, it wasn't really a joke, because she was single and had been for a very long time. Long enough she didn't have to worry about guests coming over and taking the spot away from her skeleton boyfriend.

Among the spooky décor, Kellen worked at her writing desk tucked into a corner, with her hair piled atop her head. Her rectangular, purple-rimmed reading glasses were perched on her nose. She wore lavender pajama bottoms and a matching long-sleeved shirt. The fact her clothes matched was a miracle.

A stack of children's books sat beside the computer monitor. She was in the midst of cranking out her next book when her cellphone sounded. After checking the caller ID, she answered the call with a smile. "Hey, Twinie."

On the other end, Jensen laughed. "Don't you think we're too old to use that term?"

"What? Never. We'll be twinies even when we're old and gray and living in a retirement home together."

"If we end up in the same retirement home, I'll be moving out."

"Party pooper."

Jensen chuckled. "What are you doing?"

"Writing. What else?"

"Well, the Halloween party starts in an hour. Usually, you're here by now. The kids keep asking where you are."

Kellen glanced at the time on her phone "Shoot." Phone in hand, she leapt to her feet. The computer chair rolled behind her as she hurried away. In her bedroom, a superhero costume waited on the bed. She kicked off her fuzzy slippers. "I'm getting ready now. I'll be there soon."

"Okay. See you."

"Bye." She tossed her phone onto the bed. Ten minutes later, she stood in front of the mirror, studying the brown leather costume of a certain fierce Amazon warrior. She adjusted the metal bracelets on her arms. Her golden skin made her resemble her niece's favorite superhero. With shield in hand, she could even fool herself. When she ducked to climb into her little car, though, the shield collided into the door frame, making her giggle. A superhero would be much smoother than that.

On the way to Jensen's house, Kellen admired the trees along the road bursting with autumn colors—rustic orange, red crimson, and golden yellow. The rays of the setting October sun sent spears of light through the foliage, creating a magical, festive scene. She passed houses decked out to the nines with spooky decorations. Jack-o'-lanterns with jagged teeth and triangle noses lined sidewalks. Candles inside the hollowed-out gourds made their eyes and mouths glow.

Kellen pulled up to Jensen's two-story house. Out of all the houses on the street, this one was the one with the most Halloween spirit. White bed sheets covered plastic heads and dowel bodies to form a ring of ghosts around a maple tree. Their hands were the corners of the cotton sheets knotted together, so they looked to be holding hands.

A blow-up phantom next to the driveway bobbed in the breeze, bending toward her and reaching out for her. Fake gravestones scattered over the lawn, and plastic skeleton arms stuck out of the ground, as if they were digging their way to the top. Spiders dangled from trees, and silky spiderwebs covered the bushes along the front of the house. The door displayed a plastic cover of a grim reaper with a sickle. The scenery sent a delicious shiver down her spine. She rang the doorbell.

A moment later, the cast from a favorite childhood movie stood before her. Jensen wore a suit and a skinny mustache stuck to his bronze upper lip. Dana, his wife and Kellen's best friend, wore a fitted black dress with tendrils of silk around her feet. A black wig covered her blonde hair and stretched to her hips. She had even dusted white makeup in a strip across her eyes. And their children, a boy and a girl—twins, of course— portrayed a spooky brother and sister duo with black hair and pale skin who enjoyed morbid things.

"Aunt Kellen!" Weston and Roxon jumped and waved their arms.

"Hey, kids. Tell me, do you two like Amazons?"

"Yes," they shouted in unison.

"Good. Come on." She held their hands. "Show me the spookiness."

They led her through the house, pointing out all the new party decorations.

Pumpkins of all sizes, painted black and white with stripes and polka dots, covered the counter. Rubber spiders dangled from the ceiling. In the dining room, goodies packed the table. Black caramel apples the kids claimed were poisonous, pumpkin pie bites, and cookies in the shape of crescent moons were among the desserts. In the center of it all sat a bowl with dry ice fog spilling over the rim.

After their Samhain family dinner, they welcomed the guests arriving for the afterparty dressed as everything from superheroes and scary creatures to clever last-minute concoctions. Once the party was in full swing, Kellen picked up a toxic-green margarita. She sipped on the drink in a corner while watching couples dance to Halloween-themed music.

Jensen joined her. "I don't think superheroes are supposed to be wallflowers."

"I'm not a wallflower. I'm a writer. People watching is what we do." Kellen peered around the room again, searching for a man in an expensive suit. "Where's Shawn? I hope he's dressed like the uncle." Seeing the buttoned-down, serious Shawn with a bald prosthetic cap on his head and wearing drab, rotting clothes would be the highlight of her evening.

Dana shimmied over. "Shawn couldn't come. He's working late."

That didn't surprise Kellen. Shawn was always working. She usually only ever saw him during their family Christmas Eve parties. He hadn't even attended their Juneteenth celebration that year. He lived in Boston, whereas Kellen lived in Cauldron,

Massachusetts, with Jensen, Dana, and the twins. Her apartment was ten minutes away. She liked being close and a part of their lives, but she suspected Shawn liked being at a distance. Working…always working.

"I wish he could've come, though," Dana said. "The twins would love to see him."

Kellen watched Roxon sneak up on Weston and attack him with a can of purple silly string.

In retaliation, Weston whipped around and nailed Roxon in the face with a hit of green silly string. Giggling, they chased each other around the house, sending strings shooting into the air. Many innocent bystanders got hit in the skirmish.

Kellen couldn't help but smile. "Why don't we video call Shawn? Bring him some Halloween fun?"

"He'd be beyond annoyed by that." Dana grinned. "Let's do it."

Kellen followed Dana into the kitchen where she retrieved her cellphone and activated video call. Together, they waited. Kellen peered over Dana's shoulder, staying clear of the screen so Shawn wouldn't catch a glimpse of her costume. After a moment, his face popped up on the screen—neatly combed dark brown hair, kind green eyes, a crisp jacket, and pale blue tie. He looked handsome. He always looked handsome…

His face split into a grin. "That suits you, sis."

"Ha ha."

As the twins bounded into the kitchen for more treats, Kellen caught them. "Your Uncle Shawn is on video call," she whispered. "Say hi."

They flanked Dana to see the screen. "Happy Halloween, Uncle Shawn."

"Hey, Happy Halloween."

The twins bounced up and down and showed him their empty candy buckets. "We're going trick-or-treating with Aunt Kellen."

Shawn's smile faltered a fraction before he caught it.

But Kellen had seen the slip and frowned at his reaction.

"Oh, is Kellen there?"

"Of course, I am." She slung an arm around Dana's shoulders.

Shawn's eyes widened ever-so-slightly.

Was that good or bad? Being a writer, she might notice things, but understanding what those things meant was not her strong suit.

"What are you supposed to be a warrior princess?"

"An Amazon, actually."

"Ah. Should've guessed. You are a wonder woman."

Kellen smiled. "When will you come to one of our Halloween parties, huh?"

"Eh." He lifted a hand. "Halloween isn't my thing."

"Come on, Uncle Shawn." The twins pouted.

"Okay, okay. Next year, I promise."

Dana grinned. "You'll have to wear a costume."

He grimaced. "I'll come wearing sweatpants, with a TV remote control in my hand. It's basically a costume."

Kellen shook her head. "That doesn't count."

"I know," Weston shouted. "A superhero."

"Yeah." Roxon's eyes lit up. "And then Aunt Kellen can dress as one, too."

6

Dana's grin grew. "It's settled. You're coming next year, and Kellen will be your date."

Kellen's gaped. How did next year's Halloween party turn into a date between her and Shawn?

He blinked. "Wait. What?"

Kellen wagged her finger at Dana. "No."

Dana winked. "Yes."

"Noooo."

"I'm gonna go while the two of you debate that. Happy Halloween!" And just like that Shawn ended the call.

Kellen was left to listen to Dana's laughter.

She didn't have any plans for next Halloween. After all, that was a full three hundred and sixty-five days away, but she was certain she would not be Shawn's date, even if he did attend the party.

Dana adjusted her wig. "Well, my job is done here. I better get back to the guests and be a good hostess."

"You're the best hostess," Kellen called after her.

The twins tugged on Kellen's arms. "Aunt Kellen, can you take us trick-or-treating now? Please."

She peered at Jensen as he filled a bowl with more tortilla chips. "This must be how our parents felt whenever we ganged up on them to get what we wanted."

"No kidding. I get this every day."

Kellen smiled at Weston and Roxon. "All right. Let's go."

The twins dashed for the front door.

Kellen followed them outside and down the driveway. A few paces ahead, Weston and Roxon swung their plastic pumpkins back and forth by their handles.

The moon was bright, and stars twinkled above. Kellen inhaled the crisp air scented with pine and earth. Children, in a variety of costumes, skipped past her on the sidewalk as she enjoyed the autumn night. A gentle breeze rustled the dry leaves on the ground. Their crinkling sound sent chills down her arms, but in a good way. A cozy, happy sort of way.

Weston's and Roxon's laughter surrounded Kellen. The sound of their joy made her smile. She waited at the foot of driveways while they begged for candy. At the end of the street, when the time came to turn around and visit the houses on the other side of the road, Kellen stared at the moon. "Oh wow."

"What?" the twins asked.

"A bat flew across the moon."

Weston tipped his head back. "Where?"

She bent down to their level and pointed. "Right there. Maybe it was a vampire bat." She gasped. "Do you hear that? I heard it squeak. I think it's close."

Weston and Roxon scanned the night sky for a blood-sucking nocturnal creature.

Kellen peeked at the twins out of the corner of her eyes. Discreetly, she snuck her arms behind them. Then she grabbed them. "Boo."

They flinched and let out little screams. Then they fell into her, bursting with guffaws.

She joined them in their laughter until they held onto their sides. "Come on. Let's get the two of you some more candy."

Continuing on their way, Roxon skipped along. "Aunt Kellen, do you have a boyfriend?"

Kellen thought of her skeleton boyfriend, bumming it out on the couch. Best not to bring him up to her nine-year-old niece. "No. Why?"

"Do you like Uncle Shawn?"

"Sure." She glanced at Roxon, wondering where this was going. "Why?"

"I heard Mom say to Daddy that she's going to hook you and Uncle Shawn up if it's the last thing she does."

Kellen choked on her own spit.

Weston danced over after kicking clumps of leaves in the road and pounded her on the back a little too hard to help her coughing fit.

"What does 'hook up' mean?" Roxon asked, unfazed by Kellen's near-choking.

Kellen cleared her throat. "It means to hang out."

"Oh. Well, that's not so bad." Roxon waved a hand in the air. "You've hung out with Uncle Shawn before."

If only you knew the truth, kid.

Roxon peered at Kellen. "I wonder why Mom said that."

"I don't know."

But I'd like to find out.

"Why don't you visit this house? They always have full-size candy bars."

That had the twins racing off, hopefully forgetting about the conversation they'd been having, but Kellen wouldn't forget so easily, though.

By the time they returned to the house, the twins' plastic pumpkins were full of candy.

They hurried into the kitchen, dumped out their loot on the table, made piles of each different kind of candy, and traded each other for the items they wanted.

Kellen remembered doing the same thing with Jensen.

Eventually, the party wound down, and the twins slunk off to bed.

Kellen helped clean the mess left behind by the partygoers. When she finished, she met Jensen and Dana at the front door. She couldn't get over how great they looked together—completely in love and utterly happy. As a writer, Kellen spent most of her time inside, working. She didn't have a social life outside of their family get-togethers.

Years ago, she had accepted she'd be single for the rest of her life, but seeing Jensen and Dana as in love now as they were in high school made her yearn for what they had. If one twin could find love, surely the other could do the same. Right? "The party was great. But a little tip for you both, don't meddle in a superhero's love life by hooking her up with anyone named Uncle Shawn."

Dana gasped.

Kellen pointed. "Yup. The kids snitched."

"Rats," Dana hissed.

"Let that be a lesson."

Chapter Two

Shawn was still grinning after he beat a hasty exit from the video call. Aside from his horror at the idea of dressing in a superhero costume, seeing Kellen's reaction to being a couple next year made him chuckle. Until he thought too much about it.

Kellen's aversion to the possibility of a date was like a sucker punch to the gut. She clearly hadn't liked the idea of the two of them being a couple, even for something as silly as a Halloween party where they'd be dressed as superheroes. Her rejection, quite frankly, sucked.

He thought back to one of the last Halloween parties he'd attended during his freshman year of college, sixteen years ago, when Kellen herself had been sixteen. She'd dressed in a yellow motorcycle suit with black stripes and a fake samurai sword. She'd even worn a short, choppy blonde wig with bangs to complete the costume. Shawn had gone in his first-ever suit, which he'd found at a secondhand store, and a briefcase with a scuff on the back, also from a secondhand store.

Kellen eyed him up and down. "What are you supposed to be?"

"I'm a businessman."

She laid the edge of her plastic samurai sword to the side of his neck. "I should put you out of your misery now."

"Very funny." He pushed the sword away.

"If this was a real sword, you would've just sliced your fingers off."

"If that was a real sword, I'd have to take it away."

"You don't take away BK's sword."

He lunged for it.

Kellen hopped backward "So, you want to go up against me?" She brandished her sword.

He dropped his briefcase. "Yes, I think I do."

And the game was on.

Kellen whirled around and let out a squeal.

"A skilled assassin wouldn't squeal," he shouted as he gave chase.

"She would if she wanted to trick you."

"*You're* the one running from *me*."

Kellen dove through the opened sliding glass door, the screened patio door, and outside to the backyard. Then she vanished around the corner of the Collinses' house.

He followed her. They cut across the driveway between guests' cars.

She was a few steps ahead when she shot around the other corner, aiming for the backyard again.

He sprang around the corner and skidded to a stop.

Kellen stood there with her right arm extended, pointing the tip of her samurai sword at him, which was inches from the middle of his chest. "Yeah, running you into a trap," she sneered, breathless from the race.

Panting, he stared. Her cheeks were flushed. Blonde bangs were fluffed around her face. She radiated energy, and that drew him in like a bee to honey. He lifted a hand and pushed the blade to the side.

"And now you have no fingers."

He took a step.

Her brows lowered. "What are you doing?"

"Advancing." He stepped closer.

"I can see that. Why?"

Another step. "Because BK could end me, so I have to move slowly."

A step remained between them. He smoothed the blonde wisps from her forehead.

She watched him with wide eyes, unmoving, unblinking. Possibly not breathing.

This could be her first kiss, he realized. She was sixteen, and he was nineteen. A year ago, his feelings for Kellen had changed. No longer was she his kid sister's best friend. She was his kid sister's gorgeous and funny and smart best friend. He understood immediately that his new feelings were forbidden. Not only did an age difference exist—he was in college and three years older than her—but the older brother couldn't fall for his younger sister's best friend. Just couldn't.

Who did that? Younger brothers were allowed to crush on their older sister's best friends. Even a brother who was a year older could get away with having a thing for his sister's bestie, but not when three years divided them. He remembered her before puberty. He remembered her braces and seeing her in dorky pajamas, dancing to choreography she and Dana created to popular pop songs. He remembered it all. But things changed last year, and he'd seen her with new eyes.

While away at college, he thought he'd meet a girl his own age who would take his mind off Kellen, but that hadn't happened. He missed Kellen more than he missed his family. In fact, he only attended this Halloween party so he could see Kellen. Seeing her now, he couldn't deny his feelings.

The urge to kiss her burned inside him. He advanced the final step, making his intentions clear. The woman she was dressed as wouldn't have let him get so close. "May I kiss you?"

She blinked.

Possibly her first blink since he'd approached.

She didn't say anything, but her head jerked ever-so-slightly.

"Was that a nod?"

She moved her head again in what appeared to be an involuntary twitch.

A grin formed on his face. Taking that twitch for a nod, he raised a hand to her chin and lifted her head as he leaned forward. She touched his arm with her free hand. That touch, though soft, encouraged him. It told him she did want this to happen. She *did* want this kiss.

Her breath warmed his lips, but Jensen shouting Kellen's name had her springing away from Shawn. "I-I have to go." And just like that, she was gone in a flash of yellow.

During the rest of the party, Kellen avoided him.

Utterly disappointed and beating himself up, Shawn returned to college the next day. Trying to kiss her, showing his cards like that, had been a huge mistake. To get her off his mind, he focused on his studies like never before. He aced every single one of his exams and had the highest GPA of his class.

The next Halloween party at the Collinses', Kellen pretended as though that near-kiss a year before had never happened.

After that, Shawn didn't like to attend anymore. He stayed at college. His major, which he changed from design to tech and business, became his one goal. Eventually, he avoided any event where Kellen might be in attendance, which became difficult when Jensen married Dana and any family gathering automatically included Kellen. As much as he wished he could, he couldn't avoid her all the time. Skipping out on Christmas, for instance, was not acceptable, and now Dana and Jensen hosted Christmas at their house because of the twins. The merging of their families meant the Collinses' obsession with Halloween became a priority for the Callaghans, as well, and his absence hadn't gone unnoticed.

If he didn't go to next year's Halloween celebration, then Dana would be pissed, and he did not like dealing with Dana's wrath. So, he might just have to put up with being near Kellen next Halloween. And he'll have to be dressed as a superhero.

He let out a groan. Why couldn't he dress in full body armor and a mask? At least, no one could tell it was him.

His phone chimed, notifying him of a text. He checked it to see Dana had sent him a photo. He opened it, expecting to see the twins. What he found instead was Kellen in her costume, posed as if she were running at the speed of light. His heart skipped a beat. Stunning. If he were there right now instead of working late, he'd want to kiss her just as he had all those years ago. This time, though, he wouldn't let anything stop him.

He swallowed. *Better that I'm not there.*

A knock sounded on his office door.

He glanced up. Who else was still there? "Yes?"

The door opened, and his boss, Mr. Harris, stepped in. His suit appeared wrinkle-free as if he hadn't worked a fourteen-hour day. "Shawn, always working." Mr. Harris's white teeth flashed, and dimples appeared in his brown cheeks.

Shawn stood and buttoned his jacket. "Always, sir."

"I wanted to let you know that I'm composing a team to help me with the next stage of Global Imagination. I want to join forces with Tokyo App. They could elevate Global Imagination to the next level. My goal is to make this happen in a year. I want you on my team for this. What do you say?"

Shawn couldn't believe it. His system vibrated with excitement. Mr. Harris asking Shawn to join his team on such an important project meant a great deal. "I'm in." He shook Mr. Harris's hand.

A year from now, everything could be different.

Chapter Three

Eleven Months Later…

The second-best day of the year behind Halloween was here—the First Day of Autumn. On this day, ever since Kellen's childhood, her family would decorate for the spooky season. Kellen had kept that tradition for her studio apartment, and Jensen had brought that tradition to his own family.

Kellen carted out the plastic containers from her storage closet, hauled them to the living room, and popped off the lids. Fred, her skeleton boyfriend, grinned at her with his toothy mouth. "Fred, my love, it has been far too long since you've graced me with your presence." She lifted him out of the box. His plastic limbs unfolded and clanked together hollowly. She draped one of his arms around her neck and held his skeletal fingers in her hand. To her Halloween playlist, she swayed around the room, imagining him to be a prince and she was a princess, dancing in the woods. Round and round they went in circles that had Fred's plastic legs flying out.

Suddenly, the prince in her mind became Shawn in an expensive suit, holding her close as they spun in each other's arms. She closed her eyes, letting herself fantasize to the tune of Kesha's "Supernatural."

She hadn't fantasized about Shawn since they were

kids and she'd had a massive crush on him. Realizing he might forever think of her as his kid sister's BFF, she set aside her childish crush and moved on. It hurt, but at least she still had him in her life as a co-brother-in-law. She cringed at that. Admittedly, that wasn't what she had envisioned, but it was all she had, and she'd take it. Already their conversations were awkward whenever they interacted.

When did things get so weird and strained? When did he stop teasing her? When did the little, harmless flirtations end?

Right around the time he landed his job at Global Imagination. That was when he had withdrawn from her, Dana, and everyone in favor of career and success.

A clattering sound prompted Kellen to open her eyes. She looked down to see Fred's right leg at her feet. "Oh dear. A prince you are not." She set Fred on the couch, in his favorite corner. "Hold on." She retrieved his leg. Sitting beside him, she stuck his leg bone into his hip bone. "There. All better. You don't even have to get an X-ray."

Fred tipped over to the side, leaning onto the armrest with his head back as if to say, "Seriously. You've got jokes now?"

"Oh, don't be like that, Fred." She righted him and resumed pulling Halloween decorations from the box. "I am now officially the weirdo who dances with and talks to fake skeletons." With a grin, she snapped straight and pointed at Fred. "Better a fake skeleton than a real one, though, am I right, Fred?" She bent over the box. "I'm right."

She unwrapped the pieces to her ceramic haunted village and tossed the newspaper all over the floor.

Soon, the floor was covered with rumpled sheets of newspaper, some of which were slightly yellowed with age and torn from repeated usage. She shuffled her feet through the newspaper sea every time she moved around her apartment to set up or hang a new decoration.

She stretched fake spiderwebbing across the kitchen cabinets she never opened and placed her cast iron witch's cauldron in the middle of the coffee table. Now, she'd have to go to the store to buy bags of candy to fill it. Candy often sustained her during her writing sessions and gave her something to munch on when she suffered from writer's block.

The witch's cauldron was the last decoration, so she gathered the newspaper wads and stuffed them back into the plastic containers. Then she stood in the middle of her apartment, basking in pride at her ceramic pumpkin collection, sugar skulls, and the broomsticks she'd made out of tree branches and pine needles.

Her cellphone alerted her to a new text.

—*Autumn Solstice decorating at the Collinses' house is commencing. Get your butt over here.*—

She grinned at Jensen's text and fired off a reply.

—*I'm coming!* —

Everything about Halloween was taken seriously in her family. And she wouldn't want it any other way.

Kellen arrived at Jensen's house to see plastic containers scattered across the lawn, the twins doing cartwheels, Dana untangling a strand of pumpkin lights, and Jensen plugging in the inflatable phantom. She parked in the driveway and hopped out.

The twins rushed over. "Aunt Kellen." They leapt onto her.

"Whoa." She laughed. "The two of you are excited."

"What's not to be excited about?" Jensen called out. "It's the First Day of Autumn, for goodness sakes—"

"The second-best day of the year." Kellen joined Jensen on the grass as the phantom inflated. "So, this guy again, huh?" Hands on her hips, she watched the phantom come to life.

The phantom rose partially, as if the blow-up was kneeling. Then taller and taller it grew until the phantom towered over her.

Jensen stood beside the phantom. "Hey, he's my bud." He rubbed the grim reaper's side.

"Your bud?" Kellen snorted with laughter.

"Yeah. He guards the house."

"From what?"

"From…you know…stuff."

Weston bounced beside her. "I wanted to get the big dragon."

"A dragon would've been so cool," she said.

They high-fived.

Jensen laid his right hand to the middle of his chest in mock-hurt. "What's wrong with my phantom?"

She shrugged. "I don't know. It just gives me the creeps."

"Am I wrong, but aren't Halloween decorations usually creepy?"

"Yes, but he's…" She stared at the phantom. It bobbed toward her. "I just don't like him."

Jensen gasped. "Don't listen to my evil twin." He gave the soft nylon a pat. "You're perfect just the way you are."

Amused over how she talked to a fake skeleton and Jensen talked to an inflatable phantom, she joined Dana, who was draping the pumpkin lights over the trimmed bushes in front of the house. The two of them finished distributing the lights on bushes and around tree trunks. With the last strand in place, she glanced around the yard, noticing someone was missing yet again.

Kellen dug into one of the containers of decorations, finding the fake gravestones and plastic limbs. "Have you heard from Shawn recently?"

"We talked for a few minutes yesterday. He's in Tokyo for business. He'll be home in two days."

Kellen blinked. She had no idea Shawn wasn't even in the country. "What's he doing in Tokyo?"

Dana set a fake skull on the grass. "He's trying to get a big app company there to join forces with the company he works for. I don't know all the details. You know how he gets when he starts talking about techy stuff."

Kellen made a snoring sound.

"Exactly."

She examined a gravestone, figuring out a way to make their fake graveyard different than what they did last year. Perhaps they could construct them in a section of the yard and surround them with plastic garden edging to make it appear like a real, old-fashioned cemetery. She wondered if they could put piles of potting soil or mulch in front of the gravestones to resemble freshly made graves. The fake limbs and mannequins would, of course, be bursting from those graves as zombies.

Dana pointed a skeleton hand at Kellen. "You

know…you ask about my brother a lot."

Kellen glanced up. *Oh no*. "Huh?"

"Don't play coy with me. You know what I mean."

Kellen placed a mannequin head on the ground. "Am I not allowed to ask about Shawn? I've known him practically my whole life. He's a part of the family."

"You're not fooling me." Dana leaned closer. "You still have feelings for him, don't you?"

Heat blazed across Kellen's cheeks. "I have friendly feelings toward him. That's all."

Dana eyed her. "You and Shawn belong together."

Kellen pulled out a giant spider from another container. "No, we don't. We've never even *been* together."

"But the two of you *should* be together."

"Why?" Kellen faced Dana. "Because *you* think we should be together?"

"No, because you do."

Kellen stared, speechless. How could Dana know that? Kellen hadn't so much as uttered a word about her feelings toward Shawn since they were kids and she'd made the mistake of telling Dana about her crush. Afterward, she had to deny it vehemently and claim she'd outgrown that silly, puppy-love crush. "No, I don't," she lied.

Dana continued to eye her. "And because he does."

That statement shocked Kellen to her core. "Did…did he tell you that?"

"No, but I can tell. He's never been able to keep a secret from me." She picked up a fake arm and poked Kellen in the side with a plastic finger. "Just like you can't."

Kellen lowered her head. "It's not meant to be. He's too busy. I'm too busy. *He's* too busy." She dropped her voice to a whisper. "It's not meant to be." Hoping to bring an end to the conversation, she stuck her head inside another container full of decorations. She discovered the outfit for a scarecrow that the twins would put together later with Jensen and a plastic jack-o'-lantern that'd be the scarecrow's head. When she peered up again, she found Dana playing with her smartphone. "What are you doing?"

As if in reply, Shawn's voice emitted from the speaker. "Hey, sis."

Dana grinned over the phone at Kellen. "Hey, Shawn. Guess what we're doing."

"Annoying me?"

"We're decorating for Halloween. Guess who's here helping us."

"Jack Skeleton."

"That's not his name, and no, but she did dress as Sally once." Dana rotated the phone so Kellen could see Shawn on the screen.

Kellen waved, hoping her cheeks weren't as red as they felt.

"Oh, hey," he said.

She smiled. "Hey."

Dana rotated the phone back. "Don't forget that you're supposed to come to our Halloween party this year as a superhero. *With* Kellen."

Kellen ducked her head and laid a hand to her forehead. *This is not happening. Please tell me this isn't happening.*

"Remember the photo of Kellen in her costume that I sent you?"

Kellen's eyes widened. *Oh my God*, she mouthed.

"Um…Yeah, I remember it." Shawn sounded worried.

Kellen was worried.

"Remember how hot she looked in the leather skirt?" Thankfully, Dana didn't wait for Shawn to answer that. "Well, just wait until you see Kellen in a certain superhero's iconic red skirt and boots."

Kellen's eyes widened. She dove for Dana, wrestled the phone out of her hand, and jabbed the end call button. "I can't believe you said that."

Dana smirked wickedly. "He's definitely coming to our Halloween party now. He'll want to see you in that little red skirt."

Chapter Four

Stunned once more from Dana's call, Shawn leaned against the counter in his hotel bathroom. The last thing Shawn had seen before the video call had cut out was a partial, blurry view of Kellen's face.

Dana's words returned. *Remember the photo of Kellen in her costume that I sent you*?

He sure did. He opened the photo app on his phone and scrolled back to the photo of Kellen from last year's Halloween party.

Remember how hot she looked in the leather skirt?

That leather skirt...her long, tan legs...her shapely thighs. Everything about her on a normal day was beautiful, but throw in a warrior's costume and she was stunning. He jabbed the photo app closed. Pressing the phone to his forehead, he squeezed his eyelids shut.

Don't think about her. Don't think about her.

If his mantra hadn't helped him yet, he was fooling himself into thinking it'd start now, but the chant was all he had. One day, maybe he wouldn't think about Kellen Collins. Today, however, was not that day.

He checked his watch. If he was to arrive at the meeting on time, he needed to get going. A glance at the mirror told him he was ready. Everything about him was groomed to the tee. Not a single bit of stubble dotted his chin, and product kept the hair at the top of his head slick and in order. Even his three-piece suit was wrinkle-free, and his shoes gleamed with a spit-shine. Anything less would've been viewed as disrespectful. His job depended on this trip.

He had come in the place of the head app creator of Global Imagination, who was retiring. Shawn hadn't been given the title of his predecessor yet, but he was in the running with a few others for a job he had aimed for his entire career, but whether or not he had a chance for the promotion rode on this meeting.

Outside his hotel, paid for by his work, he climbed into the waiting car, also paid for by his work. He forced Kellen from his mind and went through his talking points. Moments later, Shawn stood in a boardroom with a spectacular view of Tokyo's bustling life; he stood before a long table lined with distinguished and honorable businessmen and women at Tokyo App.

And the man at the head of the table, silently regarding Shawn, was the CEO and man in charge, Mr. Takahashi. He would be the man who would grant or deny a partnership with Global Imagination. If he granted it, that would be a one-way ticket to Shawn's promotion. If he denied it, Shawn would be responsible for losing a partnership that would hurt Global Imagination and Shawn's standing in the company. They needed this deal to increase their foothold in the app world.

Shawn carefully but eloquently gave his presentation, highlighting the benefits they'd both reap from a partnership and the success of the apps they've created thus far.

At the end, the room was silent.

The board members glanced at each other.

Mr. Takahashi didn't reveal a single thought on his chiseled face.

Shawn held his breath captive in his lungs.

After a tense moment, Mr. Takahashi nodded a few times. "You have done well, Mr. Callaghan. A partnership will be of great value. You and Global Imagination have a deal."

Stunned, Shawn bowed slightly at the waist. "Thank you, sir."

"And tell Mr. Harris that I would like for one of his best techs to work in Tokyo as a representative of Global Imagination. The Global Imagination tech will work directly with the Tokyo team to make sure this collaboration runs smoothly."

"Yes, sir, I will let him know. Thank you."

Mr. Takahashi rose from his chair, and everyone else stood, too. One by one, they followed Mr. Takahashi out of the boardroom, leaving Shawn alone.

When they were gone, he pumped his fist at his side in victory. "Yes," he whispered. In a single moment, his life had changed. Or, more precisely, his life *could* change. This could lead to what he'd always wanted.

A flash of Kellen's face blazed through his mind. She was smiling from ear to ear. Wind blew her hair back. Golden sun lit strands of her hair into a sea of browns and auburns. He shook his head. *No. No, that's not what you want.*

Yes, it is, another part of his mind told him. *And you know it.*

That other part of his mind was right. He had wanted Kellen for years. He allowed himself a moment to fantasize about living in Tokyo, working at Tokyo

App, and coming home to Kellen, who'd be tapping away at her laptop, writing a book. They'd be doing what they love, and they'd be doing it together. If only that could become reality, but not all fantasies were meant to be real. That was why they were fantasies to begin with.

Shawn returned to his hotel. Upon entering, disappointment hit him. Picturing Kellen sitting cross-legged on the white couch had been easy. He studied the couch in question and imagined her there now with her laptop on a matching pillow, a scarf over her hair, and wearing pajamas. She'd be cute, comfortable, kissable. Yeah, he'd kiss her every morning before heading off to work and every evening when he returned home.

Okay. Stop thinking about her. Right. Now.

He pulled out his cellphone and called his boss. "Mr. Harris, I have great news. Mr. Takahashi has agreed to the partnership."

"That is excellent." Mr. Harris's deep voice exuded happiness. "I was right to have sent you."

"Thank you, sir." He had to restrain himself from doing a little victory dance. "Mr. Takahashi also said he'd like one of your best techs to work in Tokyo as a representative for Global Imagination."

"Everyone will covet that position."

"Yes, sir."

"I will send the best of the best to Tokyo."

"Of course."

"And Shawn?"

"Yes, sir?"

"You are at the top of a very short list."

Shawn gripped his free hand into a fist. Everything

he'd been striving for was within reach. "I appreciate that, sir."

"Come back home. We have a lot of work to do."

"I'll get the first flight out. Looking forward to returning home and getting to work."

"See you soon."

"Bye, sir." Shawn hung up. He set his phone onto a sleek, white tabletop and beat his hands on the surface with an upbeat tune of celebration. Everything was falling into place. *Almost* everything.

He lowered his gaze to his phone. Except one piece might forever be missing. He picked up his phone and typed out a text.

—What was all that about with my sister earlier?—

A moment later came Kellen's response

—She got into the Solstice candy. She knew not what she was saying because of a sugar high.—

Shawn snickered and tapped out:

—Sounds like Dana.—

He debated over his next question, whether he should ask it or not. Taking a deep breath, he went for it.

—I have a weird question... If you could live and write somewhere else, anywhere else, would you?—

The three little dots didn't appear.

Shawn shook his head. *That's what you get for asking a weird question. People then think you are weird and don't answer.*

But the three little dots did appear.

He held his breath, hoping to see a *yes*.

—Why would I want to go anywhere else? I have everything I need right here.—

Her response evaporated the tiny dream he'd dared

to envision of the two of them together. He nodded. Of course. She had everything she wanted. She didn't have these strange and inappropriate fantasies about him as he did for her. *Time to move on.* After all, he might be moving to Tokyo, to live and to work there. Alone.

Permanently.

Chapter Five

The next day, Kellen sat at her desk, staring at the blinking cursor. "If I was a great children's book idea, what would I be?" she mumbled.

Her publisher wanted a new children's book before Halloween, but she was having trouble coming up with a good idea. Over the last hour, she had typed four little words, *Once upon a time*, but nothing more came to mind. She highlighted the few words and hit the backspace button, erasing them. Now, the page was blank. She let out a sigh. Working under deadlines stifled her creativity. She had four weeks left to write her next great children's story. Knowing that added to her stress.

When she saw Jensen's name appear on her phone's screen, she pounced on the distraction. "Hey, Twinie."

She could practically hear Jensen's smile through the phone. "Considering you answered my call on the first ring, I'm guessing you're still stuck on your story."

"Yeah." She trailed the tip of her index finger down the colorful spines of her children's books. "After publishing ten children's books, I feel as though my well of ideas has dried up. The ideas I'm coming up with are pathetic."

"Like what?"

"Like a talking sock that hates stinky feet."

"Oh."

She groaned. "I told you it was terrible."

"How'd you even think of that?"

"Yesterday…at your house…when you removed your shoes."

Jensen chuckled. "I guess you can't babysit then, huh? Dana and I are going out on a date tonight. A quiet dinner with just the two of us."

"I could." She loved spending time with Roxon and Weston.

"No. I'd be enabling your procrastination. Off to work with you!"

Kellen smiled, grateful for his support. "But what about the twins?"

"I'll call their usual babysitter. I'm sure she'll want some extra cash. I'll talk to you later."

"Okay. Bye."

"Bye."

She ended the call and sighed again. Pushed back from her desk, she pondered an idea for a story about twins. She wanted to write a cute story, one that would make kids laugh, maybe even wish they had a twin to get into shenanigans with. After all, she had gotten into a lot of mischief with Jensen as a child, but none of her memories were story-worthy. How could she make an adventure out of all the little moments of fun they'd had?

Maybe I'm thinking too hard and need to get my mind off writing for a while. Usually when she was stuck, she'd step away from her project to do something else, like take a walk, and her brain would work out the kinks in her story without any effort. She hoped that would work this time. As she switched off the computer, she told herself she was not procrastinating. Nope, she was trying a technique.

She took a walk. She washed dirty dishes. She dusted. She reorganized and decorated her bookshelves. Finally, she returned to her desk. Unfortunately, no words came.

The time on her phone showed it was almost dinnertime. Perhaps she could drop in on her parents. They'd welcome her, and she'd get a home-cooked meal. Her mouth watered at the mere thought of Wanda's cooking. In her freezer, she had cardboard boxes that contained little trays of food. Most nights, she'd pop one of those into the microwave and make a salad. Most nights, she was lazy.

She changed out of her writing uniform—red flannel pajama bottoms and her dingy slippers. They were more of a gray now, not the pure-white they had been when she first bought them. No matter. No one ever saw them but her muse, who seemed to be on a vacation, anyway. She put on jeans, a T-shirt, and sneakers. Before she left, she remembered to wash away the blue ink smeared across the side of her right hand from her hard work earlier. Who was she kidding? She didn't do any writing. That ink was from doodling swirls, smiley faces, and flowers.

Moments later, she knocked on the door to her parents' house.

Wanda answered it.

"Kellen, what a surprise." Her dark eyebrows lowered over her brown eyes. "Writer's block, huh?"

Kellen couldn't believe her power. "What do you mean?" She feigned ignorance. "I'm just stopping by for a visit. And"—she sniffed the air wafting through the front door—"is that beef stew?"

Wanda stepped aside.

Kellen walked into the warm house. She inhaled again, enjoying the savory scents lingering on the air. Onions, garlic, red wine, and browned meat had salvia pooling inside her mouth. The aroma made her parent's house that much cozier. She removed her light jacket and draped it over a peg on the coat rack by the door. A bowl of Halloween candy sat on the oak stand beside the couch. She snatched up a mini chocolate bar and smiled at her surroundings.

Not much had changed since she had gone to college. The floral couch was the same one she had laid on when she was home sick from school. The wooden coffee table was where she'd do her homework, sitting on the floor. In the dining room, the table was also the same. Growing up, she'd had every meal at home there, seated across from Jensen with Wanda and Jasper on either head of the table. If she crawled under the table, she'd find her name carved into the wood next to Jensen's name. This was her childhood home, and she was glad it hadn't changed. Except for her old room, which was now a guest bedroom.

Jasper entered the living room. He had a bit of brown sauce glistening on his graying whiskers.

Wanda tsked. "Jasper, have you been sampling the stew?"

Jasper shrugged. "I don't know what you mean."

"You have leftovers on your chin."

He swiped at his chin. "Oops." He smiled at Kellen. "It's good to see you, sweetie." His arms came around her in a hug. When he stepped back, he held her by the shoulders a minute while his blue eyes studied her. "Uh-oh, writer's block, is it?"

Kellen threw up her hands. "How do you two do that?"

"You twist your lips to the side when you're thinking hard on a story."

"I do not." She caught herself as her lips shifted to the side and pressed them together. She smiled instead, showing off all her teeth. "See?"

Jasper shuddered. "Scary."

Jensen had definitely won Jasper's sense of humor in the parental jackpot.

She had inherited Jasper's eyes, while Jensen had Wanda's dark eyes.

"Come on, honey." Jasper held out an arm to Kellen. "Let's steal some more stew. We can eat straight from the pot, and your mother will never know."

"I will, too," Wanda shouted from down the hall. "It'll be ready in a minute. Kellen, keep your father away from that stew. The last time I made it, he had eaten all the beef from the pot before I could even serve it. We ended up having vegetable stew that night."

"Don't worry, Mom, I've got my eyes on him."

Jasper sighed. "Where's Jensen? I need another man in this house. I'm feeling ganged up on."

"Jensen and Dana are going out for dinner today."

"Oh, that's nice. I used to take your mom on dates when you kids were little. We liked to go out every Friday. Couples in love should do that, you know. They need time alone."

She remembered. After their date night, Saturday was pizza and family game night. Sunday was always a big dinner before school and work resumed on Monday.

Jensen and Dana followed in her parents' footsteps; they were a lovely family.

Sitting on the couch, Kellen chatted with Jasper and kept him from sneaking off to taste the stew. Her stomach growled when she heard Wanda announce dinner was ready.

She occupied her usual spot at the table. The chair on the other side was empty. Memories of sitting there every night, telling her parents about their school day and sharing jokes, came back as if they had happened yesterday.

The stew was better than Kellen remembered. The flavors danced on her tongue, and the beef practically melted in her mouth. She scooped up chunks of potato and carrot and slurped the delicious broth. Beside the bowl was a glass of red wine and a nice, crusty roll. She tore off a chunk of the roll and sopped up juices from her bowl. She washed it down with a swallow of wine—a burst of flavor. Boy, she missed eating at home. Her tiny apartment kitchen didn't see much action, unless she stood in it while waiting for the pot of coffee to brew. She wasn't completely inept at cooking, though. Wanda had taught her how to make several meals, but she never had any occasion to cook them—not a meal for four when she was only one. Kellen ate her fill, and then she plopped down on the couch, content.

"Would you like coffee?" Wanda asked.

"Coffee sounds good."

"I'll get it." Wanda half-rose from her chair.

But Kellen stopped her. "No, let me. You made a fabulous dinner. The least I can do is fetch the coffee." In the kitchen, Kellen set the coffee pot on a tray with three mugs, saucers of milk and sugar, and three spoons. She hefted the tray and carried it into the living room. As she bent down to set the tray on the coffee table, she gasped from the sensation of her heart stopping. Her legs weakened, and she dropped to her knees. The dishes clattered, but she was close enough that they didn't fall to the floor. Splotches of white light exploded in front of her vision. Her head spun.

She desperately sucked in air, forcing herself to breathe. Once she managed to get oxygen into her lungs, she pressed a hand where her heart punched her chest, beating terribly fast. She gripped the sides of the table to stop the spinning.

"Kellen."

Wanda and Jasper sprang to their feet.

"Jasper, get water. Quick." Wanda rubbed her back. "What happened?"

"My heart s-stopped." Kellen rubbed a hand to her chest, fearing she'd pass out. Her body shook uncontrollably. Her voice quivered. "I don't feel right. I think s-something is wrong."

Jasper hustled back with a glass. Water sloshed at the rim as he hurried. "Here. Take a slow sip."

Kellen accepted the glass with a trembling hand. She could barely draw any water into her mouth because her hand shook so much. What little water she did manage to sip, she choked down. "Something's very wrong." She rubbed her chest. "I can feel it."

Jasper paled. "Do you think she's having a heart attack?"

"At her age?"

"Maybe we should call an ambulance."

"Let her just calm down." Wanda stroked her arm.

"Breathe in through your nose and out through your mouth."

Kellen focused on breathing until her heartrate leveled out and her shaking stopped, but she couldn't dispel the feeling something was terribly, terribly wrong. She lay on the couch, as she had when she was a kid with a cold or upset stomach.

Wanda laid a cool cloth on her forehead. "Rest for a little while. Maybe you just had too much wine."

Kellen wanted to tell them she wasn't even tipsy, but she was still so shaken from what had happened that she couldn't find her voice. She lay on the couch for an hour, waiting for that sinking feeling to dissolve, but it lingered.

The house phone rang with a loud shrill, causing Kellen to flinch.

Wanda answered it. "Hello? Yes, this is Wanda Collins."

A brief silence stretched, creating a buzzing sound in Kellen's ears. And then—

"Oh, my gosh." Those words came out on a gasp, but what followed was a yell. "Jasper!"

He popped out of his recliner and hurried into the kitchen. "What is it? Who's on the phone?"

Kellen pulled herself into a sitting position. From where she sat, she could hear Wanda's words.

"Something happened. It's the hospital." Wanda paused when her voice caught. "Jensen…"

Tears filled Kellen's eyes, because she knew. Her heart had known the moment it happened. Her chest felt oddly hollow, as if her heart, which had been racing so violently before, had disappeared, leaving behind a tangle of arteries.

In the kitchen, her parents' voices became murmurs.

A few minutes later, they entered the living room, holding hands.

Wanda sniffed. "Kellen, I have to tell you—"

"I know." The tears Kellen had been holding back spilled down her cheeks. "I already know. Jensen died."

Wanda covered her mouth with a hand.

Jasper lowered his head.

Kellen felt numb all the way to her toes. The instant Jensen died, it had sucked the life from her, replacing it with something less. She took a deep breath, grateful she could still do that, but she didn't know how the rest of her body still functioned. She rose to her feet and found them sturdy, even though she felt as though she floated. "I'm gonna go to the hospital. Dana needs me." She wanted to be with her best friend and to hold her while she cried.

"Sweetie." Wanda's voice was a rasp, but as loud as a bell. "Dana died, too."

Caught off guard, Kellen faltered her steps. She grabbed the couch's armrest to keep herself steady.

"They were in a car accident. They didn't make it."

Kellen lowered onto the armrest and cried into her hands.

Wanda sat on the couch, wrapped her arms around Kellen, and pulled Kellen onto the cushion.

Kellen cried on Wanda's shoulder.

Jasper sat beside them.

The three of them cried together, as one entity, sharing the same pain and the same sorrow. The tears falling down Kellen's cheeks were also her parents' tears. And they were Jensen's tears.

Growing up, they often knew when the other was hurt or scared. Many believed twins had this power, a connection they acquired while in the womb. Although she hadn't seen Jensen fall from the jungle gym and break his arm, Kellen had wailed. After doctors X-rayed both of them, they discovered Kellen was fine. Fine, except she had felt Jensen's pain. And when Kellen's heart was broken in high school, Jensen knew. He called her right away. He and Dana had been together and madly in love, but he was full of angst and despair—*Kellen's* angst and despair. They were the same in many ways—bonded mind, body, and soul.

She never thought she'd feel the instant of Jensen's death, but she had. If anything, she figured they would die together, but she was still alive. Alive and twin-less for the first time in her life.

And Weston and Roxon were parentless for the first time in their lives. Kellen gasped. "The kids. I have to go to them."

"They're probably in bed," Wanda said. "It's eight o'clock."

Kellen snatched her jacket off the rack, almost knocking it over. She tugged it on and picked up her purse. "A babysitter is watching them. I have to tell her. And I need to be there in the morning."

Wanda nodded. "Okay. We have to go to the hospital. We'll call Dana's parents."

"I'll call Shawn on the way."

Jasper kissed her temple. "Drive carefully."

Kellen paused on the doormat. They had just lost a child in a car accident. They didn't need to lose their last child. "I will. I promise." In her car, she locked the seatbelt around herself and shut off the radio. She scrolled through her list of contacts, pausing at *Dana* and then *Jenson*. Tears clouded her vision. She blinked them away. After hitting the icon to call Shawn and the speaker button, she set her phone in the center console. Her car filled with the monotonous rings. She drove carefully, keeping to the speed limit.

The ringing carried over to Shawn's voicemail. She didn't want to leave a message, though. This sort of news shouldn't be delivered through voicemail, so she tried again. The rings seemed to go on forever. At a red light, the robotic tone once again told her to leave a message.

Dana had said Shawn was in Tokyo. What time was it over there? What day was it? Should Kellen call in the morning? Or would he be sleeping then?

The beep sounded, and she let out a breath. She didn't know how to reach him. Texting was an option, but a bad one. Leaving a voicemail was the next best thing to actually talking to him, but she dreaded being the one to leave it and tried to picture him the moment he listened to it. Where would he be? Would he be alone? Even as she did it, she hated doing it this way.

"Shawn, it's Kellen. Something bad happened…" Bad wasn't even the right word for it. Awful was a better choice. No, terrible…life-changing…disastrous. "Jensen and Dana were in a car accident. They didn't make it." She choked on the last three words when tears clogged her throat. She inhaled a faltering breath. "I'm on my way to their house. The kids are with a sitter. I'll have to tell them in the morning." She paused. Already she didn't know what to say to Shawn. How would she ever summon the right words to tell the twins?

"I don't want to do it alone," she whispered and

was taken aback she had voiced that longing out loud to Shawn. She hoped she had said it soft enough he wouldn't hear it. "Please call me the moment you get this message." She was about to hang up, but before she did, she added, "I am so, so sorry for telling you this way. Please forgive me." And she jabbed the end-call button on the screen.

The traffic light turned green.

She drove the rest of the way to Dana and Jensen's house where all the Halloween decorations were still up. The gravestones and skeletons, ghosts and reapers were suddenly too morbid. Her brother and best friend had died tonight, and their home was covered in ghoulish creatures and symbols of death. The decorations sent shivers down Kellen's spine. She hurried out of her car and dodged the phantom she now believed was really trying to grab her. She hesitated before knocking on the front door where the grim reaper grinned.

The door opened.

A teenage girl with a face full of freckles stood at the threshold. "Oh, hi, Kellen. I thought you were the Collinses."

"They won't be coming." Kellen peered at her feet. "They were in a car accident. They…they…" Telling someone to their face was much harder. If she couldn't even tell the babysitter, how would she tell the two people who meant the most to Dana and Jensen? She gazed into the girl's eyes. She shook her head, letting the silence say what she couldn't.

"Oh." The girl swallowed. "I'm sorry."

Kellen nodded and dug out cash from her purse to pay her for babysitting. "You can go home now. I'll stay tonight." When she stepped inside the house, Kellen stood motionless in the hall. She didn't know what to do. All around her she could feel Dana's and Jensen's presences.

Normally, the house burst with life and activity, but now quiet consumed it.

She tiptoed up the stairs and peeked into Roxon's and Weston's rooms, needing to see them. They were tucked into their beds—safe and sound. The sight of them reassured and frightened her. They were okay, but they would be waking to a world that didn't have their parents.

Downstairs, she rotated in a full circle, noticing the Halloween decorations. She knew what she had to do— remove anything that depicted death. She carried in the boxes from the garage and set to work. The first thing she did was unplug the blow-up phantom and throw out the grim reaper door cover.

Chapter Six

In his first-class seat, Shawn stretched his legs. In minutes he would be landing in New York City for his layover flight home. He still had a high from the work he'd accomplished in Tokyo. Even though he was exhilarated after his trip, he fought against heavy eyelids. He asked a flight attendant for coffee. While gazing out the window at the clouds, he nursed the cup and sipped the dark roast. The caffeine gave him a slight buzz thanks to his empty stomach.

The plane landed with a bump, and he was one of the first ones off the flight. Holding his black leather briefcase and a small travel bag, he made his way through John F. Kennedy International Airport to his terminal. As he walked, he dug his phone out of his pocket and pressed the button at the top. The screen changed from black to white, and it buzzed in his hand. App icons filled the screen, revealing two missed calls and a voicemail notification. Seeing Kellen's name in the missed calls section surprised him. He expected the caller to be Gina or Dana since they were the only ones who called him. As pathetic as that sounded, it was true.

In the bustling airport, he listened to Kellen's message.

"Shawn, it's Kellen. Something bad happened…"

Her voice was soft and wet.

"Jensen and Dana were in a car accident. They didn't make it."

He halted, and the world stopped moving around him. The sounds of the airport dropped away. The people rushing past him became invisible. He was all alone in a busy airport.

"I'm on my way to their house. The kids are with a babysitter. I'll have to tell them in the morning."

A long pause followed her words. He thought he heard her say something in the background, but he couldn't make it out.

"Please call me the moment you get this message. I am so, so sorry for telling you this way. Please forgive me." The message ended abruptly.

With the phone pressed to his ear, he listened to the options to delete or save the message. He ended the call and dropped into a stiff chair.

Kellen's words rang in his head.

A clenching sensation in the middle of his chest stole his breath. Dana? His little sister? How could she be gone? From the moment she was born, she'd been precious. He doted on her, fought the kids who bullied her, and threatened the boys who wanted to date her. She was his most favorite person in the world. He texted her every day and called her as much as he could, but he wished he had visited her and the twins more.

That's what Kellen had said. Something about the kids.

He increased his phone's volume and replayed the message, listening for the whisper.

"I don't want to do it alone."

His heart tore for Kellen. She didn't deserve the

burden of telling the twins alone. He checked his watch. Early yet. He doubted she'd be awake, but he tried calling her, anyway. The call went straight to voicemail. "Kellen, I'm in the airport. I'm catching my flight home. I'll be there as fast as I can." He hung up, knowing he wouldn't make it in time. The kids would be up in a couple of hours for school; Kellen would have to tell them then.

His flight was announced, and he walked to the opened door with his ticket. On the plane, he sat in a daze. Dana had died while he was on a flight. He never realized how quickly you could lose someone you love. He boarded a flight and Dana was alive. He exited that same flight and Dana was gone. Forever.

Feeling immobile, although the plane was moving, he stared out the window at the cloud formations. Tears stacked in his eyes. He fought to keep them from escaping, but they plunged down his cheeks and dripped onto the lapel of his designer jacket.

The plane ride was excruciatingly long.

A lump of tears lodged in his throat. Every time he blinked, he saw Dana's face in the blackness beneath his eyelids—her wide eyes, dimples, and pointed chin that made her look like a pixie. A pang stabbed him in the middle of his chest. She was the sweetest person, genuinely good, and the best sister and mother. He couldn't understand why someone so pure had to be taken away. What was the reason? What was the purpose? He swallowed hard and felt as if he was choking on the bitter taste of sorrow.

When the plane landed, his soul felt ancient, as if he had aged an eternity. With his travel bag and briefcase, he hurried to the parking lot and found his car. He climbed into the driver's seat and turned on the ignition. The air conditioning and radio came on, but he didn't put the car in Reverse. Being alone, enclosed, he laid his head on the steering wheel and allowed himself to break. Like the thin, elastic layer of a water balloon, the emotions he had bottled up on the plane popped and poured forth, washing him out as if a tsunami had swept him up, pummeled him, and left him stranded on a deserted shore. He gripped the steering wheel on either side of his head and squeezed his eyelids shut. Water leaked from his eyes—warm and wet.

He stayed that way for several minutes, until his eyes felt like red-hot, swollen beach balls about to burst in his eye sockets. He inhaled deeply, filling his lungs. Using the sleeve of his jacket, not caring about wrinkles or getting it dirty, he rubbed the evidence of his emotions from his face. He extracted his phone from his pocket and called Kellen.

She answered on the second ring. "I'm so glad it's you. Did you…did you get my message?"

"Yeah." His voice was hoarse. He cleared his throat and tried again. "Yeah, I got it. I'm sorry you had to leave a voicemail. I was on an overnight flight." He listened to the silence on the other end.

"The twins will be up any minute." Kellen's voice was thick with tears. "I don't know what to do."

"I'm on my way. I'll be there in an hour." He ended the call and backed out of the parking space, wanting to be there for Kellen and the twins.

Chapter Seven

Kellen paced in the kitchen and wrung her hands. Jensen and Dana's kitchen was massive, about four times bigger than the tiny kitchen in her apartment. As a matter of fact, their entire home was big, making her feel microscopic, especially with the weight of what she had to bear on her shoulders pushing her down.

She opened and shut cabinets while on the hunt for supplies to make pancakes. Busy work. That's what she needed to keep her mind off the inevitable. She sifted together flour, sugar, baking powder, and salt. In a well in the center of the dry ingredients, she poured in milk, melted butter, and cracked in the gooey insides of a large egg. She mixed it until the batter was smooth.

On a hot gridle, puddles of white batter sizzled. Little bubbles formed, and she flipped the cooking cakes. The undersides were a perfect golden. She was piling the pancakes onto a platter when two doors opened upstairs.

Twins. She shook her head with laughter and sadness. Jensen and she had the same biological clocks while growing up, too. They'd wake and fall asleep at the exact same moment.

Two sets of feet padded down the stairs.

Kellen steeled herself.

The twins hurried into the kitchen. Roxon wore pink leopard print pajamas, and Weston wore superhero pajamas. Roxon's hair stuck up in all directions, and crusty sleepies were still stuck in the corners of Weston's eyes. But when they saw her, their faces split into smiles.

"Aunt Kellen!"

Their excitement struck her in the gut.

Weston bounced on his feet. "What are you doing here?"

"Making pancakes." She waved the spatula in the air like a fairy wand. "Do you want a few…hundred?" She forced a smile.

Their eyes lit up. "Yes."

She gave them two pancakes each and let the twins drown them in powdered sugar and maple syrup.

They cut into the cakes enthusiastically and shoved giant bites into their mouths.

Kellen picked up a pancake and bit into it without syrup. It wedged into her throat, so she gulped coffee. She recalled the breakfasts she had with Jenson before school, slurping milk from their cereal bowls and picking at eggs. Pancakes had been their favorite, too, with lots of sugary-sweetness on top.

She handed the twins napkins to clean the powdered sugar and syrup from their sticky mouths. "Okay. Get ready for school." She turned on the faucet to wipe off their plates.

"Where's Mom and Dad?" Roxon asked.

Kellen stilled her hands in the act of washing. She couldn't lie. Telling them a fake story now until they got home from school and she had support would be easier for her, but they wouldn't forgive her for that once they found out the truth. She faced them. "Something happened last night."

Even those words made her cringe. *Something? Something? Everything had happened.*

"What?" they asked together.

"Your parents were in a car accident."

Roxon's eyes widened. "Are they okay?"

Throat tight, Kellen shook her head.

Weston peered at the ceiling. "Are they upstairs?"

"No." The word stuck in Kellen's throat.

Roxon covered her mouth with a hand. "Are they in the hospital?"

Kellen stretched across the counter and held their hands. "Your parents were hurt too badly. They didn't survive."

Their faces were blank as they digested what she had said.

She held her breath and waited.

Tears beaded in Roxon's eyes. "They're dead?" Her voice was soft.

Unable to speak, Kellen nodded.

"No, they can't be," Weston shouted.

"I'm sorry." Kellen squeezed their hands as tears formed in her own eyes. "I'm so, so sorry. They loved you so much."

Roxon shook her head. "They shouldn't have gone out yesterday."

"It was an accident, sweetie. It wasn't anyone's fault."

Weston's chin quivered. "What will happen to us without them?"

"I'm here. I won't leave you. I promise."

"I don't want you," Roxon yelled. "I want Mom." She yanked her hand free and dashed out of the kitchen. Her feet pounded up the stairs.

A moment later, a door slammed.

Kellen and Weston stared at each other.

Silence stretched.

Quiet tears flowed.

Then Weston extracted his hand gently from hers and escaped upstairs to his room.

Their rejection, her grief, and the weight of what they'd all have to face next rooted her to the spot. Even so, she crumbled under the weight of it all and collapsed onto the counter. With her hands stamped over her mouth, she muffled her sobs.

****

A mere ten minutes later, a silver sports car pulled into the driveway.

Relief descended upon Kellen. From here on, she wouldn't be alone in all this. She set her cup on the counter, rushed out the door, and met Shawn in the middle of the driveway. He was rumpled, unshaven, and crestfallen. She slung her arms around his neck.

He embraced her in return and rubbed her back.

He smelled like cologne and coffee. "I told them," she whispered.

Shawn eased back.

From this distance, the red streaks in his eyes were visible. "It didn't go well." She wrapped her arms around herself. "How could it?" A sigh slipped from her lips. "They've locked themselves in their rooms." She peered over her shoulder at the upstairs windows, wishing she knew what to do.

"Let's go inside," he offered.

In the kitchen, she poured him coffee.

He wrapped his hands around the cup. "Thank you."

They stared into their drinks.

The silence between them was overwhelming. Kellen exhaled, hoping to expel her grief. "Should I tell the twins you're here?"

"No. They already know I'm here."

Kellen thought of the windows overlooking the driveway and figured he was right.

"I'll give them a bit of time and then I'll see if they want to talk to me."

"Okay."

For the rest of the morning, Shawn tapped away at his laptop at the kitchen counter, and Kellen wandered aimlessly through the house. She found one of Jensen's ties on the dryer and Dana's lipstick by the front hall mirror and wondered if Dana had slicked on that lipstick before leaving for their dinner date. Heart heavy, she gathered the items, and then she made her way upstairs, tiptoeing.

The sound of sniffling and muffled weeping floated down the hall.

She faced Jensen and Dana's bedroom, a place she hadn't ever stepped foot because the space was private, only a place where the couple and the twins belonged. She eased open the door, and the musky scent of Jensen's cologne bombarded her. Stepping inside, she felt like an intruder. Not wanting to disturb anything, or be somewhere she wasn't supposed to be, she set the items on the dresser. Then she backed out and closed the door behind her.

At lunchtime, she made peanut butter and jelly sandwiches.

Shawn ate his in front of his laptop.

She was beginning to think the laptop was a part of

him. Being a writer, she could understand that, but not now. Even if she tried, she doubted she could form a single sentence. As it was, she didn't even want to sit in front of her laptop.

She situated two plates with sandwiches, sans crust, and two glasses of milk on a tray. At the top of the stairs, she set the tray down and knocked on their doors. "West, Roxy, I brought lunch."

No sound.

"Peanut butter and jelly sandwiches."

Nothing.

"And milk."

Who was she luring out with milk? Cats? If they didn't budge at the mention of PB&J, what made her think milk would do the trick? "I'll leave it in the hall. You can get it when you want it." She set a plate and glass to the right of their doors and hefted the tray back downstairs.

Two hours later, she collected the dishes, except they weren't empty. The sandwiches didn't so much as have a bite missing. She poked the bread and found the sandwiches to be dried up. Unsure of what to do, she collected the untouched milk and sandwiches.

"They didn't eat?" Shawn asked.

She dumped the room temperature milk down the drain. "No."

"When they get hungry enough, they will. I'm going up now. See if they'll let me in."

She nodded. "Do you want me to come?"

"No, thank you. I'll do this alone." He left the kitchen.

Gripping the counter, she listened to Shawn knock on their doors and call out their names. *Please, let him get through to them. Please, please, please.*

He stayed up there for several minutes, attempting to get the twins to open their doors, but he was unsuccessful. "Your aunt and I are here whenever you need us." He returned to the kitchen with a shake of his head.

She sighed. "Have you heard from your parents?"

"Yeah. My mom said they're working out the funeral plans with your parents, and our job is to be here for the twins. They have everything handled."

Kellen nodded again. She wished she could be there for her parents, but she knew they'd rather have her here instead. During the rest of the day, she made phone calls. The first was to the twins' school to notify the principal and their teachers they would be absent for the rest of the week. Then she called Jensen's and Dana's employers to let their bosses know what had happened. After that, she flipped through their phonebook calling their closest friends to break the news. By the final call, hours later, exhaustion and emotions left her raw to the bone.

"I could've helped with that." Shawn stood in the doorway to the dining room.

He had ditched his jacket and tie a long time ago. The sleeves of his button-up shirt were rolled to his elbows, and the first two buttons of his shirt were undone. With the five o'clock shadow darkening his jawline and chin, he didn't quite resemble himself. He looked...handsome. More so than usual when his appearance was sleek and shiny, a corporate worker with a condo and expensive car. Now he appeared like a normal, everyday guy. She shrugged. "You looked busy."

"Yeah." He joined her at the table and took the chair next to her. "I was informing my co-workers about the details of my trip and requesting time off."

A scent of cloves and cinnamon touched her nostrils. It warmed her and reminded her of the lovely season upon them. She inhaled, savoring the smell and hoping not to be obvious.

"Are you okay?"

She opened her eyes. "Yup." Her stomach growled. "Actually, no, I'm starving."

He held up his phone. "I can help with that. Pizza?"

"Sounds good."

The pizza arrived, and Kellen called up to the twins.

Their feet didn't scurry on the floor above. Not a single door opened.

She met Shawn's gaze. "They haven't eaten since breakfast."

"I'm sure they have their solstice candy in their rooms. They've probably been pigging out on chocolate and licorice all day."

Kellen groaned. "I hope not." She could only imagine the massive tummy aches that would cause.

"They'll be okay."

Kellen and Shawn ate pizza at the dining room table.

"It's weird not having Jensen and Dana here," Shawn said.

"I know. It is weird." Kellen glanced around. "I keep expecting them to turn the corner and grab a slice." She stared at the slice on her own plate. "Halloween is in four weeks. It won't be the same without them."

"I guess that means the Samhain feast and Halloween party won't be here this year, unless you do it."

Kellen jerked. "What?" The thought horrified her. The most she did was take home leftovers. She specialized in that.

Shawn smiled. "Hosting a party can't be that bad."

She raised a brow. "Have you ever made a feast?"

"No, can't say I have."

"Until you have, you can't say it's not 'that bad.' " She took a bite of her cheesy pizza and thought about Halloween. *I'll never make the festivities as good as Dana had.*

Change could be tough on kids, though. Maybe it would be better for the twins if everyone gathered at the house on Halloween as they usually did, but she didn't want to ruin anything. Would it be against the rules if she bought the dishes pre-cooked?

While pondering that, she carried a plate of pepperoni pizza and a can of soda up the stairs with Shawn. Once again, she knocked on their doors. "We have pizza." She listened. "Extra pepperoni."

Not a peep.

Shawn tapped her elbow with his. "Let's just leave it."

They set down the food and drinks and retreated downstairs. After some time, they ventured back up to check on the twins' dinners. The plates were still on the floor, but the pizza was gone. And the cans of soda had been drained.

Kellen faced Shawn with a grin of triumph, and they high-fived quietly.

That night, Kellen slept in the guest bedroom, and Shawn slept on the couch. Kellen had a hard time falling asleep because she kept imagining Shawn scrunched up on the couch, struggling to find a comfortable position.

In the morning, she couldn't wait for coffee and was pleasantly surprised to find the coffeepot already full to the top.

Shawn entered wearing jeans and a white T-shirt.

She hadn't thought he owned any blue jeans, and he looked good. Her cheeks heated.

"Morning," he said.

She cleared her throat. "Morning. Thanks for making the coffee."

"No problem."

She poured herself a cup and sipped. "Mm." The brew had a touch of flavor to it that tingled her taste buds. "Did you add something?" She pointed to her cup.

"Oh, yeah. A dash of cinnamon and nutmeg. Do you not like it?"

"No, I do." She recalled how he had smelled like cinnamon yesterday. Her throat constricted again. "It's good. Um. Do you want breakfast? Scrambled eggs? Toast?" She opened the fridge to see what she could make. Then, out of the corner of her eye, she noticed movement. The sight of Weston and Roxon standing together caught her off guard. She offered them a cautious smile. "Good morning."

"Morning," they mumbled.

She ticked her gaze over to Shawn.

He gave her a tiny nod.

"Do you two want omelets?"

Weston and Roxon exchanged glances.

"With cheese?" Weston asked.

Kellen smiled. "With lots and lots of cheese." She set to work on cracking eggs. Cheese omelets weren't much, but they were a start.

Chapter Eight

Two days later, Shawn waited by the front door for Kellen and the twins. He fidgeted with his silver cufflinks. The sound of heels clicking on the tile had him raising his gaze.

Kellen walked toward him wearing a black dress, tights, and ankle boots—beautiful, even in all black. Her dark, wavy hair settled on her shoulders, and her shapely lips were painted a deep red. He picked up her black coat from the rack and held it out.

She hesitated before she slipped her arms through the sleeves.

As he fixed the coat on her shoulders, the ends of her hair brushed his fingers. He stole a whiff of her perfume—sandalwood.

"Thank you," she said. "Weston, Roxon, it's time to go."

The twins shuffled into the hall.

Weston stared at his shoes. "Do we have to go?"

Kellen knelt down. "If you don't go, you might regret it later, and it might make you sadder."

"But we don't want to say goodbye," Roxon mumbled.

Kellen's eyes exuded helplessness when she sought Shawn out for assistance. Shawn didn't often talk to children. He could charm executives and all the higher-ups in the company, but talking to kids was another thing altogether. "Hey." He lowered next to Kellen. "You're not really saying goodbye. Their energy is all around us. It's that energy that makes us whom we are, and that energy can never go away. We might not see them, but they are there as an energy that can love us throughout the day, and even at night when we're asleep." He paused. "Does…does that make sense?" The concept of energy could be a bit over their heads.

But they nodded.

"They'll be with you everywhere you go," Kellen added. "Forever."

Weston and Roxon looked at each other and clasped hands.

Then Kellen rose to her feet.

Shawn followed suit and opened the door.

On the sidewalk, Kellen paused next to him. "Thank you for that. What you said was nice."

He stared after the twins as they dragged their feet to her car. "It was what my parents had told me when my grandpa died. I was a couple of years older than they are now. The explanation helped me, so I hope it helps them."

Kellen's lips lifted at the corners, and she tilted her head. "I think *you* will help them."

Except, he wouldn't be here to help them. He planned to leave after the funeral, only he hadn't told her or the twins yet. In the city, he had a job and a life. And his boss wanted employees vying for the Tokyo position to pitch him new app ideas. The employee with the best app would not only see that app come to life but would also get the promotion of a lifetime. He couldn't just stay in this small town. Not when he had so much at stake.

****

Large oak trees lined the cemetery. Sunlight beamed through the leaves and shone onto gravestones. Two mahogany coffins hovered over large, covered holes. Beautiful, flowered wreaths draped over their centers.

Shawn stood beside Kellen while the minister spoke. He didn't know what the minster was saying, because he couldn't take his gaze off the smaller of the two coffins. His throat constricted. *My baby sister.* Those words repeated in his head again and again. He angled his head toward Kellen.

Silent tears drizzled down her cheeks, leaving behind wet tracks.

Her sadness only made his own more pronounced. Seeing her crying gutted him. Dana wouldn't want her best friend to hurt alone, and Shawn wanted to offer Kellen all the support he could for the short time he had left. He shifted his hand until the smooth skin of Kellen's hand touched his finger. Then he laced his fingers with hers.

She squeezed his hand.

He squeezed back. Her hand was cold, but it warmed in his, and he didn't let go. Not even when the four of them stepped up to lay white roses on the coffins. They backed away together and turned as one. Their hands disconnected only when Kellen hugged their parents.

"We'll see you at the house," Wanda said.

Their footsteps were heavier leaving than when they had arrived, for they all knew…this really was goodbye, despite what he had said earlier.

Seeing Kellen falter, Shawn laid a hand on her

lower back to guide her. She walked easier then. At her car, he held the door open.

Before she climbed in, though, she roped her arms around his neck and whispered, "Thank you."

By lending her a hand to hold and a hand to support her, he had given her exactly what she needed to get through. And in doing that, he had made the funeral bearable for himself. But in minutes, he would be heading back to the city. In minutes, he'd be breaking her heart all over again. He swallowed down his guilt.

As he stepped around the car to the driver's side, he lowered his shoulders in an effort to dispel that guilt. During the drive, he couldn't form the words to tell them. Minutes later, he pulled into the driveway. Time was running out.

Kellen secured an arm around each of the twins and headed to the door.

Shawn stayed on the driveway, with the keys to his car in hand. He shuffled his feet and cleared his throat. "Hey, everyone." They looked so worn that he regretted the next words that came out of his mouth. "I'm leaving." He didn't think it would be possible for their faces to drop any more than they already were, but they did.

"What?" Kellen's voice was flat, emotionless.

Shawn's palms broke into a cold sweat. "I'm going back to the city."

Kellen's eyes widened. "Right now?"

He nodded. Seeing the expression on her face robbed him of his voice. Silence stretched between them.

Then Roxon's face became hard, and she shouted,

"Everyone leaves us."

The twins broke off from either side of Kellen and bolted into the house, leaving her on the sidewalk.

The front door banged shut, making Shawn flinch. Worse yet was Kellen's disappointment.

"A whole bunch of people are headed over here right now, and you're leaving this second?"

"I have to get back to my job." Work was a lame reason. But for years he strove toward the place where he was finally at, and he didn't want to jeopardize that by being away for too long.

"I can't believe you're doing this," she whispered.

"My life is in the city."

Kellen peered over her shoulder at the house.

When she faced him again, her eyes were dry, but something else was there—a calm, quiet rage but no less dangerous.

"What's sad is you don't realize you have a life right here." She shrugged.

That simple action, and the meaning behind it, was like a punch to the gut.

"Bye, Shawn." And just like that, she pivoted on her heels.

"Kellen."

She didn't so much as pause.

He had known leaving would be hard, but he hadn't known it would be this excruciating. Sighing, he got into his car and started the engine. The time he had already spent out of the office was too much. This Tokyo promotion was what he wanted. Wasn't it?

It's too late to take it back now. He backed out of the driveway and kept his gaze from the rearview mirror as he drove away.

Coming down the road at the same time were all the cars headed to the reception.

He passed each one, feeling more and more like a massive jerk.

Chapter Nine

Leaning against the closed front door, Kellen plastered a hand to her mouth to smother her cries. How could he do this to them? To the twins? To her? Just when she thought he was being compassionate and caring—and she *thanked* him for it—he pulled the rug right out from under her. She hadn't expected him to stay forever or even for a week, but to leave moments after they had buried their loved ones? She had not seen that abandonment coming. It hurt…a lot. A part of her felt as though he had disrespected Jensen and Dana. And the other part of her was outraged he could do this to the twins after they had already lost so much.

Tears leaked down her face. Taking a deep breath, she dashed away the wet tracks on her cheeks. Dozens of people were on their way and would arrive any minute. She didn't have time to wallow. She hurried into the kitchen and pulled platters of meat, cheese, fruits, and veggies out of the fridge. She removed the covers and set them out on the counter with a ton of clear plastic plates, utensils, and cups.

A car door slamming outside made her jump. She scurried to the coffeemaker and switched it on. In the hall, she shouted up to the twins' bedrooms. "They're here."

A knock sounded.

She swiped her hands over the front of her dress

before opening the front door.

Two hours later, the twins never came down.

Kellen leaned against the kitchen island. Her parents and Shawn's parents, Gina and Stephen, crowded around the counter space. Exhaustion filled her from head to toe. Her feet felt like blocks of pulverized meat, and her eyes were gritty from crying. Even her cheeks hurt from pasting on a fake smile. She kicked off her shoes, and a sigh escaped her lips. The cool tile refreshed her stocking-covered feet.

She stirred a spoon slowly in the coffee she had added milk and sugar to. Even lifting the cup to her lips was tiring, but she took a long sip, savoring the calm in the house and the closeness of family.

"I can't believe Shawn wasn't here." Gina shook her head. "He didn't even tell us he was leaving."

Kellen eyed her coffee a moment before peering at Shawn's parents.

Stephen brushed a hand over his trimmed brown beard. "He disappointed me."

The green stare that met hers was identical to his son's.

Kellen shrugged, but this time, it had far less attitude than the shrug she had given to Shawn. This shrug was one of defeat. "He's doing what he needs to do." For him.

"Sweetie…" Jasper cleared his throat. "Dana and Jensen made me the executor of their wills. I already filed them. We should all get together soon to go over their last wishes."

Her throat tightened. "Okay."

"When would you like us to read their will?"

Never. She'd rather not have to hear their last

words at all. She'd rather have Dana and Jensen alive. "Two days." Two days from now, nothing would be different, but maybe two days from now the task would be easier.

****

The rest of the day, visitors kept Kellen busy. Every ten minutes or so, friends and neighbors stopped by to express their deepest sympathies and to push pre-cooked meals and baked goods into her hands. She was figuring out how to shove four pans of meat lasagna and chicken casserole into the freezer when someone else rang the doorbell. She withdrew her icy hands from the freezer. While rubbing the feeling back into her numb fingers, she hurried to the front door.

Mrs. Spencer, a neighbor from down the street, smiled.

"Hello, Mrs. Spencer."

"Hello, dear. I brought meat loaf."

Kellen forced her face to stay relaxed and not to scrunch up. Meat loaf was not her favorite. "Thank you, Mrs. Spencer. How kind of you." She held the aluminum tin in her hands.

"What you're doing for your niece and nephew is wonderful."

Everyone who stopped by expressed something along the same lines. Kellen told Mrs. Spencer what she had told the others. "Thank you." That seemed easiest.

"Well, dear, if you need any help, you can call me or stop by."

Kellen presented her with the same smile she showed everyone else as they departed. Another "thank you" left her lips. Then she transported the meat loaf into the kitchen and set it on the counter.

"Ew. What's that?" Weston's nose was crinkled in the same way Kellen had wanted to do a moment ago.

She laughed. "It's meat loaf. You've never had it before?"

He eyed the pan as if he wanted to poke the meat loaf with a stick. "Nope. Never. And I don't think I want to try it now."

Kellen mashed her lips together to keep her laughter at bay. "Don't worry. We won't, because, and this is a secret…I don't like meat loaf, either."

Weston giggled.

The doorbell rang again, and Kellen groaned.

"Why is everyone bringing us food?"

"Because they think it's helpful."

"Well, maybe we should give them a menu of what we like before they bring anything else over."

Kellen tugged his earlobe. "I don't think it works that way, buddy. Why don't you escape upstairs before I open the door? I'll give you a three-second head start. One…"

Weston was gone in a shot.

She opened the door to Mrs. Bloom, who held a two-layer vanilla cake decorated with sliced strawberries. Now *this* Weston would like. The next delivery, though, made Kellen's eye twitch from straining to keep her face passive—lime gelatin with pineapple chunks. She jiggled the bowl in her hands, making the mold wiggle back and forth.

Roxon joined her. They both eyed the moving dessert.

"What flavor is it? Green apple?"

"No such luck, kid. It's lime."

Roxon's face scrunched up. "Why would anyone

think lime is a dessert flavor? Yuck."

"I have no idea." Kellen set the gelatin aside. Another knock made her whimper. "No more."

Roxon patted her arm. "You're on your own."

Mrs. Dawson had a turkey casserole. "You know, if you can't manage a turkey, this is a great alternative for the holidays."

Kellen's smile twitched. *Please don't remind me.*

Several more concerned people dropped off food. The final one turned out to be key lime pie. Kellen carried it into the kitchen where the island and countertops were packed. She held the pie, unsure of where to set it.

"Whoa." The twins showed up, one on either side.

Roxon peeked beneath aluminum foil. "What will we do with all of it?"

"Well, some of the casseroles and such will come in handy, but we definitely don't have room for it all. Maybe we can donate the rest. Many churches serve hot meals. I'm sure they'll appreciate this. Even the meat loaf."

"I say we keep all the desserts," Weston announced.

Kellen couldn't help but chuckle. Talking about the donated food was easy, and they needed easy right now. "I'm sure you would like that."

"Except the gelatin."

Roxon nodded, agreeing with Weston's wise ruling over the lime gelatin's fate.

"And this—" He stole the key lime pie out of Kellen's hands. "I have an idea about this."

"Oh, yeah? What?"

The pie flattened into Kellen's face. Whipped

cream oozed around the sides of the pie tin, getting into her ears and hair.

The twins squealed.

Kellen pried the pie tin off her face, and the whipped cream made an odd sucking sound. Globs of pie fell to the floor. A big clump plopped onto her right foot. She pushed her tongue through the remains of the dessert so she could talk. "That's not what I had in mind." Whipped cream sputtered from her lips. With her index fingers curled like hooks, she used them to swipe the gunk from her eyes. Her eyelashes were caked together and heavy, but she was able to see. "You." She pointed at Weston. "I'll get you back."

Weston hopped onto the balls of his feet. "No, you won't." And he was gone in the blink of a pie-covered eye.

Kellen fully intended to get him back.

****

That evening, Kellen sat on the couch, penning a story and failing miserably. She crossed off the paragraph she had just jotted down, using way too much ink in her frustration.

Roxon joined her. She picked up six balls of waded paper. "What's this?"

Kellen sighed. "Failed attempts."

"Being a writer looks hard." Roxon piled them onto the coffee table.

She smiled at her niece's observation. "You have no idea. Writing the story is just the start."

"If it's not easy, then why do you do it?"

"Because I love to write." Kellen set her pen down. "And the things we love to do the most are never easy. Our passion makes the hard parts worthwhile, though."

"Dad used to say something like that whenever I had a hard time remembering my lines for school plays." A hint of longing softened Roxon's voice.

Kellen couldn't be their dad, or their mom for that matter, but she could be herself, and she had many of the same values as Jensen did. She could still teach those values to the kids, as Jensen would've done.

"What are you going to do with these?" Roxon attempted to juggle three of the paper balls from Kellen's failed efforts. She missed a ball, though, and it bounced off the top of her head.

The two of them collapsed into giggles.

Kellen picked up a couple of paper balls and grinned. "I have an idea." She grabbed a stack of office paper from the recycling bin from the garage. "Let's make ammo." She crumpled a piece of paper with Shawn's name. Seeing it reminded her of the hours he had spent on his laptop, printing off reports and emails while he was there. And he left to do more of the same. Her anger made the ball of paper a little more compact than was necessary.

"Ammo for what?" Roxon balled a piece of paper in her hands.

"Let's have a paper ball fight. Us against West. This is payback for the pie to the face."

Roxon grinned. "Yes!"

By the time they finished, they had a mountain of paper balls between them.

"This will be our bunker." Kellen flipped the coffee table onto its side.

Roxon lowered onto her hands and knees behind the coffee table.

"Ready?" Kellen asked.

Roxon loaded ammo into her arms. "Ready."

"Hey, West," Kellen shouted. "Can you come into the living room please?"

Weston's response arrived a moment later. "Coming."

Snickering under their breaths, they listened to him clomp down the stairs. The second she spotted him, Kellen yelled, "Fire." And they tossed the paper balls. One hit him on the top of the head. Another whacked him on the shoulder. More sailed past him than made contact.

He burst into laughter and collected the paper balls that landed around him. He chucked them back. A ball bopped Kellen in the middle of her forehead.

That had Weston howling.

Kellen pitched a ball, and it hit Weston in his stomach.

"Oh, you've got me." He grabbed his belly. "Kidding. I have on a bulletproof vest." And he threw an armful of paper wads.

Yelping, Roxon and Kellen dove behind the coffee table.

Paper pelted their backs.

The three of them played until they were too tired to throw another ball of paper. And for that bit of normalcy and fun, Kellen was grateful.

Chapter Ten

For the first time in Shawn's life, each work day dragged on. He'd be immersed in his work, and then the twins and Kellen would blaze through his mind and he'd lose all train of thought. All week he'd battled the disruption.

During a morning meeting about the partnership between Tokyo App and Global Imagination, which he helped secure, he found himself tuning out.

"Shawn, do you have anything else you'd like to add?"

Mr. Harris' voice snapped him back to reality.

Everyone in the meeting was staring.

He glanced at his laptop. He hadn't written a single note. "No, you covered everything."

Mr. Harris nodded. "All right. I think we're good today. Thank you, everyone."

With a glance at his watch, Shawn gathered his laptop and headed toward the exit.

"Shawn?"

He turned back. "Yes, sir?"

Mr. Harris studied him from the head of the table. "Are you sure you're ready to return to work? You lost two loved ones. You have the right to take a few days off. And you can."

A lump formed in Shawn's throat. He hated how everyone at his job knew about his sister and brother-in-law. "I appreciate that, sir, but this is where I need to be."

Mr. Harris tilted his head to the side. "Shawn, your job and position are secure here. You don't have to worry about losing your project or jeopardizing any promotions you could be up for."

Shawn swallowed. *Could* be up for? That didn't sound like he had the promotion in the bag anymore.

"You can take a little time off to deal with everything," Mr. Harris continued.

Shawn slipped a hand into his coat pocket. "Thank you, sir, but I'm doing okay."

"All right. Just remember what I said."

"I will." He returned to his office. Once there, a Sky call was coming in on his computer. He rushed around his desk. Dropping into his desk chair, he snatched the computer mouse. He tapped the button repeatedly to activate the call.

An image appeared on the screen.

The entire family—minus the twins—gathered in the den at Dana and Jensen's house. Everyone stared at the screen, including his parents, but not Kellen, as if she didn't even want to see him through a screen.

He cleared his throat. "Sorry. I was in a meeting."

Kellen looked at the ceiling, an act that said, *Of course, you were.*

"That's okay, Shawn." Jasper picked up a stack of papers. "Shall I begin?"

"Yes." Kellen's voice sounded small.

Shawn set aside the items he still clutched from the meeting. His hands shook, something he had long learned to control. To steady his hands, he gripped the armrests of his chair and scooted closer. "Yes."

Jasper flipped through stapled papers.

Shawn shifted his gaze to Kellen.

She sat stiffly beside Wanda, breathing deeply.

To his eyes, she appeared as though she was barely holding herself together. *I should be there with her, not here in my office.*

Jasper looked up from the papers. "First, and most importantly, they wanted both of you to be Roxon's and Weston's legal co-guardians."

A moment of silence followed that news.

Shawn gaped at the screen. *They want me to be the twins' guardian?*

Then Kellen shifted in her chair. "*Both* of us?"

Jasper nodded once. "Yes." He pulled out two envelopes from the file. "They wrote the two of you letters to explain their decisions." He passed one of the envelopes to Kellen.

She pulled out a letter and unfolded it. "It's from Jensen. 'Dear Kell—' "

"You don't have to read it now," Shawn said. "It's personal. Just for you. You don't have to read it in front of me."

For the first time, she connected her gaze with his through the screen, from miles away. "I want to." She peered back at the letter. " 'Dear Kellen, if you're reading this, then something none of us expected to ever happen has happened. I'm no longer with you.' " She paused and took a deep breath.

The emotion in her voice had tears biting Shawn's eyes.

" 'But don't worry, Twinie, because I live inside you.' " Kellen dropped the letter to her lap and covered her face with her hands.

Through the speakers, her muffled sobs met his ears.

Wanda hugged her as they wept.

Jasper passed them a tissue box.

Kellen tugged a tissue free and wiped away her tears. Then, clutching the tissue, and sniffing, she picked up the letter again. " 'And that's why Dana and I are granting you co-guardianship of Roxon and Weston. Being my twin, you embody everything I am. We grew up together and have the same values. No one knows me better than you do, and you can tell the twins all about me, what we were like as kids, and remind them of their father whenever they need it…whenever they need me. You will be the mother figure they need in their lives, but you will also be the closest thing to their father left in this world. We love you, Kellen.' " She refolded the letter, stuffed it into the envelope, and clutched it in her hands.

Beside her, Jasper held the second envelope—the letter for Shawn. He wanted to hear Dana's words as he had heard Jensen's voice while Kellen read her letter. He'd have to wait until he received the letter in the mail before he could read it, though, and that would take too long. "Kellen." His voice was low. He waited for Kellen to meet his gaze through the screen. "Can you read mine? Please?"

After a second, she acknowledged his wish with a small nod. She opened the other envelope. Before she started, she met his gaze.

He inclined his head. "Go ahead."

She inhaled a slow breath. " 'Hey, Big Brother, I know this is coming as a shock that Jensen and I want you to help raise Roxon and Weston, but, Big Brother, you helped raise me, so I know you can do it. You are gentle but strong, smart but silly, and that is the kind of male role model we know the twins will need if we're gone. We understand you've built your life in a specific way and children are not a part of that, but we thought long and hard about this decision. And while we realize the twins would need you to keep them stable, we also thought you could use them in your life just as much. You must think we're nuts, but I think we're geniuses. Just think about it. With love. Forever. Dana.' "

Kellen slipped the letter into its envelope.

When she looked at the screen, her gaze burned into him. Dana had seen a grand design for him and his life, if he were to accept the responsibility, and he had already thrown it away. He peered at his hands, needing relief from Kellen's glare. She had said much the same before he left, and her gaze screamed those words again. That, on top of Dana's words, was a one-two punch to his gut. He was ruining his little sister's dream out of selfishness. But did he have to lose everything he had worked for in return?

"Would you like me to continue?"

The calm voice made Shawn lifted his gaze.

Jasper held the file in his hands and waited for Shawn's answer.

"Yes, please."

Jasper flipped a page. "Dana and Jensen left both of you the deed to their house, which is paid off."

Shawn blinked. *They'd paid off their mortgage already*? But that wasn't the most important question. He leaned forward. "Meaning?"

A smirk formed on Jasper's face. "Meaning they hoped the two of you would live in their house, under the same roof, while raising Roxon and Weston."

Kellen's jaw dropped. A little squeak escaped her mouth.

Shawn's own eyes bulged in shock.

"Obviously, they can't force you to live in this house together, even with their will, but cohabitation would go over better with a judge. Being a stable environment and all."

Shawn shook his head. "But I have a condo and a job in the city."

"You can commute." This came from Kellen.

Did she really want him living under the same roof as her? "You think this is a good idea?"

She let out a little chuckle. "Not necessarily, but it was their wish, and doing so would help our case. That's what's important. We could deal…to honor them and to do what's right for the twins."

Shawn combed his fingers through his hair. *Was* he right for the twins? He wasn't so sure. "I think…I think it would be better if I remained their uncle. Only. Not their guardian."

Kellen's mouth opened. She stared.

Silence buzzed in Shawn's ears. He would've preferred her to say something, anything, tell him he was selfish, stupid, taking Dana's gift for granted. Then again, she didn't have to voice any of that. Her shocked expression said it all.

Jasper glanced at Kellen and cleared his throat. "Well, you don't have to decide right this minute. Take some time to think it over."

Shawn peered at the files on his desk. His responsibilities were already being pushed to the side. He couldn't concentrate. If he took time to think over this life-changing decision, he could lose more valuable work time. But he owed it to Dana to give their decision serious thought before he signed away his rights as the twins' guardian. "I will."

Kellen crossed her arms. "What happens if Shawn refuses? Would that ruin my chances of becoming their legal guardian?"

"No. Shawn is allowed to refuse, and in that case, you'd be their sole guardian."

"Okay." Kellen eyed the screen. "I'll do it alone."

Her words punched him in the gut.

"What do I have to do? I want to begin immediately."

Gina patted a file on her lap. "We have all the forms here. We'll help you fill them out. Then Stephen and Jasper will take you to file them, and Wanda and I will stay here to keep an eye on the twins."

Kellen faced her father. "How long until I see a judge?"

"Could be nine to ten weeks."

"And in the meantime?"

"Temporary guardianship takes effect immediately."

"Good."

Wanda held her hand. "We believe you"—she faced the computer—"and Shawn are what's right for the twins, but…" She shifted back to Kellen. "…even if Shawn decides not to be a co-guardian, we know you are the best guardian for them. We'll help you every step of the way."

"Thank you." Kellen took a deep breath. "Could you give me a moment? I'll meet you all in the dining room to fill out the forms in a minute."

Stephen patted her shoulder. "Of course."

The four of them gave her a hug one at a time before leaving the den.

Then just the two of them remained, but her back was to the laptop.

She lifted her hands and covered her face.

His heart wrenched. Why hadn't he inquired if missing the meeting would be okay? Why hadn't he done anything and everything in order to be there? At least, they could've talked things out face to face. "Kellen?"

She stiffened, as if she'd forgotten he was there.

"I'm so sorry," he said.

"Don't."

That single word was like a switchblade to his liver.

She stepped closer. "You do what you have to do. I'll do what I have to do, which I guess means I'm going it alone."

"Kell—"

"Bye, Shawn." She reached out, and the connection ended.

For several minutes, he sat with his head back and his eyes closed.

What do I do? What do I do?

He had no idea. Perhaps he should get to work. He picked up his pen and held it poised over his notepad. Nothing. Not a single thing came to mind regarding the project he needed to create to land him the promotion he coveted. He lowered his right hand to the notepad and wrote what he had on his mind:

Roxon.

Weston.

Kellen.

Seeing those three names propelled him to his feet. He knocked on his boss's door.

Mr. Harris swiveled away from his computer. "Shawn." He lifted a hand and waved Shawn into the room. "What can I do for you?"

Shawn approached his desk. "I heard my sister's will. I need the rest of the day to think things over. Is that okay?"

"Absolutely. Whatever you need. You can take tomorrow off, too."

Panic fluttered through him. He didn't want Mr. Harris to think he couldn't handle his personal life. Requesting time off could jeopardize his future. "No. I'll be okay. I just need today. I'll be back in my head space and working tomorrow."

Mr. Harris's eyes squinted for a fraction of a second. "I'm not worried about that. If you need anything, let me know."

"Thanks, sir."

Shawn drove to his condo. The walls were blinding white, and the tile at his feet was also white. The furniture was sparse, and the kitchen was all chrome and black. His condo didn't hold life. Nothing in it revealed who he was as a person—no personality, no colors, no clutter, and no mementos. Was *he* empty? Was *he* bland? He hadn't even bothered to set out pictures of his family. A picture of his parents did occupy a place on the mantel, and it shamed him to know he didn't have a picture of Dana and Jensen or the twins.

His job was his life. He spent most of his time in his office. The moments he left his office were fleeting.

The time he spent in this condo was for eating, sleeping, and getting ready for another day at work. His condo had served its purpose, but now, he recognized it as an empty shell.

With purposeful movements, he retrieved his rolling suitcase from the closet and packed his clothes. He grabbed a few suits, which he hung on the hooks in the backseat of his car. During the drive, he never once reconsidered his plan or thought he was making the wrong decision.

About an hour later, he pulled up to Dana and Jensen's house. The outside lights cast a glow. Silence dominated the night, but the house called out to him. He collected his suitcase and suits and proceeded to the front door.

This is it. He knocked briskly and waited for it to open.

When it did, Kellen stood there in her cotton pajama bottoms and a long-sleeved pink top. Her naturally curly hair was pulled into a ponytail, and her face was bare of makeup.

She looked beautiful, even with her eyes wide and her jaw slack.

"W-what are you doing here?"

"I'm your new roommate."

Chapter Eleven

Shawn slipped past Kellen into the house.

She blinked at the darkness beyond the glowing circle from the porch light. The smell of cinnamon and cloves wafted in after him. The scents wakened her mind, and she whirled around to watch Shawn making his way toward the couch with his suitcase and suits in hand. She hadn't expected this, but his decision delighted her. He must've changed his mind, saw the light, and realized how much he was needed.

Smiling to herself, she retrieved a blanket and two pillows from the linen closet.

In the living room, Shawn had stowed the suitcase beside the couch and laid out his suits over the back of Jensen's recliner.

She set the bundle on the coffee table. "Did you eat dinner?"

He shook his head. "I drove straight through dinner."

"Well, you're in luck. We had lasagna a neighbor dropped off. I'll heat you a plate."

"Thank you." He paused. "Did you file the guardianship forms?"

"Yeah." *Was he changing his mind*? "Will you...will you be signing the guardianship papers?" She diverted her gaze.

"I don't know yet."

Kellen stared silently for a handful of seconds before the tension in the air pushed her to the kitchen. She kept him company while he ate. To make the moment less awkward, she nibbled on graham crackers and peanut butter and drank milk. "So, what made you come back?"

Shawn washed down a bite of lasagna with a swallow of soda. "I can't say for sure." He paused while pushing cheese and sauce-covered meat and noodles around on his plate. "All I know is, it made sense."

For Kellen, it had also made sense. But how he could go from leaving so suddenly, being vehement he had to get back to his life in the city, to showing up on their doorstep and wanting a place in their family? Kellen shifted on the stool. *Our family*? The four of them were indeed family, but were they *a* family? She didn't know. She drank the last of her milk and dusted graham cracker crumbs from her hands. "I'm off to bed. If you need anything, let me know."

He inclined his head.

She left him to the remains of his meal. Upstairs, in the guest bedroom, with its calming, pale yellow walls and bedspread, she lay down, anticipating the twins' reactions upon seeing their uncle had come back home. That last bit made her swallow. Calling this house his home wasn't fair yet. It might be her home, but he could end up not wanting it for his own.

Come morning, she was skeptical. Would he stay or would he go?

Shawn sat at the island with a coffee cup when she ventured down for breakfast.

She filled her cup. "Did you sleep okay?"

"I cricked my neck." He wrenched his head from side to side to undo any painful knots he gained from sleeping on the couch.

Kellen pursed her lips as she stirred sugar and a splash of milk into her caffeinated concoction. The couch was definitely too small. "Maybe we can switch. I could sleep on the couch until we figure out better arrangements, and you can take the guest bedroom. You'd be more comfortable there."

"No."

Kellen looked up at his quick answer and sharp tone.

"You might think I'm a jerk because I left, but I was raised to be a gentleman. The room is yours."

She gave him a small smile.

Upstairs, a door opened.

They turned their attentions to the ceiling and listened.

Small feet treaded across the floor as the twins stirred.

"What should we tell them?" she whispered. She wasn't positive what to call this situation herself.

"We don't have to define it or explain it just yet."

"Okay." Giving everyone time to cope with the changes happening was the right thing to do.

She scrutinized the cabinets for the makings of breakfast. She found a bottle of vanilla and ground cinnamon and lined them up next to a bag of white bread. From the refrigerator, she selected three eggs. Being careful not to get a single fragment of eggshell in the bowl, she cracked open the eggs. She whisked in a sprinkle of cinnamon and a dose of vanilla to make French toast.

Behind her, a skillet sizzled with butter. She dipped a slice of bread into the eggs until it soaked up enough of the mixture. The soggy bread threatened to fall apart as she transported it to the hot skillet. Instantly, the smell of sweet vanilla and cinnamon circled around her, filling the kitchen with its deliciousness.

The padding of twin feet coming down the stairs had her turning toward the entry way.

Roxon and Weston froze at the threshold between the two rooms. Then they launched forward. "Uncle Shawn." They flanked his chair and threw their arms around him.

Their delight brightened Kellen's mood.

"Are you back?"

Weston's innocent question and wide eyes made her heart stutter.

"I'm back." Shawn looped an arm around them, returning their embrace.

Those two words held so much meaning for the twins, so much promise of having a complete family, as broken as it might be without their parents. Hoping those words would last and he'd stay for a long time, Kellen faced the skillet and flipped the French toast so their undersides could become a beautiful golden brown. "Who wants French toast?"

"I do." The twins raised their hands.

"Whatever scraps they leave, give them to me," Shawn said.

"Would you like it in a dog bowl?" Kellen teased.

"Nah. You can just plop it onto the counter here, and I'll eat it with my mouth."

The twins howled with laughter. By the end of breakfast, they had syrup sticking to their mouths and chins.

"Go upstairs, wash your faces, and change. We have to drop off all that food at the church. But first—" She popped open a vitamin container and plucked out two chewable tablets. "Here, have your vitamins."

They each snatched one before scurrying away.

Kellen glanced at Shawn as he carried the twins' plates to the sink. "Do you want to help us deliver the food? Or do you have to work?"

He returned to his place to continue eating. "It's the weekend."

"Well, I figured you worked on the weekends."

"Nope. Even I need a break from work."

Kellen mulled this over while rinsing off the plates. "What about your condo?"

"I suppose I'll sell it. Or I can rent it."

"And your girlfriend?" She picked up her coffee.

"Will I rent my girlfriend?"

Kellen almost spat out her coffee. She covered her mouth as she coughed and laughed. "No." She gasped. "I meant what does your girlfriend think about all this?"

"I don't have a girlfriend."

"Really?" Kellen had imagined many women in his life—sophisticated women in expensive clothes, shoes, and jewelry with sleek hair and manicured nails. She peeked at her own nails. On her right hand, three of her nails were stained with blue ink.

"I'm focused on my job," Shawn said.

"I see." And she thought she did; Shawn didn't care as much for relationships as he did his career.

He narrowed his eyelids. "And where's *your* boyfriend?"

Kellen thought of her skeleton boyfriend waiting

faithfully for her to return to her apartment and binge-watch TV. She couldn't very well tell Shawn about him, so she stuck a hand on her hip. "I don't have much opportunity to meet guys when I'm locked up in my studio apartment writing."

At least, not ones who aren't plastic.

"So, you're saying we're *both* workaholics."

Meaning they worked so hard they didn't have dating lives. Well played. "I'm not a workaholic," Kellen objected. "I get out a lot. Who here flaked out on last year's Halloween party?"

Shawn wagged his fork. "Family functions don't count. Who can you meet at a party with only family?"

Her cheeks burned. She couldn't help but think of when they were kids and she'd had a huge crush on him, and then the awkwardness that had consumed her when Jensen started to date Dana. By marriage, the two of them were technically family. She swallowed. "Friends were there, too."

Shawn laughed. "Jensen's and Dana's work friends and the parents of the twins' friends from school."

She folded her arms. "Are you calling that slim pickings?"

"It's just not for me."

"And how has meeting someone at your job worked out, Mr. Workaholic?"

He smirked.

"So? Do you want to come with us to drop off the food at the church? You could meet someone."

"So could you." He winked before leaving.

She glared after him. *Smart aleck.*

Then she became aware of a pair of eyes watching her, and she found Roxon smiling mischievously.

"What?"

"You don't have to go out to meet anyone, Aunt Kellen," Roxon said. "There's a man living right under this roof."

Their niece had heard their conversation. Nothing could mortify Kellen more.

Roxon giggled and skipped out of the kitchen.

Kellen stared blankly at the wall with her mouth hanging open. She stood there a while, disbelieving her ten-year-old niece had just given her dating advice.

"When I did that once, a fly flew into my mouth."

Kellen snapped her mouth shut and peered at Weston in the kitchen's entryway. "What is it with you and your sister this morning?"

Weston shrugged. "We had our vitamins."

Who knew vitamins could make kids feisty?

****

With the trunk of Shawn's car packed, Kellen sat in the front seat while Shawn drove to the church Kellen and Jenson had attended as children. One by one, she and the others carried in the frozen meals and desserts.

Carrie, a petite woman with bronze skin who operated the pantry and daily free soup kitchen, shook their hands. "This is wonderful. It'll really help out. Thank you."

"You're welcome. Everyone's intentions are kind, but we really had more than we could handle."

"I understand, and I'm sorry for your loss."

Kellen smiled, accepting her sympathy and adding it to the already teetering tower of apologies and grief she'd received thus far.

Carrie pulled a hairnet over her black bun. "Would

the four of you like to stay during lunch and help serve this food?"

Kellen peered toward Shawn and the twins. "You know, I think that'll be good for us. I'll go tell them." She joined the three of them. "Guess what? We've been invited to help serve today's lunch."

Weston and Roxon exchanged looks. Their faces scrunched up and their brows lowered.

"You mean to homeless people?" Weston asked.

"They're not all homeless. A lot of people are just down on their luck and going through a tough time. But even if they are homeless, they are worthy, and we shouldn't judge them or their circumstances. One hot meal can really make a difference. Come on. What do you say? Do you want to make someone's day a little bit better and fill some hungry bellies?"

Shawn held up a hand. "I'm game."

His willingness surprised Kellen.

The twins stared, too.

She figured the twins were just as surprised, but perhaps they'd change their mind if their cool uncle was up for serving food to strangers. "Well, what say you?"

They sighed. "Okay."

Wearing aprons, hairnets, and gloves, they stood behind the counter, ready to serve food. Shawn manned the warming trays containing the main courses—a choice between spinach and cheese lasagna or meat loaf. Weston held clear, plastic tongs to pass out rolls. Roxon stood guard at the dessert counter where slices of vanilla cake sat on paper plates.

Kellen occupied the sides' station. She studied her helpers with pride, but the sight of Shawn made her snort with laughter. The hairnet covered his perfectly groomed hair, and the elastic cut across his forehead, making him look absolutely silly. Never would she have expected to see business-suit Shawn sporting soup kitchen attire.

"Are you laughing at me?"

"You and your hairnet."

Shawn adjusted the hairnet. "I'll have you know, I am rocking this hairnet."

Weston and Roxon laughed and so did Kellen. The longer she was around Shawn, the more she glimpsed another side other than the businessman—the fun side. And she enjoyed it as much as the twins did.

Carrie opened the doors to the cafeteria.

A flood of people entered.

Kellen had a startling moment of clarity right then. She'd had no idea how many people in her community went to bed hungry every night and relied on the soup kitchen to fill their bellies at least once a day. People of all ages were there—the elderly who should have someone looking out for their well-being, people her age who were promising individuals but got struck a blow, and an eye-opening number of college students who couldn't afford to eat but needed food to nourish their minds.

One gray-haired woman with a walker said she trekked from her home each day to get a meal, and she had such bad knees that she fell a lot.

A young mother, holding a baby to her chest, didn't have the sort of help all mothers should be blessed to have and prayed for enough gas in her car to get her to the church for a tray of food and a bottle of milk.

Three children circled around a couple, who had recently lost their jobs.

Kellen peeked at Weston and Roxon to see them share a quiet glance. In that moment, Kellen had a feeling they were counting all the things they were grateful for, in light of their deep, life-altering loss.

Roxon politely asked the children if they wanted cake, using a voice that sounded as if she was talking to a younger sibling she doted upon. She received eager nods and passed the kids thick slices of cake.

Kellen enjoyed the time she spent serving lunch. She piled mashed potatoes, mac and cheese, and vegetables onto the plates presented to her and spoke to many different people of all races, faiths, and ages. They shared their stories of what brought them there that day. Each story touched her heart.

College students shared their struggle with loans and how they were unable to balance working hours with their heavy course load. Each of them strove toward degrees that would later impact the world and help many people, maybe even save lives.

A man in his early thirties told her the tale of how a fire that started in another apartment wiped out his apartment and everything he owned. To add insult to injury, his job cut his hours so he couldn't afford to save for another place to live. Right now, he was sleeping on someone's couch, but that person restricted him from eating the food in the fridge because he couldn't contribute.

Kellen shook her head at his plight and gave him an extra serving of mac and cheese. She stole glances at Shawn throughout. No longer did he have the face of a privileged man who never had to worry about where his next meal would come from. Now he resembled a man impacted by the people around them. She hadn't realized how this would affect Shawn. She thought it would be good for the twins to see many people were without the things they've always been privileged to have in their lives. Not every child had a cell phone, toys, a bed, or food. Sometimes, their only meal came from the school cafeteria.

She recalled how, when the twins were younger, they had been confused over the fact Kellen didn't have a credit card. They had seen their parents using them and innocently assumed everyone had one. They also couldn't understand why she didn't have all the gadgets they owned, and she had to explain not everyone had the money for things like cell phones, tablets, and flat screen TVs. This was the first time she noticed understanding dawn in their young minds.

Kellen gave the last person in line a helping of all three sides and leaned against the counter. While peering out at the room, she sighed, satisfaction filling her. Hands lifted forks to mouths as the attendees devoured the food Kellen and the twins had rejected out of selfish dislike or because they couldn't fit it in the freezer. Laughter and smiling faces existed now that hadn't been there when they were waiting in line.

The children skipped around the room, playing a game of tag and being as lively as all children should be.

Still wearing her apron, Kellen wrapped an arm around the twins. "Do you see that?" She indicated the crowd. "We did that with the food we didn't want…meat loaf…green bean casserole." She scrunched up her nose and smiled. "But do you see how happy that food is making everyone else?"

The twins nodded.

"Makes you realize how what you have and might not want can be everything someone else needs, doesn't it? That we are privileged enough to turn up our noses at certain foods, but there are people out there who would be so grateful for it."

The twins nodded again and smiled.

Carrie joined them then. "Did you work up an appetite?"

Weston patted his tummy. "Yes."

"You all can grab yourselves some food. Volunteers eat for free."

The twins scurried over to fetch a tray.

Carrie laid a hand on Kellen's arm. "You, too, honey."

"Oh, no, I'm okay."

Carrie settled her fists on her hips. "You gave us all that food we set out today, plus more. And what's left will spoil, so eat up." She eyed Shawn. "You, too."

"Yes, ma'am." He picked up two trays and gave one to Kellen.

The four of them finished off the lasagna and sides, and the twins snagged the last of the dessert. They sat at the table where the family of five ate their meals.

The twins scarfed their food, not caring they had vetoed this same food as a potential meal at home. As soon as they finished, they ditched Kellen and Shawn to play with the three other children—Nick, Danny, and Renee.

Seeing their childish delight made Kellen smile. This experience taught the twins a valuable lesson and rewarded them with three new friends. "If you ever want to have a playdate, let me know," Kellen told Imani, the mom of the three kids.

"Oh, I will." Imani pointed at her children. "I haven't seen them that happy or having this much fun in a long time."

Kellen gave Imani her number and a parting hug.

In the car, the twins jabbered away about their new friends.

"And they go to our school," Weston said.

"That's awesome. You could see them on Monday."

Roxon clapped her hands. "I can't wait."

Their excitement to return to school for the first time since the funerals relieved Kellen. She hoped it'd last, but when the car pulled onto the driveway, Kellen found an array of potted plants and bouquets of flowers—gifts from well-meaning individuals that made reality come crashing down. Standing in front of the welcome mat, the four of them stared at the collection.

Roxon sighed. "Even if we put them in water, the flowers will die."

"And the plants could die, too, even if we plant them," Weston said.

Kellen swallowed. She looked to Shawn for assistance.

"Maybe not," he said. "We could place the potted plants in a secret spot and come back later to see how they're doing. Only we will know where they are, and they'll do much better in the wild."

"That's a great idea," she said. "We can make a fairy garden in the woods with glass gemstones and a decorated bird house. There are other plants inside and a bunch of vases of flowers. We could donate those to a nursing home."

Weston and Roxon peered at one another.

"Mom would like that," Roxon finally said. "She believed in recycling and giving to others. She often volunteered at the nursing home to read to the residents there."

Kellen nodded. "Your mom was an amazing person." She aimed her smile at Shawn, who had helped Dana become the woman she was by being such a caring brother.

"We have a bunch of craft stuff," Roxon offered.

Weston pointed to the backyard. "And there's an extra birdhouse in the gardening shed."

They gathered paint containers of every color of the rainbow and sat at the kitchen island. Kellen and the twins dipped paint brushes in colors of their choosing and designed the four walls of the birdhouse. They made it resemble a real house by painting on windows and curtains, flowers and grass along the edges, and a roof that replicated the sky with fluffy clouds and a couple of bird silhouettes.

While they worked, Shawn sat off to the side, texting the entire time.

Kellen supposed his time away from work had been too long.

The twins kept glancing at him, too.

But he was too consumed in whatever conversation was unfolding on his phone to notice.

When they finished the birdhouse, they loaded their fairy garden supplies, small shovels, and all the plants and flowers, including the vases, into the car.

"Is Uncle Shawn coming, too?" Weston wanted to

know.

"I don't know. I'll go ask." Kellen returned to the kitchen to find Shawn still engrossed with his phone. "Hey, the twins want to know if you're coming."

A few seconds went by before Shawn looked up and peered around. "Uh…"

"Nice to have your attention. Are you coming to the park with us?"

"Um." He glanced back at his phone.

"It was your idea. It'd be good if you were there for this. And you said you don't work on the weekends."

He gripped his phone. "I know. I just have something I need to take care of."

"Okay, well, I guess we'll be going then."

He nodded absentmindedly.

But he had already dismissed her. Whatever his job required of his time at that moment, she hoped it would be worth it. She stepped outside and saw the twins' disappointment in the way their shoulders lowered when Shawn didn't come out of the house behind her. "Your uncle has some work to do, but we'll do this ourselves. It'll be fun." She rubbed their shoulders. "I promise."

****

The trees in the park were lush with the rustic colors of autumn and a few bright green leaves scattered throughout. Some of those leaves speckled the ground like Mother Nature's jewels.

Weston pointed. "They look like juicy, chewy candy."

Beneath Kellen's feet, the grass was soft. Each step had the soles of her sneakers sinking an inch. She drew in as much of the fresh air as she could. "You smell that?" Kellen and the twins paused in the middle of the autumn wonderland and inhaled. "That lovely, earthy smell is autumn, my friends, the season where Mother Nature begins to hibernate for its long winter's nap."

Roxon bent down and picked up a red sugar maple leaf. The edges were curled, and it crinkled in her fingers. "But isn't it all dying?"

Kellen winced. *Why did I say that?* Reprimanding herself, she set the box of supplies on the ground and lowered to her knees to be level with their faces. "It appears that way, but these trees are strong and healthy. And even the flowers that seem to wither will bloom again in the spring. They're called perennials. Their bulbs stay in the ground, and they know when to grow every year."

Weston blinked wide eyes. "Kind of like magic?"

"A lot like magic."

"I wish people could do that," Roxon whispered.

Kellen squeezed their hands. "Me, too." Deciding against talking about reincarnation, she hefted the box again and led them to the woods. A chippering sound caught Kellen's attention. She scanned the roots of a tree to see a squirrel holding a pinecone. With a finger to her lips, she indicated for the twins to be quiet and pointed at the furry critter going about its business. They spied on it as it dug a shallow hole, stuck the pinecone inside, and covered it with leaves.

Its little arms reached here and there, and the squirrel patted the leaves into place with frantic movements, as if getting everything perfect, every leaf, every grain of dirt.

Behind their cupped hands, they giggled.

"Does he think it's a nut?" Weston wondered.

"Apparently."

When the squirrel finished, it scurried up the tree and disappeared into the colorful canopy.

They continued their leisurely stroll, winding this way and that.

Kellen enjoyed the natural sights around them. Pine trees shot to the sky. Pomegranate shrubs with bright-yellow leaves carried red-skinned fruit in pairs of two. Late-season monarch butterflies with their fiery wings drifted on the breeze.

After a while, they stepped off the path and journeyed through the woods until they discovered a clearing not visible from the trail. Kellen set the supplies on the ground. "This is a good spot."

One by one, they worked the potted plants free, loosened the roots, and stuck them in fresh holes. They arranged the plants into the shape of a heart. In the middle sat the birdhouse, now renovated as a fairy home, and they scattered the glass stones throughout the rest of the space. The sun reflected off the glass, sending spears of pink, purple, and blue light dancing among the leaves.

Kellen sat for a long time, imagining the beams and orbs of light were fairies. Reluctantly, she packed their things and promised the twins that they'd return a few times every year to revisit the magic throughout the changing seasons.

****

In their pajamas, the twins sat on Roxon's purple bed. "Are you and Uncle Shawn our mom and dad now?"

That was a question Kellen had been dreading. She

shook her head. "No one will ever replace your mom and dad. And we don't want to replace them." She glanced at Shawn, who stood nearby with his hands in his pockets.

He nodded. "That's right."

Sensing they needed more, Kellen continued. "We're your guardians. You can call us Aunt Kellen and Uncle Shawn for as long as you want to. Forever even."

The twins stared at their feet.

Their silence had Kellen chewing on her bottom lip.

Then Weston nudged Roxon.

They shared a look and nodded at each other.

Roxon gazed at Kellen with her wide brown eyes. "Are you going to get married?"

And just like that, the twins' eyes lit with the possibility.

Kellen, on the other hand, sputtered. Her cheeks blazed with heat, and she wished she could hide their embarrassed color.

"Whoa." Shawn held up a hand. "Let's not get hasty."

"Y-yeah," Kellen said, "marriage is a big deal. We don't have to be married to care for the two of you. We'll still be a family, though."

"But the two of you are living together," Roxon pointed out.

The statement reminded Kellen of what she had said that morning about there being a man under this very roof...a man Kellen could date. Kellen rubbed her burning cheek. "We're roommates. That's all."

Shawn stepped closer. "Men and women can be

roommates without being in any sort of relationship, but we are friends, and we already are family. That's enough."

Kellen frowned. *That's enough?* She forced a smile. "Yes, that's enough. Isn't it?"

The twins nodded.

"Okay, it's time for bed." She gave them each a hug. Once bedtime prayers were recited, Kellen stepped out into the hall at the same time as Shawn. They stood there, avoiding eye contact. Finally, Kellen wished him goodnight.

He stammered the same back.

She beat a hasty retreat to the guest bedroom. On the other side of the door, she listened to his footsteps as he climbed down the stairs. She no longer knew what she expected from Shawn, but he clearly didn't want any kind of commitment. She wondered how he'd commit to these kids. Or if he even would.

Chapter Twelve

Sunday morning, Shawn woke to Kellen hauling a Christmas tree box into the house from the garage. He rubbed the sleep from his eyes. What kind of woman wrestled a Christmas tree box into the house at six o'clock in the morning? And in September? Kellen did. He shuffled past the kitchen and into the little hallway that led to the garage door, which was open.

Kellen was attempting to shimmy the box for an eight-foot tree through the small entrance. She let out a grunt. When she tugged it, she ended up stubbing her toe on the bottom of the box. She hopped in place. "Ow."

Shawn stifled a laugh. "You know people are sleeping, right?

A clump of dark hair had fallen loose from the messy bun atop her head. She let out a huff that lifted the hair from her face, but it settled over her right eye. "Yes, I know, which is why this is perfect. I want to set up the tree before the twins wake up. That is, if I can get this enormous box through this door. I swear the doorframe is shrinking."

Shawn scratched his head. "Isn't it a couple of months too early?"

Kellen wiggled the box another inch. "Yeah, but I thought it would be fun to decorate a Halloween tree."

Shawn couldn't deny the logic. Christmas trees

were fun, even when decorated for other holidays. Not that he'd had one in years, but still. "Okay. Here, I'll help." He wrapped his arms around the box and gave a great heave that caused the box to tip backward, sandwiching them to the wall.

"I can't breathe," Kellen rasped.

Shawn shoved the box off them, but he gave a little too much oomph. And since they were both holding onto it, they tipped forward and nearly tumbled through the open doorway, but he righted them again. "Well, that didn't go too well."

Kellen let out a breath. "No kidding."

"Let's just do your little shimmying technique. I'll maneuver this side, and you can do that side." He pointed to the opposite end.

She slipped between the box and the wall to get to the other side.

Working together, they rotated the box slightly from side to side. A few wiggles and they maneuvered the box squarely in the middle of the hallway, but the box was so wide and the hallway so narrow that they had to continue to inch it along, more often swaying it from side to side. With the tight space and moving backward, he stubbed his own toe several times.

They finally succeeded in getting the box to the living room and laid it flat on the carpet. Now they were staring at it in matching poses, with their hands on their hips.

Kellen peeked from beneath heavy lashes. "So...would you like to assist me with getting this huge tree up?"

Shawn stared. He didn't know a thing about artificial Christmas trees or real ones, for that matter.

From his childhood, he remembered having to take out the metal and plastic branches one at a time and organize them in piles by letters, which indicated the size. After all the branches were in place, then came the fluffing process, which he disliked the most because of how the bristles would scratch his skin and make him feel itchy all over. And that was why he hadn't bothered with a tree as an adult. He hadn't needed to when his parents continued to host Christmas at their house. Then when Dana had a family, she gladly picked up the task.

Just thinking about Dana caused a pang in his heart. She had made the holidays special with truckloads of cookies, gallons of hot cocoa and eggnog, and decorations that would put the North Pole and Santa's workshop to shame. Without Dana and Jensen, this year would be different. And their absences would be felt by all. Every holiday would be different. But first, they had to get through Halloween. "I don't like putting these things together."

"These things?" Kellen chuckled. "No one really likes the hassle of putting up Christmas trees, but how pretty they are once they are up and decorated and sparkly is worth it. There's a reward at the end of the task. Besides that, the tree is massive. I could use a hand."

He let out a breath. He couldn't very well let Kellen struggle under the weight of an eight-foot fake Christmas tree. What kind of gentleman would that make him? Not a very good one. "All right."

Kellen's smile magnified in wattage. "Thank you." She ripped off the tape securing the box and flipped the flaps to reveal branches with tiny pinecones. When she lifted out a branch, she hauled out a whole section of the tree. "Oh wow." Straining, she pulled out what appeared to be a baby Christmas tree but was really just the top. "Look at this. It's pre-lit."

"Thank goodness." Half the battle was already done.

"Are you a Scrooge?" She gave a teasing smile.

"No, I appreciate the holidays. I just don't decorate."

"Do you work on Christmas?"

"Define 'work.' "

She let out a breath that lifted that clump of hair. "Paperwork, emails, phone calls, and texts related to your job."

With his hands in his pockets, he shuffled his feet. "Sometimes." Saying it out loud filled him with a great deal of shame. "But I'm always present at the party." *I am, right?* Swallowing, he thought back to last Christmas Eve. Had he taken a call during the gift exchange? Guilt filled him. He needed to move on from this conversation. "Um. Let's get this tree up."

At least the tree was easier to assemble than what he remembered from his childhood. A step ladder and a few pieces later and the tree was up. It just didn't look so great since the branches were all clumped together, showing holes and bare spots. He did his best to spread the bristles around and make the tree appear fuller, but Kellen ventured around to his section and rescued him.

Upstairs, one door opened, followed by another.

Kellen gasped. Her eyes lit up.

She bounced on her feet as if she were a child and this was *her* surprise. Then she scurried around the tree and plugged in the lights.

The twins came around the corner and halted. On their faces wasn't surprise. Their faces were blank.

Right away, Shawn realized something was wrong, and he could tell Kellen noticed it, too, because her happiness was rapidly deflating.

"We always decorate the tree in November with Mom and Dad," Weston said.

"I know." Kellen's voice was small. She glanced at the glowing Christmas tree beside her.

"But I thought it would be fun to create a Halloween tree. We could spend the day making a bunch of silly decorations, and we can cover the tree."

"There's no such thing as a Halloween tree," Weston said.

"Actually, there's a book called *The Halloween Tree* by Ray Bradbury. I could read it to you, and we can watch the movie, too."

"No," Weston shouted.

Kellen jolted.

"You're ruining everything." Weston spun on his heels and stormed up the stairs.

A second later, a door slammed.

"We did the tree with Mom and Dad the first full day of our November break. It was our tradition." Roxon shook her head at the tree. "This is stupid."

With that, she left.

Kellen stood there, looking stunned. Her shoulders had dropped several inches.

Shawn shifted in place. Kellen radiated defeat, and he didn't know how to fix that. The silence from upstairs was troubling, too. They did one right thing to help the twins, and then they were knocked back a dozen steps. They were on a teeter-totter with this whole guardianship thing and could fall off at any moment. From here on out, everything they did or said would impact the twins, and that was a big responsibility.

"I guess we should take it down." Kellen didn't face the tree when she said it, though.

He studied the tree. The twinkling lights were charming. Despite himself, he liked it. "Let's leave it for now. The twins might come around."

Kellen glanced at him.

Her eyes emitted more sadness than he liked to see.

"Okay," she whispered.

The rest of the day, the twins stayed upstairs.

Kellen sat in front of her laptop, typing a few words at a time and backspacing to delete those very same words.

Shawn replied back to emails while watching football.

The twins didn't even come down for lunch or dinner.

They left plates of food and waited for them to emerge.

That evening, Kellen carted a bunch of craft supplies to the kitchen island. Alone, she painted small foam balls and stuck fuzzy, black pipe cleaners into them for a spider's legs.

Seeing her making decorations by herself pulled on Shawn's heartstrings. So much so that he did something he hadn't done in forever and put his phone on silent. To top it off, he flipped his phone over onto the coffee table, hiding the screen, and he left it there when he shuffled into the kitchen. He sat on the stool across from Kellen and picked up a popsicle stick. "How exactly do I make a Halloween decoration out of this?"

Kellen gave him a small smile. "I'll show you."

With her instructions, he crafted small spiderwebs with popsicle sticks and white yarn. The last time he had done any arts and crafts was in elementary school, and he was one of those kids who used too much glue or loaded on more glitter than was necessary. He preferred digital art, but he found himself having fun and laughing along with Kellen when she giggled at his poor attempts. He scrutinized the tree. "Aren't popcorn garlands too Christmasy?"

"Not if we swap out the cranberries for candy corn. Jensen was obsessed with candy corn. He bought enough to last him a year. A few bags are in the cabinet."

"Good. I'll make a bag of popcorn. My skills might be better at stringing."

"Are you sure? Stringing involves a needle. Needles have pointy ends."

"I'll show you. You'll be impressed."

"Put the popcorn where your mouth is." She fetched a wrapped bag of popcorn from the pantry and tossed it to him.

He stuck it in the microwave and listened to the explosion of each little kernel. The microwave beeped, and he pinched the ends with his fingers to remove the steaming bag. Upon opening it, the delicious aroma of popcorn burst forth and seeped through the air. The smell was so intoxicating that his mouth watered instantly. While piercing kernels with a clean needle, he munched. One kernel for the string and three for his mouth. Not exactly the best way to string popcorn, but it worked. And it certainly made his stomach and taste buds happy.

But the popcorn had a stronger power than that; it lured the twins downstairs.

Out of the corner of his eye, he spotted them peeking around the corner.

The twins watched them for several minutes before stepping into the kitchen.

"Can we help?"

Kellen jumped at Weston's voice. "Yeah, of course."

The twins crept closer, showing the first signs of eagerness at the idea of making spooky ornaments. Kellen demonstrated how to make bats, witch's hats, monster faces, and fall leaves, and Shawn fixed the twins sandwiches to fill their empty bellies.

Once they had a mountain of strung popcorn and piles of handmade ornaments, they carried armloads of decorations into the living room. First, they wound the popcorn-and-candy-corn garland around the tree and stretched silk spiderwebbing across the branches. Then they began covering the Christmas tree with the decorations they'd made, with no strategy behind any of it.

The twins hung the ornaments anywhere and everywhere they could reach, Shawn helped to hook ornaments on the top, and Kellen stuck an orange crepe paper pumpkin on the highest bough. Afterward, they sat on the couch to admire their handiwork.

Shawn shifted his gaze to the mantel. A framed photo of Kellen and Shawn together occupied a spot above the fireplace. Shawn didn't even know when that photo had been taken. In the snapshot, his arm was around her shoulders, and Kellen's head was back as she laughed. He wished he could conjure that moment to the front of his mind, but no matter how hard he tried, he couldn't.

"It looks cool."

Roxon's voice drew Shawn's attention from the photo.

Yeah." Weston glanced shyly at Kellen. "Sorry for what I said earlier, Aunt Kellen. I didn't mean it."

"I'm sorry, too." Roxon pouted.

Kellen locked her arms around them. "It's okay. I understand. It'll be really different, and at times, it'll be sucky, but we have each other."

Everyone was silent for a moment before Roxon said, "Mom would've liked this. She loved to do art projects."

Unlike Shawn, Dana had always enjoyed art class and would have pieces honored in school art fairs. "Your mom was the Queen of Arts and Crafts. Although, I don't think she would've allowed us to string popcorn. A waste of food and all, and not to mention they can attract bugs."

"Bugs!"

The twins had opposite reactions. Roxon shivered in disgust while Weston's eyes grew big at the prospect.

Kellen laughed. "We won't get bugs. We can remove the popcorn from the strings later and give the pieces to the birds and squirrels. And we can still eat the candy corn." She patted the twins on their knees. "Okay. Time to get ready for bed. Upstairs."

The twins bounded away in a much better mood than they had started the day with. Kellen's idea to make ornaments and decorate the tree Halloween-style had been a good one. He wondered what he could do for the twins next; he didn't want Kellen to come up with everything herself or think he didn't care enough to do something on his own. But what *could* he do?

In front of the mantel, he eyed the framed picture of the two of them. "Hey," he called out to Kellen as she started up the stairs. "Do you remember when this picture was taken?"

"Sure. It was a few days after my college graduation when we had a family picnic. You told me I should write a story with you as the protagonist. You insisted it would be a bestseller. Dana snapped this picture right when you were saying you'd make the best book boyfriend of all time. I couldn't stop laughing."

As the memory returned, he smiled. That was a month before he landed his job at Global Imagination. He had a feeling that was the last time he had teased Kellen. Could he get that part of himself back? Could he be the man he once was? Lighthearted, cracking jokes, and not all-consumed in work?

The thought of the promotion he'd been striving toward for years slammed into his thoughts like a freight train. How could he be that man and work on the other side of the world? He couldn't. He'd have to choose one or the other. Which was more important? His job or being the man Dana would approve of? She'd be happy if he won the promotion, but she, not so secretly, had always held out hope he'd become a family man one day. And now…for the time being, he was one.

But not everything was meant to last.

Chapter Thirteen

Hours after everyone else went to bed, Kellen stayed up writing a story. Come morning, she doubted it was any good. To her, the story felt like the same ole, same ole, nothing special, nothing new or different. She rolled over in bed to check the clock on the bedside table and gasped when she realized she had slept in. According to the time, the twins should've woken a half an hour ago. Now she wouldn't have time to make them breakfast. She tossed off the covers, shot out of bed, and hurried to the twins' rooms, but their beds were already made.

Downstairs, she found the twins and Shawn in the kitchen. "I'm sorry I woke up late." She headed for the coffeepot and selected a cup to fill. "Did the two of you have breakfast?"

"Yup."

Coffee in hand, she studied the twins. The matching grins they wore had her narrowing her eyelids.

They hopped off their stools and skipped out of the room.

That was when she spotted the candy bar wrappers on the countertop. She glared at Shawn. "You let them eat candy for breakfast?"

"It had peanuts in it. Peanuts are protein." He smirked from over his own coffee.

"Peanuts don't count as nutritional when they're atop a thick layer of nougat and coated in caramel."

"Chocolate is healthy, though."

"Dark chocolate is healthy." She picked up the wrapper of one candy bar. Sticky caramel touched her fingers. "This is milk chocolate." Using her foot to step down on the lever, she opened the trash can and threw away the candy wrappers. Sweetness stuck to her fingers, so she licked it off. Although she wanted to do what Dana and Jenson would do, and they definitely wouldn't allow candy for breakfast, she couldn't deny that the hit of sugar she got from that little taste had been yummy.

"Come on, didn't you ever have candy for breakfast when you were a kid?"

She nodded. "Jenson and I would sneak it under our parents' noses."

"Kids will be kids, right?" Shawn set his coffee cup on the counter. "Candy for breakfast once won't harm them, and I thought it'd make them happy."

She sensed more was involved than Shawn was saying. Maybe he gave them candy for brownie points. If so, she could understand that. Neither of them knew what being parents and keeping children happy required. As an aunt, the task was easy. She could dote on them, have fun with them, and then go home. But this was her home now, and she couldn't just spoil them behind Jensen's and Dana's backs anymore. Now keeping the twins grounded and dealing with the aftermath when their grandparents spoiled them rotten was her responsibility. "I guess candy this once is okay."

The twins tiptoed back into the kitchen then.

"So, Uncle Shawn's not in trouble?" Roxon asked.

Kellen chuckled and nudged Shawn. "I can't exactly ground Uncle Shawn, now can I?"

He winked.

The action caused her to blush. What was it with Shawn that made her cheeks flame like that? No one else had ever given her that reaction. Even as kids, he would tease her and have her blushing all the way to her roots. Dana would tease her even further, always saying if Kellen and Shawn dated they'd really be sisters. When Kellen and Dana were little, that was the only thing they'd ever wanted, but then Dana started dating Jensen, so Kellen got off the hook. Except, the tingles Shawn created when he smiled at her had never gone away. "Did the two of you brush your teeth? I will do breath checks, if I have to."

The twins giggled. "We brushed." And they flashed their pearly whites.

She didn't see any chocolate or caramel between their teeth, so she took their word for it. Besides, she didn't really want to smell their breaths, especially if they hadn't brushed or at the very least used mouthwash. "Okay, backpacks, and we're off."

"Um, Aunt Kellen." Roxon pointed.

Kellen peered at her attire. She wore fuzzy orange pajama bottoms with black spiders and a matching spooky top. "I guess getting dropped off by your aunt in her pajamas would be embarrassing, wouldn't it?"

"Uh, yeah," Roxon said.

"Don't worry. I'll change." She changed into jeans and a hoodie, to which Roxon gave a thumbs-up.

They left at the same time as Shawn. He held the front door open. "I know you have work to do, too, so how about we alternate days and take turns dropping the twins off at school?"

"That would be nice. Thank you."

"See you tonight."

"Yeah, see ya." She ducked into the driver's seat of her car and waved to Shawn before backing out of the driveway and heading toward the twins' school.

"Aunt Kellen?"

"Yeah?" She glanced in the rearview mirror.

Roxon tilted her head to the side. "Do you like Uncle Shawn?"

Kellen frowned. "You've asked me this before."

"That was a year ago. Things can change."

So much like Dana.

"So…do you like him? *Like him* like him?"

Kellen stared straight ahead and mashed her lips together. She knew exactly what Roxon meant, but she had no idea how to answer that. "Umm…it's more complicated than that."

"Why?"

Because she couldn't even identify how she felt toward Shawn to herself, let alone to her niece and nephew. "When you get older, relationships can get complicated."

For several minutes, none of them spoke.

"Aunt Kellen?" This time it was Weston.

Her hands tensed on the wheel. "Yeah?" She held her breath, expecting another question about Shawn.

"What if everyone at school asks us about Mom and Dad?"

This was by far a harder question to answer. "Tell them you don't want to talk about it. You can say it makes you sad."

"It does," Roxon muttered.

"It makes me sad, too. If either of you need me, you can call me at any time. And if you want to come home because you're not ready to be in school, I can check you out. We can try another day. Does that sound good?"

They nodded. At the car loop, they squeezed between the two front seats and gave her a one-armed hug and a kiss on the cheek.

She smiled. "Have a good day, okay? And search for your new friends."

Their faces brightened at that.

"Nick and Danny," Weston said.

"And Renee," Roxon added.

Kellen was awarded with seeing their renewed excitement as they bounded out of the car and joined the crowd of students entering the school. "Please help them today," she whispered. "Get them through." Throat tight, she headed back home.

She was supposed to work until school pick-up time, but she couldn't stop thinking about the twins. How were they doing? Were their friends treating them okay? What about their teachers? She didn't want anyone to treat them as if they could shatter. What they needed now more than anything was normalcy. Homework. Spelling tests. Recess. Art and music class. They needed that to get through the day, the week, the month, the rest of the year. They required that to heal.

Sitting at the dining room table, she stared at her computer screen. *Maybe I should write a story about the twins.* They would get a kick out of that, seeing themselves as illustrated characters in print. She pondered the idea for an hour, but she couldn't think of a story that would do them justice, not when she was so worried about them. Every silly story that floated forth didn't work with the current situation. Maybe that was the point, though? Perhaps she should write a silly story featuring the twins, something to take their minds off their sadness. She believed stories had that power, that they could take you away from your pain, and make things better, for as long as you were in that story's world. And she wanted to do that for the twins, but nothing was good enough.

The fear of having writer's block had her pacing the floor, circling the table again and again. Writer's block could come on any given day. Sometimes, you could write for months, years even, and not ever come face-to-face with the beast, and then one day it emerged from the shadows with teeth made out of pencil stubs, nails leaking ink like blood, a fat eraser nose, and hair of shredded paper. And many writers could succumb to that beast as it leeched ideas and words from their minds and left behind only blankness, putting up any and every obstacle to keep them from sitting at their desks. Those blocks could be mental or physical. Kellen's block was definitely mental. She could write. She wasn't fatigued or burned out. She just didn't have a viable idea.

Pacing, she begged and pleaded for an idea to fall from the sky and bop her in the head. Nothing. Before she knew it, her phone's alarm alerted her to the time; she had to leave to pick up the twins from school. With a sigh, she plucked up her keys and trudged out the door.

The only thing that lifted her spirits was the scene she found in the car loop.

Weston and Roxon were with the three kids they had met at the pantry. They were laughing, bouncing on their feet, and being as wonderfully animated as happy kids could be.

A smile pulled on her lips. After frowning all day, her lips felt alive again.

Weston and Roxon waved to their new friends and bounded toward the car. They dove inside, still bursting with excitement, and buckled up.

She glanced in the rearview mirror as she started to drive. "Hey, how was your day?"

Weston shrugged. "It was okay. Everyone acted weird at first. It made me feel bad."

Kellen swallowed.

"But then we found Nick, Danny, and Renee at recess, and we played tag. Soon, almost everyone on the playground was playing tag with us. Danny said no one used to play with them before, but because we did, everyone else did, and now they have more friends."

"That's great. You see what a good deed can do? You helped at the church and met new friends. Then you played with them in school, which led to them getting even more friends."

Roxon nodded eagerly. Then her face transformed with seriousness. "I guess they used to get bullied a lot, but we won't let that happen anymore. Right, West?"

"Right."

The pride she had for her niece and nephew was all but bursting out of her. She couldn't wait to text Shawn about it.

Weston sat forward and waved a bright orange piece of paper near Kellen's head. "Our autumn festival is next Friday. Can we go?"

She pulled up to a red light and accepted the flyer. "Of course. We won't miss that for the world."

"Do you think Uncle Shawn will go?"

Kellen set the flyer on her lap and accelerated when the light turned green. "I'm not sure. He has a demanding job. Since I work from home, it's easier for me to take time off because I'm my own boss." Except for her publisher's deadline, but she wouldn't get into that. "We can ask him at dinner, though."

And she prayed he'd say *yes*.

At home, she fixed the twins ants on a log with cut celery sticks, peanut butter, and alternated craisins and raisins to represent the ants.

Weston laughed and called the craisins fire ants and the raisins carpenter ants. He had fun crunching into the celery and pretending he was really eating bugs.

Roxon just shook her head at her crazy brother.

The gesture reminded Kellen a lot of herself and Jensen, except she was usually the one being kooky, and Jensen had been the one shaking his head in embarrassment at his weird sister. How she missed that.

She helped them with their homework and then put food in the oven—yet another frozen meal but a pizza casserole this time. Anything with pepperoni and cheese gained ample approval from the twins. And it smelled delicious, too. She warmed garlic toast, letting the smell of garlic mingle with the scents of oregano and tomatoes.

The twins set the table.

She poured glasses of milk for the twins and goblets of Shiraz red wine for Shawn and herself.

Shawn came home at the exact moment Kellen

pulled the casserole out of the oven. He set his briefcase down and wandered into the kitchen.

"Uncle Shawn." The twins leapt up from their places and raced over to throw their arms around him.

His eyes widened as he embraced them.

Everything about him screamed amazed and even a level of discomfort. Kellen knew why they were so happy to see him, though. Today had been their first day back at school and their first time away from home since their loss.

"Hey, guys." He peered at Kellen.

In his eyes, she recognized the same question she'd fretted over—whether or not they'd had a good day. Having the twins react in that way toward him could mean it went either way. They could've had a wonderful day and were beyond delighted to tell him all about it. Or they could've had a miserable day and were relieved to see him and have him make everything better.

To ease his worries, she gave him a thumbs-up.

He relaxed his body, from his furrowed brows to his raised shoulders. A smile appeared on his face. He lowered onto his chair at the table. "So, what's for dinner?"

Weston stabbed a piece of pepperoni with a fork. "Pizza casserole."

"Sounds interesting."

Throughout dinner, the twins only had great things to say about Nick, Danny, and Renee. "Renee's favorite color is purple, too," Roxon gushed.

Weston shoveled a forkful of pizza casserole into his mouth and spoke with his cheeks full. "We had an idea."

Kellen shot him a disapproving look for talking with his mouth full.

He chewed and swallowed. "Sorry." He gave her a grin that allowed Kellen to see leftovers stuck between his teeth. "We thought we could go through our toys and stuff and give them what we don't use."

Shawn set his wine glass on the table. "That's a great idea."

Warmth filled Kellen. "I'm really proud of you two. You're doing something selfless that'll make their day."

"It was something you said before, Aunt Kellen, about what we have and might not want could be what others need." Roxon scooped up casserole. "Well, we have a lot of things we don't use that Nick, Danny, and Renee probably don't have."

And her pride only expanded.

"I can bring in boxes from the garage for the two of you to fill," Shawn offered.

Kellen smiled. "And I'll call their mom and set a time for when we can drop it all off. Maybe it'll turn into a playdate."

The twins bounced in their seats.

"Oh, let's not forget. Don't the two of you want to ask Uncle Shawn something?"

Shawn peered at her with raised brows.

"Oh yeah." Weston sprang from his chair to retrieve the flyer from the refrigerator. He returned, waving the piece of paper in the air like a flag. "Can you come to this?" He presented the flyer to Shawn.

"Um…"

That one syllable had Kellen wincing and the twins deflating. She knew what that meant.

"I'm not sure. Things are hectic at work with the holidays coming up and a promotion on the line."

She shook her head, hoping to convey with that one action that his answer wasn't good enough.

He sighed. "But I can ask my boss for a couple of hours off and see if it's granted."

The twins peered at their plates.

"Dad would've gotten the time off, no matter what," Weston said.

Roxon turned to Kellen. "May we be excused?"

Kellen glanced at their half-empty plates and nodded.

The twins shuffled away.

Shawn watched them leave. "I hate disappointing them."

"I know. So do I."

"And I hate disappointing you."

Kellen fidgeted under the power of his stare. "What do you mean?"

His shoulders slumped forward. "You get this really sad look in your eyes, and I don't like seeing that. Dana had that, too, and I see the same thing in the twins' eyes."

She picked at her nails as self-consciousness bubbled through her like fizzy water. "I understand your work is important, and this is a big change for you, but I don't know what I'd do if you weren't here."

"I feel the same way."

Admitting those things to each other was a big deal and carried a lot of meaning. She didn't quite know what it meant, but how her heart skipped a beat was a sure sign of something happening deep inside.

"And thank you for texting me earlier about the

twins wanting to take a stand against their new friends' bullies. They are awesome kids."

A smile lifted the corners of her lips. His acknowledgement of the text she'd sent him filled her with happiness. As much happiness as having Roxon and Weston for her niece and nephew. "They are."

Shawn held eye contact for several seconds. In that moment, they connected as the guardians for those amazing kids, knowing they had a little something to do with that.

Kellen wasn't a mother and had never known how rewarding it would feel to raise such great young individuals, and she had only just begun. For the first time, she had a feeling she could do it. Jensen and Dana had obviously thought she could, and they had been right. They had also thought Shawn could do it, and Kellen believed they had been correct there, too.

****

The next morning, Kellen beamed at the four boxes full of toys, clothes, and shoes the twins had weeded out of their possessions. While sipping her coffee, she called Imani to ask if they could meet after school for a playdate. "The twins have surprises for Nick, Danny, and Renee."

"That would be great. I know the kids would love to have more playtime with Roxon and Weston. All they did last night was talk about them. They are the first twins they've ever met, and the first kids at school to befriend them. It's been tough for them moving and attending a new school."

"Roxon and Weston were all about their new friends, too. The thought of seeing them yesterday at school pushed them out of the car."

Imani let out a breath on the other line. "How are they doing?"

"They have good moments and bad moments."

"And you?"

She didn't know what to say to someone asking about her feelings. She operated so much on doing what she needed to do that she often didn't share how she felt. "I have good moments and bad moments."

"And Shawn?"

"Same."

"How are the two of you doing together?"

"Um." Kellen squinted at the toaster as if the device had spoken and not Imani. "We're good." She had a feeling about what Imani was hinting at, but she wasn't having any of it. The fact a woman, who was a near stranger, could pick up any sort of tension between them caused Kellen's stomach to tighten.

"Mm-hm," Imani said. "Are the two of you playing nicely?"

"Sure." Kellen pressed her lips together.

Imani burst out laughing. "That 'sure' says so much more than you want it to." Her laughter only grew louder.

Kellen waited for Imani to restrain her giggles. "You know, the twins asked me yesterday if I like Shawn…*like him,* like him. And they questioned us the night before about whether or not we'll be getting married."

"As much as I want to laugh, I understand why they desire that. They probably feel having the two of you there isn't set in stone. In their minds, if the two of you marry, neither of you can leave them."

Kellen closed her eyes. She had speculated much

the same, but hearing someone else say it broke her heart, for she had no idea what Shawn would do, what he wanted, or how he felt. Things were very much up in the air.

A door closed upstairs.

The heavier tread down the stairs tipped her off that Shawn was approaching. "Hey, I have to go. Text me where you want to have the playdate and what time, and the three of us will be there."

"Will do. Bye."

"Bye." She set her phone on the counter.

Shawn shuffled into the kitchen while rubbing the back of his neck. Pain was painted across his face. "Morning."

"Morning." Kellen grimaced. "Your neck, huh?"

"Yeah." His voice seethed between his teeth.

"Why don't you take the guest bedroom? I can fit on the couch much more comfortably. And I don't mind. Really."

"No, you deserve the guest bedroom. And if my mother knew I stole a bedroom from a woman, she'd hit me upside the head."

Kellen snorted into her cup of coffee. "Well, she wouldn't have to know, and it'd only be temporary until we figure things out."

A little voice called out from the kitchen's entrance. "You can have Mom and Dad's room, Aunt Kellen."

That statement stopped Kellen's heart. She turned toward the entrance to see the twins huddled there, poking their heads around the corner. Clearly, they had been spying. Kellen hadn't even heard them come down the stairs. "No, we don't have to do anything with your mom and dad's room. Not until you're ready."

"But we want you to." Roxon stepped forth. "You could move the stuff out of your apartment into their room. And then Uncle Shawn could have the guest bedroom."

Kellen stole a peek at Shawn, who appeared at a loss for words, too. "How about we talk about this more later? Okay?"

They nodded as they climbed onto stools.

Kellen had no idea what to do with their request. The timing felt too soon to clear out Dana and Jensen's bedroom, and she wasn't sure how she'd feel about moving her stuff into their place. She doubted she'd be comfortable there. How would she even sleep? She pondered that while she scrambled eggs and buttered toast—a meal to counteract all the sugar from the breakfast Shawn had given them yesterday.

When they finished, they headed upstairs to get ready for school.

Shawn, dressed in dark gray dress pants and a crisp white button-up shirt, continued to sit at the island, drinking his coffee and popping granola clusters into his mouth.

His cinnamon-and-clove-scented cologne found its way to her nose, teasing her with the deliciousness of the aroma. He still had a bit of a five o'clock shadow going on, and she liked it. The stubble gave him a bit of a rugged look that complimented the rest of his polished appearance. She stirred her coffee. "How's work?"

He lifted his gaze from the bowl of granola clusters and settled on her. "Good. I'm pitching a new idea to my boss today. It could be a game changer."

"A new idea for what?"

He set his cup beside his phone. "My boss wants to create an app that revolves around community, and he will promote the project winner as management of the app department. Even better than that, the corporation in Japan I had a meeting with will create the app as our companies' first business venture together."

"That would be huge. What's your idea?"

"The twins actually inspired it. The app would be community based, allowing people in need to request items. For instance, families in need can ask for gently used clothing and toys for their children, teachers can ask for supplies, libraries can request books, shelters can post a notice for bedding and toiletries, and churches can put out a call for canned goods and non-perishable food items for pantries and free lunches. Then the app will alert members about donation opportunities in their area. Upon signing up, they can choose the distance from five miles to one hundred miles from their location. If they get an alert that they're able to or want to fulfill, they then respond to the request to get specifics and find out where to drop off their donations. When someone fulfills a donation, they note that in the app. Or if a donation is an on-going requirement, which would be the cases for churches and shelters, the request will remain active and will go out to new members when they sign up and be sent back out to all members every two or three months."

Kellen loved the idea of finding ways to help her community. "Will this app just be available for people in the United States or will people in other countries be able to take part?"

He raised his cup, took a sip, and lowered it again.

"This app will be available globally, so people all around the world can register. Members can also choose to get specific requests from outside their city or state or country if they don't mind shipping costs. So, if someone in Florida wants to help military families in California or even in Okinawa, Japan, they can."

Kellen blinked. "That is amazing. To come up with all those details. Wow. I never knew what you did, but that will change so many people's lives. You should tell the twins about it. They'll be thrilled they inspired this and that it could be an app used around the world."

"I'll tell them during the drive to school."

"Have you thought of a name?"

"Not yet. Maybe the twins can help me brainstorm."

She smiled. "They'd love that."

As if knowing they were being talked about, the twins bounded down the stairs, sounding like a herd of cattle. "We're ready."

"Bye, Aunt Kellen." Weston stretched onto his toes to give her a kiss on the cheek.

Roxon lifted onto tiptoe to do the same. "Bye, Aunt Kellen. See you after school."

Shawn picked up his keys and cell phone.

What he did next shocked Kellen to the core; he pressed his lips to her cheek. Kellen stiffened and widened her eyes.

Shawn turned to go. When he registered his action, he froze. He shifted back but didn't meet her gaze. "I…uh…I don't know why I did that. I was mimicking the twins. It was automatic. Let's just pretend that didn't happen."

That'd probably be for the best. "Done."

Chapter Fourteen

Shawn beat a hasty exit.

The twins were already outside waiting by his car.

He was relieved they hadn't seen the kiss. Otherwise, they'd tease him mercilessly and pester him with a million questions about Kellen, questions he wasn't prepared to answer. But the thing was, kissing Kellen on the cheek had felt right, as if he had done it a hundred times before. He didn't know what that meant, and he was glad for the distraction driving the kids to school brought. He used the opportunity to tell them about the app.

"That is so cool," Roxon squealed.

"Can we tell our friends and teachers?" Weston wanted to know.

Shawn chuckled. "Not yet, buddy. I'm pitching my idea today. I don't even know if my company will accept the app. If they do, months will pass before the app goes out in beta form."

"Still really cool," Roxon said.

"Do you want to help me name it?"

"Us?" Weston sat forward. "We can name it?"

Shawn flicked on his turn signal, looked both ways, and made a left turn. "We can mull ideas over and see what we come up with."

"Okay."

The three of them were silent as they considered

options.

Shawn threw out a line and waited for a nibble, but nothing surfaced. He slowed to a stop when a railroad's signals flashed red and white and striped gates blocked the path.

The twins peered out the windows, searching for the train. As it went by, they counted each car all the way to the caboose.

Several minutes later, the gates lifted, and the lights switched off.

Shawn drove over the tracks to the other side of the road.

That's when Weston gasped and shouted, "What about something with 'train'?"

"There's already a lot of organizations with 'train' in the name. We'd want our name to stand out, but that's a great start, buddy."

"I can only think of individual words," Roxon said. "But none of them are turning out into anything new. Giving...hands...donation...wagon...wish...list.

"Coming up with a name is the hardest part of creating something." Shawn frowned.

"What are some other words for 'donate'?" Weston wondered aloud.

"I'll look it up on my phone." Roxon tapped on her cell phone's screen. "Give, gift, contribute, pledge, grant, deliver, present..."

"That's good." Shawn thought he was finally discovering threads that could be created into something. "What if we combine a couple of those?"

"Like Pledge a Gift?"

The car fell quiet following Weston's reply.

Shawn mulled over his suggestion. "Pledge" was

often used in conjunction with charities and donations, and "gift" elevated the act of donating something unwanted to something more intimate. Pledge a Gift was exactly what he was going for. "That's it."

Roxon clapped and cheered. "Way to go, West." She grasped his shoulder and shook him as she whooped.

Their excitement stayed with Shawn all the way to his job, and he couldn't wait to pitch the idea to Mr. Harris. He headed straight to his boss's office and knocked on the opened door.

Mr. Harris peered up from his tablet. "Hello, Shawn. Come on in."

Shawn took the seat on the other side of Mr. Harris's desk. "I'm hoping you have a few minutes to listen to my app idea."

Mr. Harris set his tablet atop a stack of papers. "I'm all ears."

Shawn pitched the app to his boss in the same way he explained it to Kellen. "And it'll be called Pledge a Gift."

For a moment, Mr. Harris didn't say or do a thing.

Not even blink. Just when Shawn felt he had lost any chance of getting the promotion, Mr. Harris's face broke into a grin.

"That is exactly what we are searching for. If you can create a demo by Friday, you can present it in consideration for the promotion."

"Thank you, sir. I'll have it ready." He departed from Mr. Harris's office, worrying over the fact he had three days to create a demo for Pledge a Gift. With that deadline, he had a lot of work to do. And Mr. Harris's words filled him with guilt, because he hadn't told

Kellen all the details behind the promotion and what it would mean for him—and for her and the twins—if he won. She had no idea he'd have to move to Japan, and he had a feeling she wouldn't be happy. Worse, she'd feel betrayed and let down, and so would the twins. They'd think he'd be abandoning them. He didn't want that. Not in a million years, but he wanted the job in Japan. If he got it, it'd change his life, giving him the title he'd always striven toward and more financial stability that he could pass on to Kellen and the twins.

No matter what, he wouldn't forget about them, but he'd be apart from them. A rock settled at the bottom of his stomach at that realization. After spending time with Kellen and the twins and knowing how vulnerable they were, he wasn't so sure he liked that thought. But he doubted they'd want to move around the world.

Sighing, he dropped into his desk chair. He couldn't think about any of that now. For all he knew, someone else would present an app a trillion times better than his and win the promotion, and then his present worry would be for naught. Powering on his computer, he put all that on the backburner to deal with later, in the event it actually happened. At the moment, he had work to do and a boss to please.

Shawn worked through lunch and was on a roll, figuring out the logistics of the app and the design. Next, he'd have to partner with someone to work out the kinks and get the app working properly with practice runs. He was proud of the work he'd done so far, though, and he owed that to the twins and their kind ways. But if Kellen hadn't looked for projects to keep the twins active and teach them about giving, the twins wouldn't have met Nick, Danny, or Renee, and they wouldn't have wanted to pay it forward. So, he owed Kellen a lot, too.

While leaving work, he had the urge to do something for the twins, to make them happy, and show them he loved them. And he had just the idea. A detour to the local animal shelter later and a five-year-old Golden Retriever named Chip sat in Shawn's passenger's seat, thumping his tail and staring out the windshield with his tongue hanging out of his mouth.

Shawn couldn't wait to show the twins their present. He hopped out of his car, left it running, and rushed up the walkway to the door. After letting himself in, he stood in the doorway. "Kell, Roxy, West," he called, "I have something I want to show you. Come outside." He hurried back to the car and waited for the three of them to emerge from the house. When he glimpsed the twins on the porch, he opened the passenger's door, setting Chip free.

Chip shot straight for the kids.

Weston's and Roxon's eyes doubled, cheers flew from their mouths, and they dropped to their knees to accept Chip's affections. They received doggy licks and tail wags.

Chip was so excited to meet his new family that he pushed the twins to the ground. Standing over them, he alternated between them, giving each a few licks before moving to the other.

The twins laughed and rolled around as if to avoid Chip's tongue, but they were thoroughly enjoying his attention.

"Shawn, can we talk a moment?" Kellen waved him over to the door.

He edged around the twins, who were rubbing

Chip's belly. The moment he stepped close enough to see Kellen's eyes, he knew she was irritated.

"You adopted a dog?" she hissed under her breath. "You adopted a dog and didn't discuss it with me first?"

And right there, he had made a big mistake. The joy he'd felt about doing something nice for the twins diminished. Once again, he did something wrong. This time, with Kellen. They were supposed to be in this together, and here he just did something pretty huge and hadn't involved her in the decision. That wasn't how parenting was supposed to go.

Wait...parenting? How could one word carry so much weight and send a wave of panic through him? In a blink, he was expected to be a parent, something he hadn't planned. He also hadn't considered being in a relationship that would require him to discuss things like getting a dog, but here he was.

"When the twins are at school, who do you think will be taking care of this dog? Me. I like dogs, but..." Kellen let out a breath. "Taking care of a dog on top of adjusting to taking care of ten-year-old twins and writing is a lot to handle at once."

"I'm sorry." Shawn dipped his hands into his pockets. "I should've realized."

Weston threw a stick.

Chip galloped after it, but instead of returning it to Weston, he laid it at Roxon's feet.

Shawn smiled. "When I left work today, I was in such a good mood, and it was all because of them. So I wanted to do something for the twins. But you're right, I should've talked to you first."

They watched the twins play with the dog in

question. He couldn't deny the delight the dog brought. A pet of some kind could be exactly what someone needed in sad times to bring them through, like a furry therapist but better—an instant companion.

Roxon accepted the stick from Chip.

Then the twins hurried over, with Chip chasing their heels. They stopped in front of Kellen. "Can we keep him?"

She looked from one to the other.

Their big, brown eyes stared, pleading.

Even Chip sat at her feet. His head was cocked to the side, and he was letting out little whines.

Kellen let out a sigh. "Okay."

The twins cheered.

Relief lowered Shawn's shoulders, and he opened the front door. "Welcome home, Chip."

****

For days, Shawn was consumed with getting his app ready for presentation. He changed the color of the logo's letters a dozen times, searching for the perfect color for the mood. After tweaking the shade again, he finally settled on lavender with a bluish hue. Roxon, a purple-lover, would approve. Next to the lavender words was a gift box cupped by two hands. Using an illustration program, he made the hands small, gave them the same golden-tan skin tone as the twins, and positioned the animated hands exactly so they were in the shape of a heart. The small gift box resting in the middle of the hands was off-white with a purple bow darker than the letters.

He tweaked many things and partnered with someone in the tech department to figure out the ins and outs to make each part of the app work appropriately. A trial run on Thursday had a few employees creating accounts and pretending to honor a gift request. And everything ran smoothly.

On Friday, the day of the autumn festival, confidence filled him while standing in front of Mr. Harris and the board. During his presentation, he walked them through the app's functions, highlighted the positive impact it would have on communities, how it was an excellent way for families to get together and make a difference, and that it was a good teaching opportunity for the younger generation. "Many people want to help out local kids and families but don't know how. Pledge a Gift will be an easy way to connect with those in need. It's also a great app for people who have piles of things in their garages or packed in their closets they have been meaning to donate but don't know where to. With Pledge a Gift, they can search for schools, churches, and shelters close to home." He ended the presentation with another view of the logo.

His boss and the other members of the board glanced at each other around the table. After a moment, Mr. Harris clapped, and the others joined in.

Shawn stepped back, amazed at their reaction. "Thank you."

"That was a great presentation," Mr. Harris said. "And this app has potential to change lives. Thank you for your time. We'll discuss Pledge a Gift and the other apps we've been presented with and get back to you by Monday morning with our decision."

Shawn nodded. "Thank you for this chance." He checked the time on his watch. If he left now, he would make it in time for the autumn festival. "Sir, do you need me for anything else today?"

Mr. Harris shook his head. "Go home. You deserve it."

"Thank you, sir." He left, excited to surprise the twins…and Kellen.

Chapter Fifteen

Shawn coming home early would've been enough to surprise Kellen and delight her, but he showed up excited, actually excited, to attend the autumn festival. She dressed in blue jeans, faded brown leather boots, and a red flannel button-up shirt—perfect autumn festival apparel.

Roxon chose overalls and added sunflower clips to her curly hair.

Weston went a little more understated with a simple orange shirt.

They were waiting at the door for Shawn so they could pile into her car when Shawn came down the stairs wearing faded jeans that fit him in all the right ways and a blue-and-white plaid shirt that hugged his biceps. The sleeves were rolled to his elbows, displaying his muscular and veined forearms, and he looked good. "All right." She cleared her throat. "Let's go."

"Sorry, Chip," Shawn said. "You're staying here, buddy."

Chip lay down with a sigh.

The twins kissed Chip on his furry head before racing off and diving into the backseat of Kellen's car. They were already buckled by the time Kellen and Shawn reached the car. Kellen sat in the front passenger's seat, and Shawn drove the short distance to the school.

The festival was in full swing when they arrived. The school's guest parking lot was packed, and cars lined the road on both sides. Shawn found a spot, and they strolled toward the school along the side of the road.

Kellen glanced at Shawn. The sunlight reflected off his hair, making strands shine like gold. "I'm glad you're here."

He smiled. "Me, too."

The school's grounds had been transformed with a Ferris wheel, a petting zoo, food trucks, and rows of tented booths. The booths boasted local artists' wares and Halloween-inspired crafts, from sugar skull décor to fairies and dragons. One booth sold witches hats—all different sizes, shapes, and fabrics. Some had silk autumn leaves and sunflowers, others had glittery spiders. A hat for everyone filled that booth.

Roxon and Kellen tried on several and took selfies together. Kellen bought Roxon a purple, curved witch hat with a pink rose at the tip that Roxon loved so much she didn't want to take off. Kellen also bought one for herself. The hat was woodland-fashioned in light brown with rustic flowers and a wacky, wavy top.

Next to that booth was one devoted to Halloween masks, from masquerade masks to monster and superhero masks.

Weston found a dragon mask with red and orange scales Shawn paid for.

The four of them ambled about the festival grounds, munching on caramel apples and salty popcorn and sipping hot cider. They played pumpkin bowling with small gourds and empty two-liters painted like bowling pins. Then the twins participated in a two-legged race they won, leaving all the other contestants in the dust.

Full of adrenaline from their race and from sugary snacks, the twins rushed over. "Can we go to the haunted house next?"

The haunted house was inside the elementary school's cafeteria, set up backstage. "Absolutely. We can't leave without visiting the haunted house."

The area behind the stage was dark. Fog billowed at their feet. Eerie music played in the background.

Ahead of them, children screamed.

The twins giggled.

"I'm so excited," Roxon whispered while holding onto Weston's arm.

Kellen ducked beneath a piece of ragged cloth. "Have you ever been in a haunted house?"

Shawn lifted a brow. "Of course. When I was a kid."

"I worked in a haunted house once."

"That doesn't surprise me."

She shot Shawn a grin, although she doubted he could see it. "I was in the very beginning, in a graveyard, hiding in a tiny space between the walls, hidden by a black cloth. I would jump out, shaking a can full of metal bits and scream in people's faces."

Shawn chuckled. "That definitely sounds like you."

Laughing, too, she nudged him. Because she'd worked in a haunted house and knew the tricks, she was able to spot all the hiding places. Even though she could find them before someone sprang out, she didn't say anything and enjoyed watching the twins jump clear off the floor and squeal.

Kellen laughed. Once, she even felt Shawn flinch.

They wound their way through the haunted house. In one section, a few students dressed as witches were cackling and stirring large wooden spoons inside a huge cauldron that spilled dry ice mist.

Someone popped out of the cauldron with a shriek.

A scream flew from Kellen's mouth before she could stop it. She laid a hand to her chest, where her heart raced. Kudos to the school staff and students; she hadn't been expecting anyone to be lurking in the pot, waiting to scare.

Strobe lights obscured the next part of the haunted house. People emerged from the shadows and crept toward them, like phantoms disappearing and reappearing closer and closer in the flashing bright lights.

Weston and Roxon latched onto each other and stepped backward into Kellen and Shawn. The four of them pressed forward after the people retreated back into the darkness.

They rounded a corner, and something leapt in front of Kellen. She reacted instinctively and grabbed onto Shawn.

He slipped his arms around her.

As soon as she realized a student dressed as a demented doll had scared the bejeezus out of her, Kellen burst into laughter.

Just as suddenly as the human-sized doll showed up, the doll disappeared.

Kellen had no idea where the student had vanished to. She twisted her neck this way and that, searching for the telltale black cloth, a slot in the walls, or something big enough to hide behind, but she couldn't detect a thing.

Roxon and Weston pulled her and Shawn forward into the next part of the haunted house.

They stepped into a room with a cardboard sarcophagus on a table and several mummies wrapped in gauze. One mummy lay inside the sarcophagus. This one was a mannequin. Another sat in a rocker...also a mannequin. The one propped against the wall lifted its arms and lurched forward with a stiff walk...not a mannequin.

"It's alive!" Weston hopped through the exit.

Kellen, Shawn, and Roxon followed him out, unable to contain their chuckles.

"That was so much fun," Roxon said. "The sixth graders worked on it with their teachers."

Kellen was impressed, knowing sixth graders had created it. "They did an amazing job. This haunted house was better than some I've gone to that had a large budget and were made by adults."

"Yeah, and they even accomplished the feat of scaring your aunt here," Shawn teased.

The twins' eyes widened. "Really?"

"Yes, and I'm not ashamed to admit it. The kid in the cauldron and the evil doll got me."

"Oh, the doll," Roxon shouted. "I think I know that student."

The twins then listed off students' names who they believed played the demented doll and shot down each other's suggestions. Their debate didn't last long when they spotted the hayride. "Can we? Can we?" they chanted together.

In the next moment, Kellen perched on top of a bale of hay on the back of a wagon next to Shawn, and the twins huddled on the other side. The green tractor started with a rumble and jerked forward, pitching Kellen sideways into Shawn.

He secured an arm around her shoulders to steady her.

The feel of his strong, sturdy embrace reminded her of how his arms had closed about her when she'd grasped him in the haunted house. His body heat seeped through her clothes and warmed her with the knowledge of how close they were.

"Sorry," Shawn muttered and removed his arm.

"No, it's okay," she whispered.

The wagon bounced.

Their shoulders and legs jostled.

Shawn secured an arm around her again. This time, though, he kept it there.

The ride was bumpy. She told herself that was the only reason why he held onto her, but deep down, she hoped another reason existed. She hoped he did it because he wanted to, because he liked it, because it felt good, natural, and right.

It did for her.

The sun was setting, painting the sky with pink and orange and yellow streaks. With the sun getting lower, the temperature dropped, but Kellen didn't mind the chill in the air. To her, a perfect autumn day or night had a chill. Also, she had Shawn to keep her warm.

Oh gosh. Did I really just think that?

She peered at their thighs, pressed together.

Yes, yes, I did.

If Dana were there, she'd be nudging Kellen or wiggling her eyebrows or giving her a not-so-discreet wink. If Dana were there, things would be different.

This might not be happening.

That realization struck Kellen in the middle of her chest. Would Shawn be here at this very moment if Dana and Jenson were alive? He'd probably be working late or coming home to his empty condo to do more work. He certainly wouldn't have left work early to attend something he'd never participated in before, no matter how many times Dana and the twins had begged and pouted.

Kellen would've been here. No matter what. She lived for all the fun autumn and Halloween activities, loved to be involved in the twins' lives, and had yearned to be a part of Jensen and Dana's family. Of course, as Jensen's sister, Dana's best friend, and the twins' auntie, she had been, but now, reality was different. Now she was their only family. Along with their grandparents and Shawn. *If* he chose to stay. If he chose them. Whether or not he'd do that was the question. A question that pestered her daily.

Will he stay or will he go?

Will he be their guardian?

Will he be my...? My what? Kellen didn't know. She didn't know how to phrase what she wanted from Shawn...or *with* Shawn. She didn't have the guts to put it into words, not until Shawn revealed, in some way, what he wanted.

A gentle breeze swept across Kellen's face, carrying the scent of fried foods from the festival, the hay they sat on, and the crispness of the air changing with the seasons. She inhaled the smell and caught the fragrance of Shawn's cologne. His cologne mingled with the autumn air, and it was utterly perfect.

The twins pointed out shadows in the woods. One

shadow by a bush was a monster. Perhaps a windigo or big foot. A shadow that darted between trees was a vampire. No, a banshee. A wavering shadow had to be a ghost. Tree monsters, as tall as the pine trees, poked their heads out from behind canopies. Their arms and legs were as skinny as tree branches. According to the twins, the tree monsters couldn't leave the trees. They had to keep touching the trunk with at least one limb or else, they'd vanish forever, but that didn't stop the twins from squealing whenever the tractor rumbled close to the pines.

Watching them reminded her of her childhood with Jensen. The two of them had had great imaginations, too. She missed that. She missed Jensen.

Sighing, she peered at the sky. Way above, far from the diminishing colors of the sunset, a few stars sparkled in the darkness. She sucked in another deep breath, drawing in autumn, the earth, and Shawn.

The tractor bumped her into him again.

This time, she didn't apologize. She didn't even bother to right herself as they neared the school. Their bodies swayed together as one. For a moment, she closed her eyes, relishing being near him without needing an excuse to be so close. Shawn couldn't see her, and hopefully, the twins were too wrapped up in searching for spooky creatures in the woods to notice she had her eyelids closed.

The tractor jerked to a stop,

She opened her eyes, praying no one had caught her lapse.

The twins hopped to the ground.

Shawn stepped off first and then offered Kellen his right hand.

Weston danced on the balls of his feet. "Can we play corn hole?"

"Sure," Kellen said.

"After a good game, how about we go out for dinner?" Shawn said. "You two could choose the restaurant."

The corner of Roxon's lips lifted. "Any restaurant?"

"Any restaurant."

The twins raced ahead to the corn hole games.

Kellen and Shawn followed. After a few steps, she realized Shawn was still holding her hand. She stiffened. She didn't want to alert Shawn, though, or make him think it made her uncomfortable, so she relaxed her body one muscle at a time.

Was Shawn aware he hadn't let go of her hand since he'd assisted her off the hayride? The thought it could be intentional made her smile. But what if he didn't know? What if, when he realized it, too, it embarrassed him and he dropped her hand as if she were toxic?

The twins found a free corn hole game and took turns throwing bean bags.

Roxon tossed a bean bag at Shawn. "Your turn, Uncle Shawn."

Shawn released Kellen's hand to catch the bean bag, aimed, and sank the bag right through the cutout.

"Now you, Aunt Kellen."

She picked up a bean bag, lowered into position, and tossed it. The bean bag hit the corn hole game, slid a few inches up the ramp, and then stopped, right at the edge of the cutout. Half of it hung down, but the other half stayed put. "What?" Kellen threw up her hands.

"Seriously?"

The twins doubled over in laughter.

"I think I should get half the points," she protested.

Shawn chuckled. "It doesn't work like that."

"Half my bag fell through the cutout."

"Sorry."

She bent over and blew a breath at the bean bag.

Shawn's laughter grew. "What are you doing?"

"I can make it fall. I can do it." She waved at the twins. "Help me."

They joined her.

"On the count of three. One. Two. Three."

They blew until they were breathless.

The bean bag didn't budge.

At the end of the game, Shawn and Weston tied for twenty points, Roxon had fifteen, and Kellen had ten. So, hand-eye coordination wasn't her thing. She was a writer; she didn't need to be a corn hole professional.

While they made their way to the car, the twins announced they wanted fast food—burgers and fries and milkshakes.

Shawn obliged. He even bought himself a milkshake.

The night had been a fun one, something the twins had needed, and they all had needed to do together.

Once home, Kellen shooed the twins off to take a bath or shower. Then she tucked them into bed and kissed them goodnight.

When she entered to get a glass of water, she found Shawn in the kitchen scrolling on his phone. At the sink, she glanced back. "Thanks for coming tonight. The twins were thrilled."

"I had a blast. I can't remember the last time I had

that much fun."

She gave him a small smile. His omission made her sad. He could've been a part of many fun times with the twins, and with Dana, but he'd chosen work. "Tomorrow, I was thinking of bringing the twins to the pumpkin patch. Would you like to come?"

Shawn blinked. "The last time I went to a pumpkin patch, Dana and I were kids."

"Then it's about time you went again, don't you think?"

Their gazes connected.

"I do. All right. I'll come."

"Great." She sipped the water. "I'm going to bed. Night."

"Night."

On her way to the guest bedroom, she hoped Shawn wouldn't change his mind about the pumpkin patch. She hoped he'd come.

Chapter Sixteen

Lying on the couch that night, Shawn flexed his right hand, recalling how he'd held Kellen's hand long after he needed to. The feel of her hand...the warmth...the connection...he couldn't forget it. He'd thought about holding her hand for years, ever since they were young, but he couldn't bring himself to do it because he'd kept his feelings hidden, buried, and undetectable. If he had tried it, he imagined she'd be startled. Who the hell just held someone's hand without showing they had feelings first?

He flexed his hand again. Apparently, he did, because he'd just done it.

But Kellen hadn't tugged her hand free. She hadn't appeared startled in the least, and that gave him a bit of hope. What did he want that spark to grow into? He wasn't sure. So much was up in the air. For now, though, that spark was enough.

He fell asleep after a long time and woke to the smell of coffee.

Kellen sat at the kitchen island, sipping from a mug. She wore striped, cotton pajama bottoms and an untied, pink silk robe.

As she swallowed another sip, she appeared to be in utter bliss. He hated to interrupt the moment and her peace before the twins woke up, but before he could retreat out of sight, he saw her peer over her shoulder and jump a little.

She laid a hand to her chest. "You scared me."

"Sorry." To make it not seem as though he'd been spying, he entered the kitchen and headed straight to the coffeemaker and poured himself a cup.

"That's okay. I was thinking about cutting into the apple pie a neighbor dropped off. Apples are healthy. It's a decent breakfast."

Shawn nodded. "Pie for breakfast is my jam."

Kellen retrieved the pie from the fridge. She wiggled out one of the slices.

The twins shuffled and yawned their way into the kitchen.

Shawn snickered. "I think they heard the word 'pie.' "

"Pie?" Weston perked up.

"Well, they did now." Kellen placed the slice on a small plate. Peeled apple and sweet filling oozed from the sides. She distributed three more portions. "I'll heat these in the microwave, and if someone happens to get out the whipped cream, then I won't argue with that."

The twins' eyes lit up.

Weston scrambled off the stool he occupied, rushed to the fridge, and yanked open the door. The contents packed on the shelves rattled.

Kellen gave the twins the first two warm slices of pie.

Weston immediately attacked his with whipped cream. Being a generous brother, he did the same for Roxon's slice without prompting.

Shawn used to do the same thing for Dana when they were kids—always looking out, even when it came to whipped cream.

They ate their slices of apple pie, with plenty of whipped cream, before setting off.

The pumpkin patch ended up being the very same one Shawn and Dana, as well as Kellen and Jensen, used to go to when they were kids. Apparently, Dana, Jensen, and Kellen continued to go there, long after Shawn had decided he was too old for such things. He'd even walk past the bins inside grocery stores, because he certainly didn't have time to carve one.

The lot of green grass stretched on and on. Rows of pumpkins of all sizes and colors sunned on top of patches of hay and wooden slats. Traditional orange, red-orange, bright yellow, pure white, rustic tan, light and dark green, and blue-gray pumpkins—they were all there in the pumpkin version of Woodstock. So many pumpkins, all different, all mingling together for the same cause…for the love of autumn. Many had smooth skin. Others had bumpy skin. Some were streaked. Some pumpkins even had rotting spots. A diverse patch of pumpkin splendor.

Roxon bounced.

Weston, though, paused on the edge of the parking lot.

Shawn tilted his head. "What's wrong, buddy?"

"I…I miss them."

Shawn squatted to eye level. "I know. So do I."

"Last year, Dad and I found the biggest pumpkin on the patch."

Shawn glanced at Kellen. She stood a couple of feet away, holding Roxon's hand. The corners of their mouths were pulled down as all the happiness zapped from them, replaced with grief.

"It took Dad an hour to carve it."

"Mom liked to get warty pumpkins," Roxon added. "She always felt bad for the ugly ones because no one else wanted them."

Weston nodded with a frown pulling down his mouth. "They needed a home, too."

Roxon joined him in nodding.

Shawn hated to see them so heartbroken. "I have an idea. Why don't we search this pumpkin patch for the biggest pumpkin and get it in honor of your dad?"

Weston smiled. "Really?"

"Yeah."

"And while they do that," Kellen said to Roxon, "we can search for the wartiest pumpkin here, a pumpkin your mom would've been proud to give a home."

"Okay."

Shawn stood. "So, the plan is all set. We'll find the biggest pumpkin—"

Roxon grinned. "And we'll find the ugliest."

"And break." Kellen clapped her hands together.

Weston marched ahead, on a mission to get the biggest pumpkin before someone else could snag it.

Shawn caught up in a few strides. They wandered the rows, eyes peeled for big pumpkins. Whenever they spotted a large one, they'd pause. Hands on hips, they'd discuss whether or not it was bigger than one they'd seen previously, but every time, they decided they could find a better one.

Their hunt continued.

Shawn stopped in front of a two-foot-tall pumpkin.

But Weston wasn't convinced it was the greatest pumpkin at the patch. Weston scanned the field. "There it is." And he raced toward the end of the patch. "Come on, Uncle Shawn." Weston jumped up and down in front of a gourd. "Hurry up."

Shawn chuckled as he strolled closer. "I'm coming."

"It's huge."

All Shawn could see were orange pumpkins on either side of Weston. The pumpkin that had Weston all excited must be as tall as the kid himself. Curious, Shawn stepped beside Weston. He pulled up short and blinked. Multiple pumpkins were not in front of Weston as Shawn had thought. No, one gigantic, enormous pumpkin sat on the grass. The gourd was so massive that Shawn doubted he'd get his arms around it. In fact, he doubted he could lift the thing; it was as high as his knees. "That is…a very big pumpkin."

"Can we get it? Please. Dad would've bought it."

Like a sucker punch to the gut. "Sure. We can get it, buddy."

Kellen will kill me. What the heck can we do with a pumpkin as big as an inner tube?

His cell phone chimed. He checked it to see a text from Kellen.

—We've made our selections. Have you two had any success?—

He tapped out a response.

—You could say that. We're at the far end of the patch. Bring a wheelbarrow. —

—On the way. —

Five minutes later, Kellen and Roxon joined them. Kellen pushed a wheelbarrow with two decent-sized pumpkins nestled inside.

"Check it out." Weston sprang to the side to reveal their pumpkin.

Kellen gawked. "That is a monster pumpkin." She set the wheelbarrow down. "You don't need this. You need a forklift."

Shawn figured she was right.

Roxon bent over and hugged the pumpkin as best she could. "Will it fit in your trunk?"

"That's a good question."

"Uncle Shawn said we could get it," Weston announced.

Shawn grimaced and glanced at Kellen.

She studied the pumpkin. "Well, we did agree to get the biggest pumpkin, and this is certainly the biggest pumpkin here. Probably in the entire town."

"The state," Shawn corrected.

Weston lifted both hands in the air. "The world!"

Kellen chuckled. "That's a real possibility. Okay." She removed the two pumpkins that rested inside the wheelbarrow and set them on the ground. "I think a group effort is required. Gather around."

They positioned themselves around the mammoth pumpkin.

Shawn lowered at the knees. "On the count of three. One. Two. Three."

They heaved.

"Oh, my gosh, it's so heavy." Roxon gasped.

As one, they shuffled toward the wheelbarrow as fast as they could.

"My hands are slipping," Weston said.

Shawn lifted the pumpkin over the wheelbarrow.

"Careful, careful," Kellen coaxed.

They managed to set the gourd down without doing it too hard or fast and cracking it open, spilling its orange guts. The pumpkin filled the entire space of the wheelbarrow.

Weston patted it. His small hand made gentle, hollow thumping sounds against the orange flesh. "Isn't it great?"

"It sure is something," Kellen agreed.

Roxon lifted one of the pumpkins from the ground. "Look at ours." The red-orange pumpkin was covered with bumps. Not an inch of its surface was smooth.

"Cool." Weston stroked a hand over its pimply flesh. "Mom would love this."

"Wait until you see the other pumpkin we found."

Kellen carefully picked up the second pumpkin. She hugged it to her stomach. The side facing them already bore a face—a rotting face. Brown and black marks created two eyes and a smiling mouth.

"Cool," Weston repeated. He pointed his index finger. That finger plunged closer.

"No, don't touch—"

His finger sank into one of the pumpkin's rotting eyes.

"—it." Kellen sighed. "Your sister almost did the same thing." She eyed Weston. "*Almost.*"

He removed his finger. Gunk covered it.

Roxon scrunched up her nose. "Ew."

Weston pointed his finger at Roxon now.

"You better not," she warned.

That had Weston grinning. Having once been a nine-year-old boy, Shawn foresaw exactly what would happen next.

Weston dove for Roxon, waving his finger and threatening to wipe the pumpkin's rotting cooties all over her.

Roxon let out a scream. "Stop."

They darted around pumpkins and cut across several rows.

"No running," Kellen called out.

Weston chased after her a little longer before Roxon hid behind Shawn.

"All right." Kellen dug into her purse. "Here, West." She opened a small plastic packet and handed him a wet wipe to clean his pumpkin-infected finger.

Shawn lifted the wheelbarrow. *Wow, this thing is heavy.*

They transferred the monster pumpkin to the trunk. They really had to wedge it in there. It barely fit. At the house, all Shawn could manage was getting it to the front lawn beside the driveway. "It's just going to have to stay here."

Roxon frowned. "You mean we'll have to carve it outside?"

Shawn nodded. "I think so."

Weston leapt into the air. "Awesome."

Carving the pumpkin was an experience. Kellen had the twins put on clothes they could get dirty. Then she handed Shawn an apron before slipping into one herself. A bucket sat in the grass, waiting for the pumpkin's stringy guts. Beside it lay a plethora of instruments to scoop out those guts, from an actual triangular pumpkin scooper to gardening trowels. Even a couple of large ladles. In order to cut off the top, Shawn had to use a jigsaw. The pumpkin's intestines held on so tightly to the top that they all had to help him rip it free.

"All right. Climb on in," he said.

The twins popped to their feet.

Kellen grabbed their shoulders. "*Don't* climb into

the pumpkin." Then she whacked Shawn in the arm. "Don't tell them to do that."

Shawn grinned.

Using their chosen tools, they hacked away at the insides, but it wasn't easy. The twins practically had to dive into the pumpkin in order to scoop out any guts. The bucket filled quickly with each new handful of pumpkin intestines.

Shawn ended up having to carve out the mouth and slice away the strings keeping the chunk of flesh in place so they could reach the farthest depths of the gourd.

Over an hour later, the pumpkin was cleaned out and carved with a face.

Kellen retrieved a pillar candle from the house and placed it inside the monster pumpkin.

Shawn lit it with a grill lighter.

Then they stood back and admired the glow coming from the huge jack-o'-lantern. The rotting pumpkin and the bumpy pumpkin sat beside it in the grass.

"Today was fun." Weston's voice ended their silence of admiration.

"Yesterday was fun, too," Roxon added.

Kellen nodded and glanced at Shawn. She didn't say anything, but the look she gave him said it all. *It was fun because you were there.*

He'd had fun, too. The only problem was, he didn't know how many more fun times they'd have together. Pretending their time together wasn't limited was pointless. He knew it. They were the only ones who didn't.

Chapter Seventeen

Sunday, Kellen drove the twins to a Halloween store to pick out costumes.

Shawn decided to pass. Costumes weren't his thing, he said.

The Halloween store's entrance was framed by fake silk webbing and fuzzy black and purple spiders that dangled just above their heads. A strobe light flashed wildly, setting the mood for what they'd encounter beyond the curtain.

Kellen pulled the stringy, decaying curtain to the side.

Halloween decorations galore. Every inch of the store was decked out in Halloween magic. Instead of mannequins, skeletons wore costumes.

They strolled through the store, marveling at the decorations and pointing out things they wished they could get. This was always one of Kellen's favorite pastimes; Halloween window shopping, minus the window. She'd see all the stuff she wished she could buy one day and would add them to a mental wish list.

Oohing and aahing, they found the aisle of costumes. Nearly every costume the kids saw, they wanted to dress up as. They had two piles of costumes in the cart Kellen pushed, and the piles kept growing. An hour later, the twins had to eliminate their choices. They discarded many, bringing the count from ten to six to three. Finally, the last two.

Roxon lowered the hangers that held her costumes. "You know what'll help us make this decision? If we know what you and Uncle Shawn will be wearing to the Halloween party."

Kellen frowned. "What do you mean?"

"You don't remember? You're supposed to be superheroes together."

No, Kellen hadn't forgotten, but she was surprised Roxon remembered.

"If you and Uncle Shawn dress as superheroes, then we will, too," Weston said.

Kellen considered their costume choices. They each had one superhero costume left. "Your superheroes are from a different comic book universe, though."

"So?"

"Yeah, so?" Roxon added.

Kellen smiled. "Fine. I'll dress as a woman of steel, but I can't make any promises for your uncle."

"That's good enough." Roxon chose the costume for the genius princess of an African nation from a popular comic book series.

Weston placed his second costume back on the rack and kept the costume for the king of that same comic book series as Roxon's character. "You know what this means?" He smirked at Roxon. "You're dressing as my *little* sister."

Roxon rolled her eyes. "Whatever."

Laughing, Weston ventured off on his own

Kellen chuckled, too. "Okay. Help me find my costume."

Roxon raided the racks with Kellen.

"Found it." Roxon held up a clothes hanger.

The costume didn't come with real boots, just red leg slip-ons to be paired with red shoes. Kellen planned to buy authentic-looking boots, though, and to wear tights like Melissa Benoist's version of the character. She was adding her costume to the cart when Weston rejoined them.

He flourished a T-shirt with the legendary *S* logo on it and a pair of fake, black-rimmed glasses. "This is for Uncle Shawn."

Kellen smiled. This was the perfect understated costume for Shawn. He already owned many business suits. Add the T-shirt underneath a partially unbuttoned shirt, a jacket, and a pair of dorky glasses and you had a nerdy reporter ready to become a superhero at a moment's notice to save the world. "It's perfect. We'll surprise him with it later." Much later. Like the day of the party. That way, he couldn't back out. Or so she hoped.

****

The days blazed by as Kellen struggled with writer's block, balanced being a guardian, took Chip for walks, and tried to plan a menu for their upcoming Samhain feast. Throughout the week, the twins had playdates with Nick, Danny, and Renee and would be having another one this afternoon before the weekend. She looked forward to those playdates as much as the kids did. Imani was fun to hang out with and easy to talk to. In a way, she reminded Kellen of Dana, and she needed that friendship.

But right now, she had to plan a feast. Sitting at the kitchen island, she scrolled through a cooking website. Should she cook a turkey? She'd never cooked a whole turkey before. She'd never even cooked a whole chicken, for that matter. And turkeys were notoriously difficult to get right. They could come out dry, overcooked, burned, and undercooked. On top of that, she discovered dozens of ways to cook a turkey and hundreds of recipes.

Roasted.

Deep-fried.

Air-fried.

Braised.

Brined.

Smoked.

Glazed.

Dry-rubbed.

Grilled.

Stuffed.

Slow-cooked.

Oven bag, no oven bag, electric roaster, roasting pan, aluminum foil, no foil.

Kellen frowned. Bacon-wrapped turkey?

She blinked. Beer-glazed?

Turducken? She tilted her head. A turkey stuffed with a duck stuffed with a chicken? She shook her head. Too many calories, too much meat.

Mayonnaise-roasted turkey? She grimaced. Yogurt-glazed?

She continued scrolling. "People have way too much time on their hands to try out these wacky recipes."

Chip made a yawning noise.

She found him sitting near her feet. Well, she wasn't alone after all. "You'd probably like the bacon-wrapped turkey, wouldn't you?"

When she said the b-word, Chip scrambled onto all fours and panted.

She tried not to smile but couldn't help it. "You know what that word is, huh?" She focused her attention back to the computer.

Chip lay on the tile, set his head on his paws, and let out a whine.

"Oh, hold your horses."

Chip raised his eyebrows as if to ask, "What do horses have to do with it?"

Using her fingertip on the screen, she scrolled through the site. "Spinach-stuffed turkey." That sounded like something she'd try, but not something the twins would even want to take a bite out of. Let alone her parents. "Chip, there are so many different options. How do you like your turkey?"

That was another delicious word that had Chip's ears perking up.

"You'd probably eat turkey, no matter how it's done. Am I right?"

He gave a soft *woof.*

"Thought so." She pursed her lips.

Barbeque-spiced.

Cajun-spiced.

Asian-spiced.

Chile-rubbed.

Italian-style.

Brown sugar-glazed

Ranch-seasoned.

And so many other ways including the good, old-fashioned way. Kellen was beginning to doubt she'd find a good bird recipe when she found a recipe for a cider-glazed turkey. "I think we have a winner, Chip."

But still, she wondered if turkey would be too much to have leading up to the usually turkey-packed holiday season. Last year, Dana had made individual chicken pot pies with jack-o'-lantern cutouts in the crust. Kellen wasn't nearly as creative. Or that good of a cook. The year before that, Dana had made jack-o'-lantern stuffed peppers, seared salmon with spiced sweet potatoes, spaghetti fashioned to look like it had eyes in it with mozzarella balls and black olives, and squash soup. All of those were far too ambitious that Kellen felt even a turkey would be easier. Or something smaller than a turkey, perhaps. "Individual Cornish hens? What do you think? They could look a little Halloween-y sitting on our plates all whole like that."

Chip tilted his head.

"I'll take that for a *yes*."

Now for the sides.

Could she stuff each individual Cornish hen? Was that possible? She searched for stuffing and had no idea so many options existed. Stuffing inside the bird or prepared on the stovetop in a pot. Just as with turkey she read traditional and creative recipes.

Cornbread stuffing.

Monkey bread stuffing.

Sourdough stuffing.

And just about every wacky concoction, including strange replacements for bread, such as soft pretzels, potato bread, croissants, and crescent rolls. The flavors were just as diverse as the turkey recipes—spinach and artichoke, beer and cheese, apple and sausage, oyster, crab, mushroom, polish-style with sauerkraut, and everything in between.

Sitting back, Kellen stared blankly at the computer.

"Oh, Chip, I'm in big trouble." She shook her head. "I'm going to make a mess out of this dinner and every family dinner after that." She didn't give up, though, and that was how she came across a herb-and-apple dressing that would go perfectly with the glaze on the Cornish hens.

What else? What else?

She scoured the Internet. Luckily, Halloween parties were popular. Unfortunately, most of the ideas were finger foods. Apparently, her family was the only one who made a huge feast to honor All Hollow's Eve.

Eight Cornish hens and stuffing would be a challenge enough. Simple sides were the answer. "Hm. Could Brussels sprouts be spooky?" Probably to the twins they'd be very scary. She nixed Brussels sprouts, hoping to find something the twins would actually want to eat. She found a pasta salad recipe with broccoli, sliced cherry tomatoes, and cucumbers with carved faces as if they were pumpkins. Maybe she could get the twins to help. And she could add blue and red food coloring to the water to give the penne pasta a ghoulish purple hue.

"That sounds a lot easier than stuffing, but I'm no quitter."

She fully intended to make that stuffing. Okay. Cornish hens, stuffing, pasta salad, and…roasted acorn squash. That would be a good autumn side dish, and it wouldn't be difficult. Although, she might need Shawn to hack those acorn squashes in half.

That left dessert. Would pumpkin pie be too much with the acorn squash? Two squashes in one meal? Nonsense. She found a fabulous recipe for pumpkin pie cheesecake and thought that might be a fun alternative to the traditional.

Studying her notepad, she liked her choices, but she wasn't feeling confident in the least. The biggest hurdle was to make all those items and not ruin them, which she didn't think she had in her. Sure, she could make breakfast and pop something in the oven for dinner, but a feast for eight people was another story, and she might not be the author of that one.

Chip sighed at her feet.

"I know, I know." She hopped over to the refrigerator and removed a pack of bacon. "I got you covered. We'll have bacon and fried eggs."

Tongue hanging out of his mouth, Chip sat up.

She chuckled. "Hold on. I have to cook it first."

While the bacon fried, Shawn stepped into the kitchen. "Is Chip your buddy now?"

Chip currently sat at her feet.

"It's just because I have the goods." She pointed at the frying bacon.

"Can I get some of that? I'll be your best buddy, too." His eyes twinkled, and his dimples winked.

"I think I can spare a piece." She smiled before turning back to flip the sizzling bacon that was frying to crispy perfection.

The twins' feet pounded down the stairs, and they slid into the kitchen in their socks. "Bacon!"

Chip raced around the island three times.

The twins chanted for bacon, which prompted Chip to let out long, wolf-like howls.

Shawn sat, began rapping his hands on the island's surface, and added his voice to theirs.

Kellen threw her head back in laughter. She spun on her feet with pieces of crispy bacon laid out on a plate in her hands. "I should keep all this for myself."

They became quiet then. Even Chip.

She smiled victoriously. "I guess I'll share." She set the plate before them and selected a piece of bacon from the top. Squatting down, she held it out to Chip. "Here you go."

Chip ever-so-delicately accepted the other end of the treat and then scampered off to his bed in the corner of the kitchen where he savored the tastiness.

Today was Kellen's day to drop the twins off at school, so everyone headed out the door at the same time.

Shawn waited while the three of them trooped out the door. He touched a hand to Kellen's lower back as she stepped out.

During the entire drive to the school, she could still feel the warmth and pressure of his hand as if it was a tattoo on her skin. Then she recalled the touch of his lips on her cheek when he had kissed her the other morning. And suddenly, his lips were there again, pressing a kiss to her cheek. She swallowed and attempted to shove down the memory, but it stayed close to the surface, a reminder throughout the day.

Kellen tried to hide something was up that afternoon at the park, but she apparently was unsuccessful.

"You look like you've been daydreaming all day," Imani said. "There's a dreaminess in your eyes."

Kellen bit her bottom lip.

"Now you're blushing."

"I've had a lot on my mind."

"And who shall that be?"

"How do you know I'm talking about a person?"

"Because that blush doesn't mean you've been thinking about writing."

Kellen pressed her hands to her cheeks. "But I have been thinking about writing…" She lowered her voice. "…*and* I've been thinking about Shawn."

"Yes." Imani pumped her right arm. "Something's *there*, right?" She eyed Kellen.

"I don't know." Kellen watched the kids on the jungle gym. "Honestly, something has always been there for me. And that's the thing, I don't know if that's the same for *him*. I can't get into Shawn's head. I don't know how he feels or what he thinks about me. If he only sees me as his kid sister's best friend."

"Maybe you should ask him."

Kellen recoiled. "No, I can't do that."

Imani threw her hands into the air. "Why not?"

"I'd want to have some inkling that I'm not off base before I ask him how he feels about me. I don't want to change the nature of our relationship if he doesn't feel the same way and then becomes uncomfortable around me."

"That makes sense. Do what feels right, but I'll also say…don't let your fear keep you from expressing your feelings. Because one day, it might be too late."

Imani's words stuck with Kellen, replaying over and over again like a warning. It kept her awake most of the night. She lay on her back, staring at the ceiling and evaluating her emotions and their history. Shawn had always been easy-going around her and always went out of his way to make her laugh or smile, even when they were kids. She had never felt his attention to be brotherly in manner, but flirtatious. Surely that had to mean something.

Right?

She rolled onto her side to face the window. The blinds were raised halfway, letting moonbeams into her room. She gazed out the window, hoping the serene moonlight would wash away her thoughts and lull her to sleep.

Tiny white fairies danced in front of the glass pane. Some pressed their faces into the glass, making soft little noises as if they were tapping on the window and beckoning her to join them in their play. She crawled out of bed and knelt in front of the window. Falling from the sky was the first snowfall of the season. Snow seemed to arrive earlier and earlier every year. Already the lawn was spotted with white. By morning, everything would be covered in a blanket of snow. She scurried back under the covers and couldn't wait to wake the twins in the morning to go out and play.

She woke an hour earlier than usual, unable to sleep another wink. Excited to pry the twins from their sleep for some snow fun, she tossed off her covers and sprang out of bed. She headed to Weston's room first. "Up and at 'em, kid." She patted his back.

"Noooo," he grumbled into his pillow. "No school. Saturday. Sleep."

Kellen laughed. "It snowed last night."

Weston's head perked up. Pillow creases marred his face. "Really?"

"Yup, so get up and put your snow clothes on. We're building a scareman."

Weston frowned. "What's a scareman?"

"A scarecrow snowman."

With the promise of fun, Weston sprang out of bed and dove for his clothes and snowshoes.

Kellen went to Roxon's room next. The purple comforter was thrown over Roxon's head. The only thing that hinted at someone sleeping in the bed was the small lump where Roxon was curled up beneath the cozy, warm layers. "Hey, Roxy, guess what?"

"Whhaaat?"

Except Roxon didn't say it with enthusiasm. Kellen grinned. "I've got one word for you."

"So do I…go."

Kellen bit back her laughter. "Snow."

"Huh?" Roxon flung the covers back. Her hair stuck up in every direction. "It snowed? Already?"

"It did."

Roxon scrambled out of bed. A moment later, she tossed open her closet door and yanked her snow pants off a hanger.

"After you get dressed, grab your brother, go downstairs, and prod your uncle awake. I'm going to change." Bursting with as much excitement as the twins, she hurried to her room. From her closet, she pulled out a heavy knit sweater, a hoodie, and worn jeans. While dressing, she heard the twins race down the stairs. That ruckus alone would snap Shawn from his sleep.

"Uncle Shawn, get up!"

And if their journey down the stairs hadn't, their shouts would've accomplished the job.

She could only imagine the mini heart attack hearing his niece and nephew shrieking at the top of their lungs had caused. Downstairs, she found Shawn sitting on the couch, with a blanket jumbled around his legs and rubbing his eyes with the heels of his palms.

He peered at her with tired eyes. "I hear it snowed

last night."

"It sure did, and we have to celebrate the first snowfall. If you didn't pack anything for cold weather, you can wear something of Jensen's. Then come on out and have a Halloween-inspired snow day with us." By the state of his disheveled appearance, she didn't know if he would have the energy to get himself off the couch, but she held out the hope he would. "We'll be outside, building a scareman." She wiggled her fingers into a pair of gloves before heading out the door.

Overnight, the temperature had dropped significantly. She was glad for her hoodie keeping her head and ears warm. Clouds of breathy exhaust floated from her mouth, and the cold bit her eyes, drying out their moisture. Everything was covered with a thin layer of glittering snow, making the world appear clean, new, and pure.

The twins lay flat on their backs, working their arms and legs systematically to make snow angels. Then they scrambled to their feet to admire their creations.

"Scareman time," Kellen called out.

The three of them worked together to roll the snow into boulders and to stack them to form the scareman's body. From the garden, they found two sticks on the ground for arms and a handful of pebbles for the eyes and mouth, which they shaped into a frown.

Weston had the idea to poke twigs with leaves into the top of the snowman's head for hair.

They all giggled over the red-headed snowman and his lumpy, uneven body, which had plenty grass and dirt and autumn leaves mixed into the snow. The branch arms were so long that the tips touched the floor.

Instead of a scarf, they buttoned a large plaid jacket around him.

Roxon giggled. "He looks like a grumpy, woodsy snowman."

"He's definitely rustic," Kellen agreed. "But that's part of his charm."

"He doesn't look very scary, though." Roxon's eyes lit up. "I have an idea." She raced into the house. A moment later, she returned with three fake crows and a bottle of red food coloring. "You know that movie *The Birds*?"

"A scarecrow meets a snowman meets *The Birds*. Epic."

They planted one of the fake crows on the side of the snowman's head and drizzled red food coloring down his face. Another they set on his shoulder.

Kellen unbuttoned his jacket and shook food coloring onto his snowy chest. The last crow was on his bare bottom half, and food coloring poured over his side.

They were laughing over their creation when the front door opened.

Shawn stepped out in Jensen's old snowsuit, with a knit cap pulled low over his forehead.

Seeing him there made Kellen smile. She hadn't been sure he'd join them. She'd figured he'd decided to fall back asleep rather than leave the warmth of the house.

"Uncle Shawn," Roxon called out. "Play with us."

Without missing a beat, Weston crouched, scooped up a handful of snow, and chucked it in Shawn's direction. It hit Shawn in the shoulder and burst into drops of snow.

The evidence of the explosion stayed on his shoulder in the form of a wet spot.

Shawn eyed it. "I guess that means Aunt Kellen is on my team?"

The twins let out simultaneous war cries, "Snowball fight!" And since Kellen was standing smack dab in the middle, they pelted her with snowballs.

She let out a yelp and scampered behind the bushes for cover.

"Get him," the twins hollered.

Snowballs sailed over her head.

Then Shawn slid into place beside her. "Those kids are brutal."

"What do you say we take them down?" She held out her fist to his.

He balled his own fist and pounded hers. "I'm in."

They formed a pile of snowballs as quick as possible while dodging the twins' attempts at nailing them with tightly packed snow.

Shawn picked up a snowball. "You ready?"

She gave a brisk nod. "Ready."

"One...two...three."

Then they leapt up and sent snowballs flying. Most of them didn't come close to the twins, but that was okay.

Kellen threw a snowball that hit Roxon in the middle and had her falling backward on the ground.

Laughing, Weston grabbed his belly and pointed at his sister.

Shawn executed a well-aimed throw that had a snowball pelting Weston in the chest and had him landing on his back just like Roxon.

Kellen and Shawn laughed so hard they didn't see the twins get back to their feet and launch a double-attack. A snowball smacked Kellen in her shoulder, and another shattered atop Shawn's head.

The twins let out victorious roars, but they didn't let up on their assault.

Neither did Kellen or Shawn. They threw snowball after snowball. Half the time, they didn't even look at where the snowballs were going or where they landed. They just kept them coming, but their stash of snowy ammo dwindled.

Kellen made more.

Shawn squatted low. "Let's get them together."

They each grasped a snowball in their hands. "Now."

And they popped their heads over the bush only to nearly get hit in the face by dual snowballs. The snowballs broke apart after skimming over the top of the bush, sending a spray of snow into their faces.

Kellen fell backward.

Shawn lost his balance, too, and landed beside her.

They studied each other, with bits of snow speckling their faces, and laughed out loud.

She was still giggling when Shawn brushed away a snowflake from the corner of her mouth. The laughter coming from her caught on a gasp.

Their gazes met and held.

Shawn leaned toward her.

His intention was clear, and her heart rate picked up speed. Every one of her nerve endings awakened in anticipation. She leaned forward, too, closing a bit more of the distance and letting him know she wanted this kiss as much as he did. His warm breath touched her lips first, and she closed her eyes. Their lips brushed. And just when they were about to share their first kiss, a snowball collided into Shawn's back, ending the moment. They flinched apart in time for the twins to come around the corner and bombard them with snowballs.

Kellen raised her hands over her head. "Okay, okay. We surrender."

The twins pounced on them then, creating a dog pile.

They played a little longer before Kellen prompted them to go inside to get warm. "I'll make hot apple cider for breakfast."

That sold them, and they rushed inside.

Shawn leant her a hand and pulled her to her feet.

He didn't show any sign of wanting to kiss her again, so she had no choice but to believe the fleeting moment hadn't meant a thing.

Chapter Eighteen

What had he been thinking? Shawn couldn't believe he had almost kissed Kellen. He had felt magnetized. All these years, he'd had thoughts of what it would be like to kiss her and had even imagined himself doing it, but he had never caved to the temptation. Not after failing to kiss her during the Halloween party when he was nineteen. But one snowball fight and a couple of lucky shots by the twins had nearly broken his streak. The problem was, he still wanted to kiss her. Everything about her enchanted him, from the curve of her pink lips and the beauty of her tan skin to the smile in her blue eyes. She was gorgeous, had an infectious personality, and cared about others.

His mother would say he wouldn't find someone better, and he agreed. Kellen was special, but he wasn't sure if *he* was right for *her*.

For the rest of the day, he avoided her the best he could, if only to tamp his urge to tug her into his arms and finally share their first kiss. All night, though, he couldn't get it out of his mind. On the tip of his finger, he could still feel the heat and softness of her skin and the bit of cold wetness from the snowflake he had brushed away from the corner of her mouth. He shouldn't have done that. That single contact had unraveled everything that usually restrained him from crossing the line. But he couldn't control himself. His hand had lifted as if of its own accord.

Not only did he think about the almost-kiss, but also what Kellen had thought about it. He hadn't imagined her leaning toward him, had he?

He didn't know how he managed to fall asleep, but he did because he woke in the morning to the smell of coffee brewing. Rather than face Kellen just yet, he snuck upstairs to shower and change. If he could go without coffee, he would've done so, but since coffee was about a quarter of his blood, he had to go into the kitchen for a cup. He found Kellen in there, wearing an apron and standing with her hands in fists on her hips, eyeing a turkey breast.

"Turkey for breakfast?"

"Cereal for breakfast," she corrected. "Everyone must fend for themselves today, because I'm doing a pre-Halloween dinner."

"Why?"

"So, I can make all the mistakes now and not then. Although I'm making Cornish hen for Halloween, but there will be turkey during the holiday season, so…"

"Makes sense." He glanced at the raw, naked turkey breast resting in a roasting pan. "What's the problem?"

"The problem is, the recipe says to marinate it overnight. And I didn't do that."

Shawn poured himself a cup of coffee. "Is that essential?"

"For the flavor to get deep into the meat and skin? Yup." She sighed. "I'm already ruining this. I should've fully read the instructions."

"You're not ruining anything."

"Easy for you to say," she muttered. "You only have to eat it."

After taking a sip, Shawn lowered his cup. "Then I'll help." He picked up the other apron and slipped his head through the loop.

She blinked. "You want to help me make a practice dinner?"

Although she sounded skeptical, likely not believing he truly wanted to spend most of the day in the kitchen, he noticed relief in her eyes at the prospect of not being alone in this task. "Yeah, we're in this together, right?" He didn't know why he said that. If that was true, he wouldn't be vying for a job on the other side of the globe. "We'll make a mess out of this together." He tied the apron at his back. "It should be fun."

Kellen laughed. "Loads."

First, they made a rub. That part was at least easy, even if they had never used a food processor before.

Kellen peeled back the paper from the butter and plopped it into the mixer's bowl. To the rectangle of butter, she added salt, pepper, several cloves of garlic, a medium onion, and minced sage leaves.

The food processor made a grinding noise while everything combined into a yellow mound speckled with green. The minced garlic and onion goodness made it a little lumpy.

"The next step says we have to separate the skin from the meat. With our fingers." She grimaced. "That sounds like something straight out of a horror movie."

"It does sound very surgical. Should we wear gloves?"

"I don't have any, so our bare hands will have to

do." She poised her hands over the turkey breast. "I guess I'm going in." Her hands lowered, but she froze. Her fingers were together, as if she had to stick a hand into something icky, except she didn't have to worry about removing the turkey's neck or bag of gizzards.

Shawn stood back, amused. "If you can't do this now, eight Cornish hens will be harder."

She glared. "Why don't you do it, then?"

He stepped up. "Okay, I will." With clean hands, he dove right in. He worked his fingertips underneath the flabby skin and lifted it gently away from the pink flesh. Fitting his large hands and long fingers beneath the skin clinging to the meat was tough. The skin was cold, wet, and a little slimy, and he could feel web-like, fatty tissue that was difficult to tear away. A shiver ran through him. "This feels weird."

Kellen laughed. "But you look like a pro doing it."

"Um…thanks?" He finished the task and removed his hands. Holding them high, he mimicked a surgeon. "I believe the patient will make it."

Kellen shook her head. "Go wash your gross hands."

He was washing his hands when he saw the twins venture into the room.

Weston plugged his nose with his thumb and index finger. "What's that smell?"

"Garlic and onions," Kellen said. "We made a rub for the turkey breast. It'll smell a lot better while it cooks."

Shawn shut off the faucet. "You monsters will have cereal for breakfast. Go get your bowls."

The twins mixed several different cereals into their bowls and sat at the island to eat.

Roxon dunked a spoon into her bowl. "Uncle Shawn, you're cooking?"

"He sure is," Kellen answered.

"Cool."

"Yeah, cool," Weston said.

Shawn smiled. "I pulled the turkey's skin from the meat."

"Ewww."

"Gross."

Kellen picked up a glob of the butter and stuck her fingers far underneath the skin. Her face contorted. "This *does* feel weird." She scooped up more rub and spread it over the meat. Then she dumped the rest of the rub on top of the turkey and smoothed it evenly over the surface.

"Why do you have to do that?" Weston asked.

"Because it's supposed to give the meat and skin a ton of yummy flavor." She separated her fingers, which were caked with gooey, lumpy butter. "But it's messy."

Once the turkey breast was covered with the rub, they set it in the fridge to marinate for a few hours, which was the best they could do. During the marinating time, they each did their own thing. Kellen wrote, and Shawn watched football with the twins. At two o'clock, they reconvened in the kitchen.

Shawn fisted his hands on his hips. "So, what's next?"

"The glaze." She combined apple cider vinegar and honey in a saucepan and set it on the stovetop to boil. "Okay, the instructions say it has to reduce by two-thirds and will become syrup-like. Apparently, this can be tricky."

"How tricky can boiling apple cider vinegar and

honey be?"

Kellen was about to retort.

The twins shouted, "Aunt Kellen."

"Coming." She pointed at the pan. "Keep an eye on it." And she left the kitchen.

Shawn stirred the golden liquid. Tiny bubbles were beginning to form on the bottom of the pan and float to the surface. The smell of the vinegar stung his eyes.

Ding.

He looked toward his phone. A text had come in from Mr. Harris. He dropped the wooden spoon, leaving it in the saucepan, and shifted away from the stove to the counter where his phone lay. Taking a deep breath, he picked it up, unlocked the screen, and opened the text.

—*The board has come to a decision.* Pledge a Gift *is the app we've chosen to move forward. We were all impressed with your creativity, dedication, and passion. We are officially appointing you as the new head of Global Imagination's app department in Japan. Congratulations!*—

Shawn fist-pumped the air before dashing off a fast reply.

—*Thank you so much, sir. I am honored for this opportunity and look forward to my new position. When will I need to travel to Japan?*—

His boss's answer came fast.

—*November 1.*—

How could he leave for Japan the day after Halloween? He'd miss the holidays with Kellen and the twins, the first one without Dana and Jensen.

"What have you done?"

Kellen's shout made him jump.

"I didn't know," he said without thinking.

She squeezed past him to get to the stove. "You burned it."

He took a moment to realize what she was talking about. He peered into the pot to see the liquid had caramelized and burned in the pan.

She pried the wooden spoon out of the mess and attempted to scrape the sticky, blackened, smoking mess off the bottom but was unsuccessful. "I don't think the pan will be salvageable." She set it to the side and examined the spoon, which looked like a rancid lollypop. "I don't think the spoon is salvageable." She dumped it into the ruined pan. "We'll just have to try again." Hand on her hip, she faced him. "Why weren't you watching the sauce? The instructions say the moment you turn your back, it over reduces and burns."

"Well, you didn't tell me that."

"The instructions are right there."

He checked the tablet propped on the counter. "But if I had turned to look at that, the sauce would've burned. At least according to the instructions."

She eyed him. "Very funny. What were you doing?"

He pressed the button on the side of his phone to turn the screen black. "Checking a text."

"I hope it was important."

"It was."

But Kellen was already pulling out another saucepan.

So he kept the details of the text to himself. Now wouldn't be an appropriate time to bring it up, not while he was assisting her with a practice dinner.

Together, they managed to get the glaze right.

They used a silicon basting brush to spread the deep, golden glaze onto every inch of the turkey breast. Then Shawn slid the roasting pan into the pre-heated oven. Now they had to prep the stuffing. After slicing two baguettes into cubes, they nervously watched them bake in the oven for a handful of minutes.

When Kellen brought them out, she sighed at their golden-brown surface.

Next, they divided the chopping duties.

Kellen peeled, cored, and diced two large Granny Smith apples, the peels of which were snatched up by the twins for a snack.

Shawn's duty was to cut the celery stalks. Unfortunately, Kellen pushed the onions on him, claiming to hate the task, and opted for mincing fresh parsley and rosemary instead. So, Shawn chopped the onion. And it was a juicy onion, too. The aroma leaked into the air and attacked his eyes; nothing like the onions that the food processor had pulverized. This time, tears formed, and his eyes burned. He blinked rapidly, hoping to swipe the tears away like windshield wipers, but it had no effect. The more he cut and the more the onion's juices were set free, the worse it became.

Kellen backed away from the counter and pressed her hands to her eyes. "Oh, my gosh, it's so bad." She lowered her hands. "I can't open my eyes." Tears streamed down her cheeks.

"You told me to cut them," Shawn accused.

"The *recipe* told us to cut them," she corrected.

A blast of the onion's stench sucker punched Shawn. "Whoa." He laid down the knife and staggered back. Now *he* couldn't see. "We need to get out of here." With his arms out, he searched for Kellen and found her a few steps away. He grabbed her. Tripping over each other's feet, they battled their way through the onion's assault to the front door. He tossed the door open, and they stumbled out onto the welcome mat. Using the collar of his shirt, he wiped his eyes. "Onions are no joke."

Beside him, Kellen swiped tears from her eyes and gasped. "West, Roxy, open the windows."

Even Chip scurried out, with his tail between his legs, whimpering. He sprang into a small pile of snow and buried his head.

Kellen laughed. "Maybe snow will help."

Seeing how much chaos a single onion could cause, they burst out laughing. They laughed so hard they had to hold onto each other to stay standing. The twins found them on the porch where they were cackling hysterically and practically embracing.

"It smells like an onion farted in here," Weston said.

Kellen and Shawn howled.

"I've never heard of a single onion wreaking that much havoc before," Shawn choked out. "What kind did you get? Ninja onions?"

Kellen straightened her face. "It was organic."

For some reason, that undid them again. Even the twins giggled.

Kellen snapped her fingers. "Shoot. I forgot to light the candle."

Shawn frowned. "What would a candle do?"

"A lit candle is supposed to cut the onion's acid."

"We would've needed a really big candle."

Once the house was aired out, they resumed their

work.

Kellen lit the candle.

Shawn finished chopping the last of the onion. Surprisingly, the candle trick worked. Either that or the onion had already unleashed every drop of its killer gas.

They combined the bread, herbs, celery, and the dreaded onion into a bowl and poured in a cup of chicken stock. All of that was then transferred into a casserole dish and placed in the oven with the turkey breast.

"And just think, you not only have to do this again, but there's also the entire holiday season," he said.

"Don't remind me." She covered her face with her hands. "Why is this happening to me?"

Her voice was muffled. After a moment, though, she lowered her hands. "I know. We'll do Christmas at Grandpa and Grandma's."

"Which Grandpa and Grandma?"

"Both." She grinned. "We'll go to one on Christmas Eve. On Christmas Day, we'll open gifts here and then head over to the other grandparents' house for Christmas night. That way I don't have to cook at all." She shot her fists in the air, but her enthusiasm didn't last long. She lowered her arms to her sides. "I need a nap."

"Go lie down. I'll wake you when it's time to get the squash in the oven."

A yawn stretched her mouth. "Okay." She headed upstairs.

"You still have on the apron," Shawn called out.

"It'll be my blanket," she mumbled.

A minute later, the door upstairs clicked shut. With Kellen upstairs and the kids in the backyard playing with Chip, Shawn had his first moment alone since receiving the text from Mr. Harris. He had no idea what to do now. This was what he had wanted for so long, and finally having it felt surreal. Obviously, he'd have to tell Kellen and the twins. He could do it tomorrow after he got home from work. He also had to put his condo on the market and make sure everything was tied in a neat little bow.

Sitting on the couch, he pulled out his laptop and set it on the coffee table. To the sounds of a football game, he searched for a flight to leave the day after Halloween. He couldn't believe he was booking the flight of a lifetime. Exhilaration filled him. Japan. He would live in Japan—the culture, the lights, the technology. He couldn't wait. That high soon dissolved, because he would be leaving behind a different life than he had a month prior. He didn't want to hurt anyone, but he'd be hurting three of the most important people in his life. And a dog to boot.

He didn't want to think about that now. He found a sixteen-hour, non-stop flight to Tokyo, which he upgraded to a refundable ticket—to be on the safe side—and booked it before he could debate the matter any further. With a single tap of his laptop's mouse pad, he was about two thousand dollars poorer. Well, technically, his job would be paying for it.

As if on cue, Roxon, Weston, and Chip came in from outside. Their exuberance permeated the house.

"Shh. Aunt Kellen is lying down."

The twins tiptoed over.

"What are you doing?" Weston strained his neck to see the screen of his laptop.

Shawn lowered it. "Just a little work."

Roxon frowned. "More work?"

"I finished. I promise."

Her smile lifted her cheeks. "Good. Do you want to play a board game?"

"Sure."

They surrounded the coffee table, sitting on pillows on the floor, and played a heated game involving reality. Every time Weston landed on a property, he counted out his money and bought it. Roxon was more methodical, saving her money to buy the pricier estates with larger fees if someone landed on them, and Shawn worked on nabbing the railroads. He was having a blast with the twins.

But then Roxon sniffed the air. "Is something burning?"

Shawn shot to his feet. "Oh no." He hurried into the kitchen, shoved his right hand into an oven mitt, and yanked open the door. A few wisps of smoke leaked into the air. When he removed the turkey breast, he found the skin not golden-brown but blackened. Luckily, the entire thing hadn't burned to a crisp or caught fire.

Roxon tsked. "Aunt Kellen's gonna kill you."

Dreading this, he knocked on the door to the guest bedroom where Kellen slept peacefully on the other side. "Kellen? Umm…I burned the turkey breast."

A mere second later, the door flew open.

Kellen stood with her hair sticking up in the back and eye covers pushed up on her forehead. Her eyes were wide. "You did *what*?"

Before he could answer, she pushed past him and pounded down the stairs.

He hurried after her, worried about her reaction.

In the kitchen, she was staring at the turkey breast in the roasting pan.

The twins joined her. They were on tiptoe to see what they were all supposed to be having for dinner.

Kellen picked up a carving fork and poked it.

"I'm not eating that," Weston protested.

"No, I think it's okay. It's just a little crisp on the outside. That's all. We'll remove the skin, and it won't even taste burnt."

"If you say so."

While the squash cooked, Kellen surgically removed the crispy skin.

Underneath, the meat looked fine and edible. Shawn carved the meat into pieces, and Kellen made gravy out of spiced apple cider, milk, apple cider vinegar, and flour. She drizzled gravy over a platter of turkey meat, which joined the casserole of stuffing and cut acorn squash in the middle of the dining room table.

The four of them sat around the table, smelling the scents of new recipes never before tasted.

Roxon inspected the table. "It actually looks good."

Kellen lifted a hand to Shawn for a high-five.

"Next time we do this, though," she said, "I'll baste the Cornish hens more, and they will still have their skin."

Weston raised his fork. "And the onion won't give off an atomic fart."

They laughed.

"Okay." Kellen clapped her hands. "Dig in."

Shawn was pleasantly surprised how good everything tasted. Despite their mistakes, the dinner turned out well. They all piled on seconds.

"Aunt Kellen, Uncle Shawn, we've been thinking,"

Roxon announced.

Wondering what this could be about, Shawn glanced at Kellen.

She looked to the twins on the other side of the table. "What's up?"

"Well, we've come to a decision. We want you to have Mom and Dad's room, Aunt Kellen. You deserve it."

"And Uncle Shawn deserves a bedroom, too," Weston said. "So, he can have the guestroom."

Kellen laid down her fork. "That is very generous of the two of you." She paused. "As long as you're okay with it, I accept."

The three of them faced Shawn. He swallowed back his guilt and said what would make the twins happy. If only for a short time. "I accept, too."

Chapter Nineteen

The following morning, Kellen heard Shawn on the phone. She paused before rounding the corner to the kitchen and stayed out of his sight.

"Yes, I'm sure. I want to put my condo on the market. I won't be needing it anymore."

Hearing those words come out of Shawn's mouth gave her hope. *He really does want to stay.* If he didn't want to be a guardian to the twins, he wouldn't be selling his condo. She entered the kitchen and gave Shawn a big smile. His own smile back was hesitant, but she wrote that off as him being reserved. She chose a bag of bagels from the fridge, selected one, halved it, and stuck one half in the toaster.

"Thank you so much. The sooner the better."

That smile tugged her lips again as she took out the package of cream cheese.

Shawn set his phone down and replaced it with his coffee cup. "What are your plans for the day?"

The toaster popped up.

She set her toasted bagel onto a plate as the grief she'd tried to set aside for the twins' sakes returned. While she lay in bed last night, she'd considered the twins' idea. They were ready for the change, but she wasn't quite sure if she was. Still, moving completely would have to happen eventually. "Well, with the twins' blessings, my mom and dad will be giving me a hand with hauling the rest of my things here, and I will officially break the lease with my apartment. They'll also help me with packing Dana's and Jensen's things and putting their bedroom furniture into the garage."

Shawn's brows bunched together as he frowned and nodded. "I wish I could help."

The knife scrapped against the toasted bagel as she spread on a thick layer of cream cheese. "I know, but it's okay. Having Mom and Dad here will help. Although, I know it'll be tough for them, too."

"Of course." He sipped his coffee. "Should everything of theirs be packed up, though? Putting away all of their things might upset the twins."

Kellen sighed. "I've thought of that. I'll set aside a few of their things to see if West and Roxy want to put them in their rooms or hold onto them. And none of the boxes will be too far. We could get them, if the twins ever want something or want to see what's in them."

"Will you pack their clothes?"

Kellen swallowed down the lump of sorrow that lodged itself in her throat. Clothes were personal. Jensen and Dana had lived their lives in those clothes. They had created memories while wearing those clothes. Kellen never thought that the idea of parting with someone's clothes would hurt so much, but it did. "I think so. It's probably too soon to donate them. I don't want to do anything before the twins are ready for it to happen."

Shawn reached out and took her hand. "That's a good idea. If you need any help when I get home tonight, let me know."

She gazed at their joined hands. The contact

comforted her. "Thanks. I will."

Kellen dropped the twins off at school and then drove to her apartment. Stepping through that door again, where she had lived for years on her own, felt strangely different, as though she had lived there in another life far removed from this one.

Her apartment was just as she had left it, including her skeleton boyfriend. Although she owned everything, it felt as though the space belonged to another woman, another writer, and another lonely heart. This apartment had been her shell for so long—her happy place and safe zone.

Now, she stood in the middle of the space that had worked triple duty as her living room, bedroom, and office, and she no longer thought of it as home. Shawn hadn't been completely wrong when he hinted at the fact she also didn't have a significant other, and it wasn't only because she spent a lot of her time writing. The truth was, she hadn't wanted to be in a relationship. She had her skeleton boyfriend, after all. Other than him, she hadn't met anyone she could see herself with, and maybe that was because she still harbored thoughts for Shawn, even after all these years.

A knock sounded at the door. She opened it to find Wanda and Jasper standing there, each holding a stack of flattened cardboard boxes.

"Hi, sweetie."

"Hi, Mom." She took the boxes, set them on the loveseat, and gave her a hug. "Hi, Dad." She kissed Jasper on the cheek. "Thanks for helping."

"Of course, honey." Jasper added his cardboard boxes to the pile. "What should we pack first?"

"The thing she owns the most of," Wanda said.

They exchanged a look. "Books."

Jasper would've stacked the books in the boxes willy-nilly, but Kellen supervised, making sure the books stayed in alphabetical order. Once the shelves were empty, they loaded her two bookcases and the boxes full of literature onto the small moving truck outside.

While Wanda tackled her closet and Jasper carried out boxes, she cleared her desk.

Emptying her studio apartment didn't take long. Without a single piece of furniture or book, it really was a shell and didn't look like a place where anyone had ever lived, but someone would live there again and probably soon. And she hoped the apartment offered the next tenant as much comfort as it had given her.

After Kellen dropped off the keys with the landlord, she drove the load to the house.

Before they could haul any of it in, though, they had to pack Dana's and Jensen's things. They stood a few feet inside the bedroom, staring at the neatly made bed, the vanity with Dana's perfume, makeup, and jewelry box, the dresser with Jensen's wallet and watch set, and the nightstands on either side of the bed; one of which held the book Dana had been reading. The other displayed a portrait of their beautiful, small family.

"This will be harder than I thought," Wanda said.

Jasper rubbed her back. "We'll get through it."

Kellen laid her chin on Wanda's shoulder in an embrace. "Together." She scanned Dana's vanity first. Seeing the lipsticks and eye shadows brought Kellen back to the time when they were little girls and would play with makeup in their bedrooms. They would have a blast experimenting with purple eye shadow and red lipstick. They would even make portraits of people on paper out of makeup and nail polish, and they'd created their own concoctions by mixing together different lotions and perfumes. Whenever they had a sleepover, they'd spend hours gluing on fake nails and dolling up their faces in ways they would never have the confidence to show anyone but each other. Heart heavy, she saved the red and mauve lipsticks for Roxon, along with Dana's mahogany jewelry box and its contents.

Next, she checked Jensen's dresser. She removed the cards from his wallet and slipped them into a plastic bag, but the wallet and all of his watches she kept out for Weston. The top dresser was a catchall for change, a couple of art projects the twins had done over the years, including a piece of construction paper with noodles glued on it to resemble four people—a raw noodle family portrait.

In the back of the drawer, she found a small bundle of paper tied together with a length of red yarn. A pang struck her in the middle of her chest when she recognized them as the stories she had written for Jensen, from silly stories she'd penned as a child and illustrated with crayons to the works she later wrote in school. Every Christmas, she'd gifted Jensen with a story based on their childhoods, and those were there, too. The one she gave him last year was at the top of the stack.

Tears blurred her vision. Jensen had always supported her passion and her decision to be a writer. Seeing he had kept not just one but all her stories touched her heart.

Sniffling sounds met her ears, and she looked to see Wanda pulling Jensen's clothes out of the closet, folding them with care, and laying them in a box. Each item she set in the box, she ran a hand over, smoothing it out and feeling the fabric one last time.

Heavy with sadness, Kellen pulled out her cell phone and sent a text to Shawn's parents, realizing they should be there, too.

They arrived shortly after, exchanged hugs with everyone, and got to work.

Gina picked up the patchwork quilt folded on the end of the bed, the quilt she had made for Dana and Jensen, and held it to her chest.

Kellen squeezed her arm. "You can take it. If there's anything you want, please let me know."

Gina dashed away a few loose tears and laid the quilt next to her purse.

None of them talked. They accomplished the job as quickly as possible, packing the things that would be in a box for the time being, storing the boxes and the furniture in the garage, and hauling in her possessions.

"I can do the rest from here," Kellen told them. "How about lunch?" She fixed sandwiches with leftover turkey from yesterday's dinner.

Wanda took a bite, swallowed, and hummed. "You made this?"

Brimming with pride, Kellen nodded. "Shawn helped."

His parents glanced at each other and then at her.

"Our son helped cook?" Stephen asked.

"He sure did."

Jasper polished off the last of his sandwich with one bite. "Well, I'm not so worried about the Halloween feast anymore. That was delicious."

They lingered over coffee and chatted.

"You know," Gina began, "I thought it would've been harder to get through this task. It was difficult, don't get me wrong, but I feel lighter now. I needed to do this to move on a little bit more."

Wanda held Gina's hand. "I know what you mean."

Kellen stared at her half-empty coffee cup. "I think the twins knew it, too. I was surprised when they first brought this up. I had delayed it because I thought it'd be too soon for them, but it was really too soon for me."

"Children know." Wanda nodded. "Children know."

Kellen embraced them and thanked them for their help. She had an hour to set her new bedroom to rights. With her things in place, the room didn't look as it had earlier that day, and she figured that was a good thing. And one day, she wouldn't feel like a trespasser. One day, it would be her bedroom, and she wouldn't be sharing it with ghosts.

One day…

In the car loop, Roxon climbed into the backseat of Kellen's car. "Did you move your things into Mom and Dad's room?"

Kellen swallowed and braced for their reaction. "I did."

Neither of them responded to that, though.

Once home, Weston turned to her. "Can we see it? Their…I mean…your room?"

"Sure. Go ahead."

They rushed up the stairs.

Wanting them to see the change and register it without her, she stayed back a moment. Then she stepped in after them to see them sitting cross-legged on the end of her bed, peering around at their surroundings. "What do you think?"

Weston ran a hand over her purple down comforter. "It's nice."

"It looks a lot like your apartment," Roxon said.

"Well, my apartment pretty much was one room. I'll have to get some pretty bedroom stuff someday. Maybe you can help me, Miss Fashionista."

Roxon smiled. "That'd be fun."

Kellen peered at her things. "So, are you two okay with this?"

"Yeah," they said.

She went to the chaise, the only thing of Dana and Jensen's left in the room, and picked up Dana's jewelry box and Jensen's watch box. She handed the jewelry box to Roxon and the watches to Weston. On top of the watch box was Jensen's leather wallet. "These are for you." She tapped a finger on the smooth wallet. "You can keep your library card and school card in there and hold your allowance." Then she indicated at the jewelry box. "Two of your mom's lipsticks are in there. You can have fun putting them on at home."

Quietly, the twins inspected their treasures.

Roxon peered at the watch box. "Can I have one of Dad's watches?"

Weston held out the box.

She selected a silver-and-gold watch with a dark brown leather band.

"Can I have something of Mom's?" He pointed at the jewelry box.

"Yeah."

Weston studied the contents. He shifted around a few pendants and rings with his index finger. Then he pulled out a necklace with a smoky quartz pendent and showed it to Roxon.

"You can have it."

Weston slipped the chain over his head.

Roxon strapped Jensen's watch to her wrist.

Then they surprised Kellen by throwing their arms around her.

"Thank you, Aunt Kellen."

She hugged them back, grateful that they were stronger than her. "No, thank you."

****

The next morning, Kellen sat in the kitchen, rapping her pen against her forehead and chanting, "Think, think, think."

"Aunt Kellen, what are you doing?"

Roxon and Weston, in their pajamas, stood nearby.

"This"—she pointed at her nose—"is the face of writer's block. Look at it. Remember it. Fear it."

The twins scrambled onto stools at the counter.

"Can we help?" Weston picked up a pencil and pulled a sheet of paper toward himself.

"I'd love your help. I need to create a story that I can write and send to my publisher before Halloween, but I can't think of anything, and I want this one to be special."

The many faces of writer's block consumed them while they searched their brains for a tiny spark that could explode into a firework of an idea.

Weston propped his chin on his fist and stared off into space.

Roxon pressed her lips together and drummed her fingers on the surface of the table.

Kellen continued to tap the pen to her forehead.

Roxon perked up. "What if you write a story about an animal that's like us?"

Kellen frowned. "What do you mean?"

"Well, we're bi-racial. You could write about a mixed animal. Or an animal with two faces, like that cat with half of its face black and the other half orange."

That idea had Kellen smiling. "I like that. I like that a lot. But what can we do instead of a kitten or puppy? We need something different."

"A fish?" Weston asked.

Roxon gasped. "Oh, like a betta fish."

"That's good." Kellen jotted notes. "A betta fish that's two different colors. On one side the betta fish can be a shiny white and blue, and the other side it can be a pretty red and pink."

Roxon nodded. "In the beginning of the story, the fish could be put into a new tank with strange fish it doesn't know. And it can be nervous about having to make friends."

"Like a new kid at school," Weston said.

"I'm really liking this." Kellen clapped her hands. "And because the fish has two different colored sides, when the other fish come up to introduce themselves, they see only one side of our fish. Then when they go to swim away, our fish turns, and they look back to see what they believe is another newcomer. Our fish has to show them its two sides, and the other fish could all gasp because they've never seen another fish like that before."

"And they can be mean to our poor little fishy." Weston pouted.

"But a tiny fish, a baby, can befriend our fishy," Roxon added, "showing everyone that although our fish is different, our fish is really just like them."

Kellen smiled, genuinely touched by their message of acceptance in spite of appearance. "I'm going to do it, and you two can help me write it." She flipped her notebook around for a fresh sheet of paper. Over the next hour, she penned the story with the twins' input.

Using colored pencils and separate sheets of paper, Weston drew the white-and-purple side of Poseidon, the name they had voted on for their betta fish, and Roxon designed the red-and-pink side. They were deep in their creations when Shawn came home.

He stepped into the kitchen. "What are you doing?"

"Helping Aunt Kellen with her next bestseller," Weston announced.

Kellen laughed. "We *hope* it'll be a bestseller."

Shawn studied the twins' drawings as they told him about the story.

His eyes lit up in a way Kellen hadn't seen happen in a long time. He hadn't even appeared this captivated by his app, which was a brilliant idea.

"I do a lot of animations for my company. It's actually what I enjoy doing the most. What if I made the illustrations?"

Kellen blinked. "Really?"

"Yeah. I love this story, and I already have visions for how it could turn out with this amazing fish…" He set the two pictures the twins had drawn onto the table. "…and the other fish and aquarium surroundings."

"But don't you have work to do with your app?"

He hesitated. "No, everything's done. My boss loved it, and it's going to happen. From here on out, other people more skilled than I am will be taking the reins to build it to its fullest extent."

The twins cheered.

Kellen beamed. "Congratulations."

Weston swayed from side to side. "Is that why you're so late?"

Shawn nodded. "Yes, but I'm here now." He addressed Kellen next. "And I'd love to pitch in with this."

"I have to discuss this with my partners first." She glanced back and forth between the twins. "What do you say? Do we make this a four-way partnership?"

"Hmm." Roxon tilted her head.

Weston tapped his chin.

At the same time, they thrust their hands into the air. "Yes."

Kellen regarded Shawn. By creating the illustrations, he had shown that he was committed. His actions might not be in the way she yearned for, but it was a start. She owed it to him to trust him and his dedication. Maybe this was the start to him accepting the role of being the twins' co-guardian and being her partner in raising the twins. She held out her right hand toward Shawn to seal their partnership in more than one way. "Okay, Mr. Callaghan, welcome to the fold."

Chapter Twenty

Shawn couldn't wait to get to work the next day, and it had nothing to do with his upcoming promotion or move to Japan. No, he was excited to use his equipment to make illustrations for a children's book, which was something he never thought he'd say, let alone think. But here he was.

He spent hours creating full-page illustrations with the text Kellen had written last night. He hadn't had this much fun creating in a long time. Even though he had enjoyed constructing Pledge a Gift, the app had been for work. This was different. This was for family. More and more these days, he found he liked being at home and doing things with Kellen and the twins.

Living in Japan, where he would be having breakfast and dinner alone, would be vastly different. His place would be too quiet without the sound of the twins playing with Chip. And he'd miss seeing Kellen writing in the kitchen, at the table, on the couch, or anywhere, really.

After lunch, his assistant Molly caught him at his task. "What are you doing?"

"Kellen is a children's book author. She created this story with my niece and nephew. I'm illustrating it."

Molly smiled so wide her dimples deepened. "A family project?"

Shawn paused. "Yeah…a family project."

She stole a peek at the computer screen. "Wow. I've seen the work you've done for the company, but that's amazing."

He studied the page he had been working on that showed Poseidon, the betta fish, surrounded by a few solid-colored betta fish and a handful of other fish, all different species—a glass catfish with skin so see-through the brittle gray bones could be seen, a speckled and shiny blue gourami, and a tiny neon tetra swimming close to Poseidon's fin. "Thank you."

Molly left, still smiling from ear to ear.

Shawn continued to work. The smallest details delighted him, like alternating light and dark scales on the fish and making some sparkle. His dedication throughout the day had him finishing all the illustrations well ahead of time. He printed out the illustrations and stepped out of his office. "Hey, Molly, can you deliver these to the art department to get them laminated and bound?"

Molly accepted them. "Absolutely." She hopped to her feet while shuffling through them. "These are great. I'd love to see them in a book." With that, she scurried off to the art department.

Forty minutes later, she returned to his office. "These sure got the art department's attention." She laid the laminated and bound illustrations on his desk. "None of them had any idea you were this talented."

He smiled while holding the sample book in his hands. Seeing his artwork in a tangible format filled him with pride. "I put the digital arts behind me to do computer programming."

"Well, maybe you should bring it out more."

He gazed at the illustrations that had reignited his passion. "Maybe I should." He couldn't wait to show Kellen and the twins the finished product. This time, he arrived home before dinner.

Kellen sat at the kitchen island, helping the twins with their math homework.

The frown lines between her brows told him that she didn't quite understand their homework, either. Holding the book behind his back, he stood before them, jittering with excitement. "Guess what I have."

"A math tutor?" Kellen grumbled.

"Better." He presented the book.

Kellen's eyes widened, and she gasped. "Is that…?"

He nodded. "It is."

"Oh, my gosh." She snatched it from his hands. "Check it out." She laid it out on the table between the twins.

They *ooed* and *aahed* while she flipped through the pages.

Roxon pointed. "It's the Poseidon I drew."

Kellen flipped the page.

Weston jabbed a finger on that illustration. "And the Poseidon *I* drew."

"How cool is it to see your illustrations come to life?" Kellen asked.

"So cool," they said together.

She peered at Shawn. "How did you do all this in one day?"

"I was inspired." His throat constricted, and something tugged him toward her, as if she had caught his heart with a fishing hook and was reeling him in. "It's been a long time since I've felt this inspired." He squeezed Roxon's and Weston's shoulders. "And all because of a fish."

"A very special fish," Roxon corrected.

"That's right."

Kellen flipped through to the last page. "This is gorgeous work. I think you missed your calling."

"Maybe I did."

"I love this, Shawn. Really, I do. And I don't want to see this story published with anyone else's artwork. I want to send this to my publisher and tell her it's a package deal. *Our* story…" She winked at the twins. "…with your illustrations, or no book."

Shawn blinked, taken aback. "You'd do that? Risk your publishing deal?"

Kellen peered at the bound book. "For this, I would."

True to her word, she overnighted it to her publisher.

Knowing he could have his name listed on a book's cover as the illustrator sent a peculiar thrill through him. Kellen was already talking about doing a family book signing together. Her ideas and the twins' excitement created a vise of guilt around his throat, because he'd be living in Japan by the time the book was published.

****

Friday night, Shawn snapped open the DVD case for *The Halloween Tree*.

"Movie time," Weston shouted from the living room. "Come on. Hurry up."

Kellen's laughter floated from the kitchen.

Shawn slipped the disc into the player.

The smell of warm, buttery popcorn filtered into

the room.

With the delicious scent came Kellen carrying a large bowl of popcorn. "Hold your horses."

West wagged a finger. "We don't have any horses."

Kellen set the bowl on the coffee table and sat next to Roxon on the couch.

The only available spot left was beside Kellen. The space was so tight the two of them would be sitting more than side by side. They wouldn't have an inch between them.

He took his place. The warmth of Kellen's thigh seeped through the fabric of his jeans. Trying not to focus on it, he pushed Play on the remote. Except, being so close to her stayed in the forefront of his mind. He couldn't even concentrate on the movie.

About twenty minutes in, he realized their hands were side by side, too, and the backs of their hands were touching. He wondered what would happen if he tried holding her hand right then, without getting down from a hayride as an excuse. Taking her hand now would be deliberate. His intentions would be clear. For the first time, he wanted that. No, he needed that; he needed her to know.

Inhaling, he decided to go for it. If she didn't want to hold his hand, she'd pull free. He lifted his left hand and slipped his fingers between hers before joining their palms together.

Kellen stilled. She angled her head. Her eyes were wide.

He swallowed. Rejection had never weighed so heavily as it did in that moment. And it was all because of Kellen. She was unique, special; she was everything.

She was worth it. She mattered. If she pulled her hand away now, then he'd feel more than a sting. To his surprise, she didn't pull free.

A smile manifested on her face, and she faced the TV again.

During the course of the movie, he randomly rubbed his thumb over hers. Their hands fit together as if they were made to hold hands, and he couldn't get enough of her touch. He yearned for more. Recalling the incident in the snow when he was a breath away from kissing her, he suddenly wanted to finish what he had started that gorgeous, snowy autumn day and finally kiss her. He held off for as long as he could, wanting privacy, but the longer he thought about it, the more he struggled to restrain himself.

An hour and twenty minutes into the movie, he glanced over to see the twins knocked out. Weston was draped over the sofa's arm, and Roxon's head was on Weston's shoulder.

Seeing the twins asleep, Shawn worked up the nerve to do what he had failed at, thanks to the twins' inopportune snowball interruption. He brushed a strand of Kellen's hair behind her ear, revealing her smooth tan cheek. Then he skimmed his fingers along her jawline and pinched her chin gently to turn her face.

She gazed into his eyes.

His heart rate quickened. He leaned forward slightly but paused to be sure she wanted this kiss, not just a near-kiss.

Her hand flexed on his, and she inched closer.

Cupping her face, he brought his lips to hers. He paused, anticipating the twins to snap awake at that instant. No doubt they had some sort of radar to alert them when Uncle Shawn was about to kiss Aunt Kellen. Luckily, they didn't stir on the other side of the couch. Not so much as a peep left them. Okay, well, Weston let out a little snore, but that reassured Shawn that they were asleep and unaware.

"Please."

Kellen's whisper warmed his lips and sent a spear of heat through his body. His longing responded instantly to the yearnings she exhibited. Dear God, she wanted him to kiss her as much as he wanted it. Inside, his own hormones were begging him to continue. Now. Don't wait. No more postponing. No more regretting inaction. Now. Right now. He closed the distance between them and laid his lips on hers.

A rush of excitement zigzagged through him from scalp to fingers and toes. Velvety-soft lips. Heat. Silky skin. She parted her lips enough to let him mold his own lips around hers and really kiss her, not just give her a mere pressing of mouths. Salty buttery-ness lingered on her lips from the popcorn she'd munched on. The taste intensified his cravings. He sucked on her lips as he'd fantasized about doing since he was nineteen. The kiss was better than he ever could've imagined. Her lips were everything, but he wanted so much more.

Beneath his palm, the heat of her skin seeped into him. Her very presence filled him and became him. For so long, she had been a part of him—his dreams, his desires, his denials. How could he end the kiss and lose a vital part of himself? He couldn't. Wouldn't. He was tired of dreaming. He was tired of denying himself his desires.

He shifted one of his hands to the back of her head

and licked the space between her lips, savoring the buttery-popcorn flavor. The hot, slick wetness he sampled at the tip of his tongue ignited him. She opened her mouth wider, giving him full access. He shifted slightly, wanting to be even closer. Closer than side by side. Closer than they'd ever been before.

Music cut through his thoughts.

Their kiss broke apart.

The music was louder than the movie while the credits rolled and pried the twins from their catnaps.

Weston let out a loud yawn.

Roxon rubbed her eyes. "Did the movie end?"

Kellen laughed. "It did, indeed. The two of you missed it."

Shawn leaned in. "Technically, so did we."

She nudged him. When she faced him, laughter sparkled in her eyes. "Shh."

But her hand was still in his. The fact she hadn't let go the moment the twins woke up struck him as a powerful action. She apparently didn't care if the twins noticed and questioned their clasped hands, and neither did he.

"Okay. Time for bed. You have school tomorrow. Now scoot."

The twins clambered upstairs to their rooms.

Downstairs, Kellen picked up the popcorn bowl to dump the kernels.

Shawn followed her into the kitchen and leaned against the island. "Are you okay with what happened in there?"

After giving it a quick wash, she set the bowl upside down on the drying rack. "The movie and the gorging of popcorn? Yeah. I'm okay with that."

"I meant the kiss."

She grinned. "I figured. And, yes, I am. I'd be lying if I said I hadn't wanted it to happen."

"You did lean in."

"I did."

His heart rate increased at the lovely sight of her blushing cheeks. He maneuvered around the island. "You also said 'please.' "

She licked her lips. "I did do that."

He stopped inches away. "I didn't want that kiss to end."

"Neither did I."

"It can continue now. Do you want that?"

She bit her bottom lip and blinked slowly. "Do you need me to say 'please' again?"

"No, I just need that look in your eyes." That look that told him she wanted him. He wound his arms around her waist and pulled her flush to his body.

She let out a gasp before twining her arms about his neck.

Eyes closed, he brushed the tip of his nose down the brim of hers. Then he rubbed his cheek against hers and nuzzled her neck. He pressed his lips below her ear and along her throat to her collarbone.

"Shawn." Her voice was a mere breath.

He kissed her softly, slowly, drawing it out to savior it longer.

She pressed into him.

Having her body—soft curves and hard angles—against his was like heaven. He explored the inside of her mouth more thoroughly. Her tongue mingled with his, and her supple lips meshed with his.

A soft sound escaped her, and she eased back. "I

should check on them."

He nodded.

She headed upstairs.

The moment he never thought would happen had just happened. He closed his eyes. Had he dreamt those kisses? Perhaps he'd fallen asleep during the movie, too, and had dreamt about kissing Kellen, as he had many times before. Was he still dreaming? He pinched his left arm to be sure.

Pain.

Sensation.

Real.

"What are you doing?" Kellen's voice drew him back to the moment.

He opened his eyes. Kellen stood at the kitchen entrance, as beautiful than ever. "Just making sure I wasn't dreaming."

She tilted her head. "Why?"

He met her eye. "Because I've wanted to kiss you for a long time."

She gaped. "Really?"

"Do you remember the Halloween when you dressed up as BK? I wanted to kiss you then. And every day since."

"I-I never knew that. I mean…I knew you wanted to kiss me that day because you asked, but…" Her voice was a whisper. "Every day since?"

He made his way toward her. "Every. Single. Day."

"Why didn't you tell me? Why didn't you show it?"

As he inched closer, he noticed she appeared to be shaking. "I was stupid, Kellen. So incredibly stupid."

"I thought it was just me. I thought it was one-sided."

Emotions tightened his throat. If only he'd had the courage to show her he cared about her as more than a friend or co-sibling-in-law, then she wouldn't be questioning his feelings right now. He shook his head. "It never was. I hid it because I thought I had to. I was three years older than you and a freshman in college. You acted as though nothing had happened, so I decided it was best to do the same. So, I focused on my studies. And then…" He sighed. "And then my career dominated my life."

Tears glistened in her eyes. "I only acted as though nothing had happened because I thought you still viewed me as Dana's best friend. Nothing more."

"You were always it for me, but I convinced myself we weren't meant to be."

She swallowed. "So did I. I told Dana those exact words on the Autumn Solstice. She knew. Dana knew about my feelings for you. She said…she said she could tell you had feelings for me, too, but I couldn't. You hid them so well."

He cupped her cheeks, kissed her on the forehead, between her brows, on her eyelids, and her temples. He gazed into her eyes. "I'm not hiding it anymore."

She looped her arms around his middle and kissed him sweetly, eagerly, and wholeheartedly.

He slid his right hand to the back of her head and deepened the kiss. The sensation felt so dizzying…intoxicating…everything.

She pressed her body against his.

A groan rumbled in his throat from her form, her heat, and her scent. What would it feel like to have her in his arms, to have their bodies erasing boundaries between them, to taste her lips, and to caress her smooth skin? He'd wondered that for so long, and here he was kissing her for the third time. He wanted those numbers to be limitless to the point where he couldn't keep track of how many times he'd kissed her. He never wanted those numbers to cease climbing.

"Shawn..." His name came out on a breath. "We should..."

We should stop.

So, he stopped immediately, believing that was what Kellen wanted.

She stepped back but held onto his hand. When she switched off the kitchen light, she took him with her. When she stepped through the living room, she took him with her. When she opened the door to the guest bedroom, she took him with her. Then she shut the door quietly behind them.

As his heart thudded hard and fast in his chest and at every pulse point in his body, he swallowed. "Are you sure?"

She closed the distance between them. "I've wanted this for a long time, too."

He took her into his arms, thanking the universe for this moment.

Chapter Twenty-One

When she made her way downstairs the next morning, Kellen felt on top of the world. She hadn't felt this way before, completely and utterly in love, and she hoped to be in love for the rest of her life. In the kitchen, she stirred a clump of brown sugar into a batch of raisin oatmeal.

Shawn stepped behind her, strapped his arms around her, and pressed his lips to her neck.

"Good morning."

"Morning. Do you want oatmeal?"

"I'm not a fan of oatmeal. I'll fix a bagel, but thank you."

While he did that, the twins came in search of their breakfast.

Kellen scooped portions of oatmeal into two bowls and placed them in front of the twins. "Do you want milk to go with that?"

"Chocolate milk?" Weston gave a toothy grin.

She held up her fingers, showing a tiny gap between her thumb and forefinger. "A tiny bit of chocolate syrup." She opened the fridge to get the jug of milk and the bottle of chocolate syrup.

"Aunt Kellen, you look glowy today," Roxon announced.

Kellen pushed the refrigerator door closed with her foot. "Glowy?"

"Yeah, you look happier than usual." Roxon swirled her spoon through her bowl of oatmeal. "Don't people get glowy when they're in love?"

Taking a sip of coffee while Roxon was talking was not the right decision. Kellen coughed and spit the coffee back into her cup. "W-what?"

Roxon twisted on her stool. "Doesn't she look glowy, Uncle Shawn?"

Shawn's eyes sparkled. "Now that you mention it, I think she does look rather glowy."

Pressing her lips together to hide her smile, she shook her head. "Glowy isn't even a word."

"It doesn't have to be a real word to apply," Roxon said.

"Now who's sounding like a writer?"

Roxon batted her lashes. "I get it from my auntie."

"Touché."

Weston tilted his head. "*Are* you happy this morning, Aunt Kellen?"

She stole a peek at Shawn, who smiled at his coffee. "Yes, I am rather happy this morning. I'm with three people I love. What more could I want?"

The twins peered at one another with matching smiles.

Shawn seemed to have also caught the meaning behind her words as he fixed her with a heated gaze.

A lump formed in her throat.

Surrounding the island, they ate together, not saying a word and not needing to. Comfort, security, and, yes, love were all there. It swooped around the room and looped around them like cozy sweaters. She was sure, more than ever, that they were meant to be here. Not just for the twins, but for each other.

Weston and Roxon scraped their bowls clean and downed their chocolate milk before going upstairs to get ready for school.

Shawn followed them out of the kitchen to take Chip for a fast walk.

With the kitchen empty, Kellen washed the dirty breakfast dishes and savored the last swallows of her coffee. Today was Shawn's day to drive the twins to school, and she looked forward to having the day to herself. The best part was she didn't have a writing deadline looming over her head anymore. Her editor should be receiving the package containing *The Many Colors of Poseidon* this afternoon. She jittered with anticipation for her editor's call and her publisher's decision that would decide Poseidon's fate.

Her cellphone dinged with a text message. She plucked it off the counter and tapped in her passcode. Her phone buzzed to tell her she had input the wrong numbers. She tried again and received the same annoying buzz. Frowning, she pressed the button on the top of her phone to blacken the screen and then pushed it again to see her home screen and the text message notification. But instead of her last book's cover art, the logo for the company Shawn worked for covered the screen, and in the text message's notification box, she read:

—Your plane ticket to Tokyo has been approved. I hope you have a safe flight.—

"What?" She raised Shawn's phone closer to her face and stared at the text, not wanting to decipher it, but knowing in her heart what it meant. Her right hand shook, so she gripped the phone with both hands to keep it from falling and hitting the counter. She read the words again, sent by Shawn's boss.

Tokyo. Shawn couldn't get farther away.

The front door opened.

Chip charged into the house. His nails clicked on the tile as he scurried into the kitchen and straight to his water bowl.

The slurping sound of Chip gulping water met Kellen's ears. She shifted her gaze to Chip. His tail was curled over his backside.

Shawn stepped into the kitchen next and hung Chip's leash on the hook on the wall. When he caught sight of her, he paused. "Are you okay?"

"You got a text." She held out his phone. "I thought it was my phone. I wasn't snooping."

He took the phone, unlocked it, and read the text. Immediately upon reading his boss's words, his face became slack. He looked to Kellen. "I was going to tell you."

Breathing became difficult. "When? Last night? Before or after we—"

"I've tried to tell you since I found out." He advanced.

She retreated. "Tried. You *tried*? Were you going to tell me today? Tomorrow?"

He lifted his hands and then let them fall. "I don't know."

"When is your flight?"

"November first."

She opened her mouth but didn't know what to say. He had to leave in a matter of days, but he didn't know when he planned to tell her? "Japan." The word felt strange, as if it wasn't another country but a whole other world on the other side of the galaxy. "How could you be moving to Japan?" Then reality hit her. "The promotion you wanted is in Japan? Pledge a Gift helped you get it? The twins inspired the app that's taking you away from them?"

His Adam's apple bobbed. "Japan was what I've always wanted."

Kellen nodded. "And nothing about this past month changed your mind?" Her voice lowered to a whisper. "Or last night?"

He raked a hand through his hair. "Every day, every minute, challenged my decision. And last night..." He shook his head.

"What happened between us didn't change anything. You're still going. Aren't you?"

Silence stretched between them.

Shawn appeared speechless.

"You're leaving us?"

The small voice, choked up with unshed emotions, had Kellen looking toward the entrance.

The twins stood behind Shawn. Their eyes glistened with tears. They held hands.

"You don't love us?" Roxon's chin quivered.

Shawn knelt on the floor. He curled a gentle hand around their arms. "Of course, I do. I always have, and I always will."

Weston swiped at a tear as it zipped down his cheek. "If you loved us, you'd want to stay."

Kellen pressed a hand to her chest. Beneath her palm, she swore she could feel her heart breaking. This wasn't what the twins needed, not after all they'd lost. Each day was a baby step forward, and they still had a long way to go, but they'd been doing well. She feared that healing would vanish if Shawn deserted them.

"I can love you anywhere," Shawn said.

His statement made tears spring to her own eyes. Love from a distance wasn't the same. She had finally opened her heart and made love with him. Now she felt as though her heart was splayed out on a surgical table, and nothing could revive it.

"But we'll never see you."

"We can video call every day."

"That's not the same." Weston jerked his arm from Shawn's hold.

"Buddy, I won't disappear from your lives. I'll call you and text you all the time. I promise. Every morning and every night, we can talk."

Roxon's shoulders bounced as she sniffed. "You'll do that in the beginning, but after a while it'll be one call a day, and then once a week, and then not at all."

"That won't happen. I swear."

The twins glanced at each other.

Weston shook his head. "We don't believe you."

Tears streamed down Roxon's cheeks. "Please stay."

Shawn cast his gaze toward the ground. "I can support you three far easier in Japan than I can here."

"We don't care about money," Weston snapped. "Right, Aunt Kellen?"

Shawn peered over his shoulder.

He resembled a man drowning and in need of a life preserver, but she refused to help him. Her voice was a strangled rasp. "Right."

Shawn closed his eyes. A long sigh whispered from his lips. "I am so sorry."

Weston crossed his arms over his chest. "No, you're not." Although his posture was defensive, tears coursed down his cheeks, and his voice quivered.

"Please, don't go," Roxon pleaded.

They were the same three words Kellen wanted to say but wasn't brave enough to voice.

"I have to."

And his three words wiped out the ones screaming from her heart. Everything in her sank, like a lead weight into the deepest part of the ocean.

Neither of the twins said another word. They turned their backs to him and left.

Shawn covered his face with his hands.

Seeing him in that position made her want to place a hand on his shoulder, help him to his feet, and hug him, but she stayed put.

He rose and shifted to face her.

The pain on his face was paramount. She didn't want to feel sympathy, though, because he had caused his own pain…and the twins' pain…and hers.

"I never meant to hurt you, Kellen. You have to believe me."

She licked her lips and tasted the saltiness of her tears. "Maybe you didn't intend to, but you have." Seeing the distress stamped across his face, the sorrow in his eyes, and the slump of his body, as if he had been physically beaten, caused her chest to tighten, so she diverted her gaze away to the wall. "Why did you do the things you've done if you knew you'd be leaving?"

"You know why."

"Do I?"

"I care so much for you."

"Apparently not enough." Saying that out loud broke her. Tears plummeted down her cheeks, and her chest shivered as she struggled to rein in her emotions.

Not wanting him to see her completely fall apart, she hurried past him, dodged his outstretched hand, and ignored him calling out her name. She closed herself in her bedroom, threw herself onto the bed, hugged her pillow, and let loose the tears she'd been fighting to hold back.

Her bed rocked with her sobs. After the unbearable heartbreak of losing Jensen and Dana, this fresh loss struck her nearly as hard. Maybe even more so, considering his betrayal was a blow too close to the first.

The front door closed, and the sound of Shawn's car starting followed it. After a moment, the roar of the engine died away as the car drove out of the neighborhood. Knowing he'd be doing that soon, leaving and not coming back, made his departure that morning all the more poignant.

A knock on her bedroom door made her flinch.

Self-conscious, she dashed away the wetness from her cheeks and cleared her throat. "Yeah?"

"Aunt Kellen?" Roxon's voice reached her. "Can we come in?"

"Yeah."

The door creaked open.

The twins crept forward on soft feet. One by one, they climbed onto the bed. Roxon cuddled against Kellen, and Weston stretched out beside Roxon. The three of them lay next to each other, not saying anything, just wallowing in their shared grief.

"I need to get the two of you to school."

Weston elbowed Roxon, who elbowed him back. He took a deep breath. "Can we stay home today?"

Kellen couldn't help but smile. Having a niece and

nephew love her as much as these two did made everything better. She couldn't imagine her life without them turning normal moments into fun, memorable, exceptional moments. Even this one was sweeter with them beside her. She stretched out her arms to embrace them. "I should be the adult and drive you to school, but the thought of the two of you keeping me company today sounds really good. I might break all the rules and selfishly keep you home."

"Please do." Roxon snuggled against her. "And it's not selfish. We want to stay with you."

"It's just one day." Weston rested his head on her shoulder. "No big deal."

She sighed. "All right. I'll call your teachers later. You two are staying right here with me." She gave them a little squeeze and relished in their snuggle time.

Even Chip came over to get some cuddles. He hopped onto the bed and draped himself over Kellen's feet.

"Aunt Kellen?" Roxon asked.

"Hmm?"

"You love Uncle Shawn, don't you?"

She had been bracing for that question, but hearing it come from the mouth of her niece and having to answer it now, after coming to terms with the fact she did indeed love Shawn but couldn't pursue a relationship with him, had her wanting to hide beneath the covers like a child. She couldn't do that, though. The twins deserved to know the truth, and perhaps saying it out loud and getting it off her chest would make her feel a teensy-weensy bit better. "Yes, I do love your Uncle Shawn. Silly me, huh?"

Weston propped himself on an elbow. "That's not

silly."

"Not silly at all," Roxon agreed.

"Well, I feel silly now."

Roxon turned her head on the pillow. "Does Uncle Shawn love you?"

"I thought so, but, honestly, I don't know." And that was the hardest part. How could he if he was willing to leave without a backward glance?

"Well, *we* love you, Aunt Kellen," Weston said, which was seconded by Roxon.

"And I love you both, equally and totally." She sat up to give them a kiss on the forehead.

The twins stuck by her side most of the day, as if they didn't want to leave her alone. Frankly, she was glad for their presence and devotion. They played a drawn-out game of real estate buying until the twins had to declare bankruptcy.

For lunch, they had chicken noodle soup.

An hour before dinnertime, the twins had an idea. "We want to make dinner tonight."

Their request surprised her. "Really? Have you ever made dinner before?"

They shook their heads.

She chuckled. "Do you have any idea what you want to make?"

Weston pulled out a baking sheet. "Chicken nuggets and mac and cheese."

"And salad," Roxon said.

"Yes, and salad."

"Okay." Their desire to make dinner amused her. "You can make dinner, and I'll supervise."

Weston removed the bag of nuggets and laid out eight on a baking sheet. He zipped it closed.

"Hold on." Kellen held up her hands. "You didn't take enough out. Are we all supposed to have two nuggets each?"

"The nuggets are for you and Uncle Shawn."

"Then what will you two be eating?"

"Peanut butter and jelly sandwiches," Roxon announced from the pantry where she was removing a box of macaroni and cheese from a shelf.

"Wait a second. What are you two talking about? I thought you were making chicken nuggets and mac and cheese for the four of us."

"Don't forget the salad," Roxon said.

Kellen studied the twins while Roxon peeled open the skinny cardboard box and dug out the packet of powdered cheese. "Why aren't you having the same thing we are?"

Weston found a pot from the cabinet underneath the counter. "Because the two of you are having dinner together. Without us.

She blinked. "Excuse me?"

Roxon grinned. "We're setting you and Uncle Shawn up on a date."

Kellen widened her eyes so big they felt as though they could pop out of her skull. "You're what?"

"Yup." Roxon giggled.

"This is serious." Kellen frowned. "You can't meddle in other people's affairs."

Weston's brows scrunched up. "What does 'meddle' mean?"

"You're interfering."

Weston nodded. "Yes, we are."

And he didn't seem bothered by that in the least.

"We're doing it because we love you and Uncle

Shawn, and we want things to work out between you."

"It's not as easy as that." Kellen sat on the pool. "One dinner wouldn't fix everything, and maybe not a thing at all. This is his decision. A salad, no matter how fabulous it is, won't change his mind."

"But *you* could," Weston said.

She shook her head.

Roxon grasped her hand. "You have to try, Aunt Kellen. You love him, and if he loves you, he can change his mind."

Kellen had hoped with every fiber of her being their mutual love would make a difference and be powerful enough to sway things in her favor. But they wouldn't be in this predicament now if he loved her as much as she loved him. Except, she couldn't deny the twins' logic. Love was worth it. So, she had to try before it was too late. She sighed. "Okay. I'll have dinner with Uncle Shawn."

The twins high-fived.

With her help, they baked the nuggets, stirred a creamy mac and cheese, and chopped veggies for a large salad. Upon Roxon's insistence, she ascended the stairs to change into something less stay-at-home and more date night appropriate.

Roxon hopped to her closet and pulled out a black cocktail dress with a swishy skirt. "You should wear this."

Kellen twisted her lips and studied the dress. At least Roxon hadn't picked out a flashy dress. She glanced at her closet. Not that she had anything that fit that description. A black cocktail dress was modest but worked for a dinner date. Although it was probably too much for dinner at home that consisted of boxed macaroni and cheese.

Roxon pouted her lips and made puppy-dog eyes. "Please."

"Fine. Who would I be to go against the in-house fashionista's wardrobe choice?"

So, she donned the dress, fixed her hair, and put on a touch of makeup. Then she waited, picking at her nails, for Shawn to come home.

Chapter Twenty-Two

Dazed, Shawn drove to work. He couldn't believe how quickly things had made a turn. One second, he was happy and spinning faster than the Earth, and the next, he was plunging to the molten core of the planet, burning to a crisp. A single omission could do that. If only he had said something sooner. But if he had, he wouldn't have received the gift of last night before everything fell apart.

He had finally found the courage to let his heart speak and speak loud. His actions had been a statement of his true feelings, of what he hadn't summoned the nerve to voice yet. And that was his love for Kellen, which was far deeper, stronger, and brighter than the love of two friends who thought of each other as co-siblings-in-law. No, this was real life, soul-binding love between two individuals. He knew it, and he should've told Kellen so that morning, but his heart couldn't control his vocal cords. Now, he was terrified he had screwed up irrevocably.

Despite his best efforts, he couldn't get his mind on his work. Every time he tried, he zoned out while recalling the hurt expression in Kellen's eyes. He saw the betrayal stamped across her face on his computer screen, on his tablet, in every file he opened, and on every sheet of paper. To make matters worse, Roxon's and Weston's faces were beside hers. All three of them stared. Their looks accused him of ruining the family.

They were right. He did all that and more. The tears they shed had told him so.

He drove home, dreading what he would encounter once he stepped foot inside the house. Things were already tense when he left. He didn't know what to expect after hours had gone by for emotions to build to a crescendo. Would Kellen erupt upon seeing him again? Would the twins be sulking in their rooms, refusing to come down?

Taking a deep breath, he unlocked the door and entered the house. Silence met his ears.

No doubt everyone was upstairs, avoiding him. He set his briefcase beside the couch and headed toward the staircase, wondering if he should head up and see if he could do damage control. On the way there, he passed the dining room. A soft, flickering glow emitted from the space. He glanced into the room to see the table set for two with a couple of taper candles in the center.

And Kellen sat there.

Candlelight flashed golden splashes on her rich, brown hair and across her beautiful, tan skin. He had never seen her more stunning.

She stood, revealing the black dress she wore and her bare feet. "This wasn't my idea. The twins fixed this all up, but I did make sure they didn't burn the house down." She shifted, and the skirt swayed at her hips. "Are you hungry?"

"Starving."

She sat again and motioned for him to take the seat across from her.

At his place was a plate with four chicken nuggets

arranged in the shape of a square. Between the lit candles was a bowl of mac and cheese and another bowl with a collage of chopped raw vegetables and salad tongs. He peeked at her, but she avoided eye contact. "Why would the twins do this?"

"They…" She paused, touched the end of her fork with her finger, and pushed it from side to side on the white tablecloth. "They saw me crying…they figured it out."

She'd been crying? Knowing that hurt him. He swallowed. "Figured what out?"

She smiled at her plate. Then her gaze met his. "How I feel about you, and they…" She lifted a bare shoulder in a shrug. "…did what kids do when they are setting up two adults in the hopes that love will blossom."

"It already did blossom," he whispered.

Kellen didn't appear to be breathing. "For the both of us?"

"I think so." As soon as he said those three words, he mentally smacked himself. Think so? He thought so? Love did blossom. She had practically said it without using the *L* word, and it was true for him, too. So, why couldn't he tell her that? Why did he have to leave it open as a possibility? *Think?* He should've owned it with *yes*. One word. That was all that was required to set things straight, and he took the cowardly way out. He opened his mouth to amend his words but was too late.

"The problem is not knowing for sure. I get it." She waved a dismissive hand. "You have a lot at stake."

And there it was. The cloud hanging over them. He had spent the day trapped in the nightmare that had unfolded earlier that he hadn't thought about what he would do next in regards to his promotion. On that, he was torn. Could he give up his career for a brand-new dream of having a family? He didn't know. To decide that, he'd have to do some soul searching. The problem was, he had days left to make up his mind on such a drastic decision that would alter the course of his life.

In times like this, he longed for Dana. She might have been younger, but Dana had always been the calm figure in his life he could turn to for advice when he needed it. Sometimes she'd even slap him on the back of the head, which she would have certainly done if she had known about all the foolish things he'd been doing lately.

Kellen picked up the bowl of mac and cheese and plopped a helping onto her plate. Then she held it out.

He accepted it without a word.

She piled veggies into a bowl beside her plate. "Salad?"

"Thanks." The formality all but killed him, but he didn't know how to fix it. Every bite was hard to swallow.

Silence buzzed between them like an annoying wasp while they ate.

He didn't know what to say to fix this. Nothing he could come up with would make a difference anyway, not when *I'm staying* was what she wanted to hear and what he wasn't prepared to say. Did she not know how difficult this was? Did she think hurting them was easy? The conflict raging inside him made his stomach whirl. He forced himself to eat.

Chew. Chew. Chew. Swallow.

Try not to make eye contact with Kellen.

Chew. Chew. Chew. Swallow.

Kellen set her fork down and cleared her throat. "The twins will be disappointed to know we didn't make up." She stole a peek at him, but it didn't linger. "Maybe we should tell them we're on good terms."

The fact she didn't want to work this out tightened his throat. "I'd rather that we really were on good terms so we wouldn't have to lie."

"I don't know if that's possible."

He attempted to reach for her hand. "I'm so sorry, Kellen. You have to believe that."

"I do." She set aside her napkin. "I know you're sorry, and so am I." With that, she lifted her plate and carried it into the kitchen.

Shawn had the urge to beg for mercy, but it was too soon. How could she grant him a morsel of forgiveness when he couldn't tell her if he'd stay or go? Only then would anything be repairable between them. He recognized she needed space, and he probably needed some, too. He picked up his own plate and delivered it to the kitchen.

Kellen stood at the sink, washing the plate.

Reaching around her, he stole the soapy plate from her fingers. "I'll clean up."

She went to leave.

But Shawn stopped her. "You look beautiful."

"Thank you." With nothing more said, she disappeared upstairs.

As promised, he washed the dishes, blew out the candles, and stored the leftovers. At the bottom of the staircase, he listened but couldn't hear anything in the rooms above. Not even living in his condo had left him feeling as lonely as he did right then.

****

The day before Halloween, Shawn drove to his parents' house. Sitting on the couch beside Gina, with Stephen in his recliner, he explained what had happened over the last couple of days.

Neither of them knew about his promotion, and they were taken aback.

"Have you considered not going?" Gina asked.

A broken smile touched his face. "Constantly since I found out."

"What's stopping you from passing on this promotion?"

He shook his head. "Heading this project has been my dream for so long."

"Dreams can change. What's your dream now?"

He lifted his hands and let them fall. "I don't know."

Gina cupped his hand. "I think you do. I think you're afraid. Change can be frightening, especially when you realize your long-time dream is not what you want anymore. It can be hard to come to terms with that, but more often than not, new-and-improved dreams turn out to be better than old ones."

He did have two dreams. Part of him wanted to embrace his new dream of Kellen and the twins, but the other part of him clung to his promotion and future in Japan running app development for a leading tech company. The problem was choosing. "How do you know which one is worth pursuing?"

"You have to trust your heart."

Shawn snorted. "That's the problem. My heart is conflicted."

She shook her head. "No, your *head* is conflicted.

Your heart already knows."

Her words struck him. Kellen and the twins were his heart. His career was his head. But for so long he'd let his head run the show. He wasn't sure if his heart was strong enough to lead. "I wish Dana was here to give me a good pep talk and tell me what I don't see."

"She is here." Stephen patted Shawn in the middle of his chest. "She's right here. Did I ever tell you about the time I was offered a job to be a professor at a school across the country that would've separated your mother and I?"

That was the first time Shawn had heard about that. "No, you didn't. You almost left Mom for a job?"

"Like father like son." Gina smirked.

Stephen settled an elbow on the arm of his chair and leaned forward. "I sure did, and it would've been my biggest mistake. If I had left, we never would've married, and you and Dana never would've been born."

Shawn blinked. "Really? What happened?"

"Well, your mother and I had been dating for a year, and I was madly in love with her. A month after I proposed, I got my dream job offer to be the professor of Introduction to Logic at Berkeley. I jumped on the job before discussing it with your mother. You can imagine the fight that transpired." He eyed Gina, who chuckled.

"We sure did fight."

"I wanted her to come with me."

"But I had started my job at a wonderful therapist's office in career counseling and refused to leave it behind. Imagine that. I counseled people on their careers, and here I had a fiancé about to leave me for his."

"And I was a professor of logic, but I didn't seem to have any logic when it came to my relationship."

"We sure were a pair."

"Still are." Stephen winked.

Shawn shook his head, needing the full story. "What made you stay?"

"Your mother did something that changed everything." He aimed his smile at Gina. "Why don't you tell him that part?"

She peered at her left hand and fiddled with a diamond ring. "I gave him back my engagement ring and told him that if he wanted to leave, he'd have to say goodbye to me and any happiness we would've had as a married couple."

"She about ripped my heart out of my chest when she took that ring off and put it into the palm of my hand." Stephen laid a hand on his chest. "I spent two days wracked with grief over the thought of losing your mother. Then I woke on the third day and realized I had caused that grief. If I rejected the job, I wouldn't be losing a thing, but if I accepted it, I would lose everything I held dear and would just have a job to go to every day. I already had a job I loved, and I had someone by my side who I loved more than anything, so why would I want anything to ruin that? Yes, being a professor at a university like Berkley was a dream but so was your mother becoming my wife. And you. And Dana." He smiled. "As it turns out, the job I kept here fulfilled me in that arena and even led to me getting my tenure and winning the U.S. Professor of the Year award. Without your mother, I might not have had that, because my love for my job came from real life."

"Makes sense." Shawn faced Gina. "Did you think

he'd stay?"

She shrugged. "I had hoped he'd stay, but really I had no idea. A big part of me was prepared for him to leave, which was why I returned my engagement ring."

Her sentiments matched Kellen's, but his situation was different from his father's. He had two kids to think of now, not just the idea of them. What kind of man would he be to leave them? Not the kind of man he wanted to be.

Before Jensen and Dana passed away, working in Japan would've been the highlight of Shawn's life, everything he had ever wanted. Or, more precisely, everything he had allowed himself to want. Over the past month, he'd had his eyes opened in numerous ways. Dana and Jensen's home had felt like his own, in a way his condo never had. Then he had to consider Kellen and the twins, who were family before, but became far more than his niece and nephew and co-sister-in-law. They had his heart. If he left, he'd be heartless in Japan.

Taking a deep breath, he braced his hands on either side of his head. He had one clear option.

"Have you figured it out, sweetheart?" Gina asked.

"I have."

Chapter Twenty-Three

Knowing Shawn was off visiting his parents, Kellen drove the twins to the park to play with Nick, Danny, and Renee. Kellen sat on a bench beside Imani. She had packed a couple thermoses of hot cider and plastic cups.

The kids played all over the jungle gym, expending their limitless energy. Weston hung upside down beside Danny, who dangled right-side up by his hands. Nick, Renee, and Roxon jumped rope.

Kellen sighed into her cup, creating ripples on the surface of her cider.

Imani gave her a long look. "What's happened? No one sighs like that for no reason."

"Everything happened, and nothing happened."

Imani frowned. "Huh?"

Kellen released another sigh. "Shawn and I…we…I am in love with him. That's the 'everything.' Then I found out Shawn accepted a job in Tokyo, and he doesn't love me in the same way, so that's the 'nothing.' "

Imani peered into her cider. "That sure is a reason for sighing into apple cider if I've ever heard one."

Kellen gazed at the blue sky. "I've been waiting for him my whole life. As a kid, I waited for him to see me as something more than his sister's best friend. As a young woman, I waited for him to notice I wasn't the kid he thought I was anymore. Days ago, I waited for him to tell me whether or not he loved me. Now I'm waiting for him to simply leave. Once and for all."

Imani cocked her head to the side. "You think he will?"

"He hasn't said he won't."

Imani hooked an arm around Kellen's shoulders, drawing her close. "I'm sorry you and the twins are going through this. Have faith that Shawn will do the right thing."

"But what is the right thing? Following his dream or sacrificing it?" She held her head as guilt pummeled her. "I feel horrible for making him choose."

"*Life* is making him choose, and Shawn will have to decide. But what you call a sacrifice might just be him following his heart." Imani gave Kellen's shoulder a squeeze. "Have faith," she repeated.

"What am I supposed to do if he decides to leave?" She slumped over her cup of cider, feeling more and more at a loss. "What do I do if that's what his heart tells him to do?"

"You'll do what you've always done. You'll keep on going for you and those babies." Imani pointed toward the twins.

Kellen watched them play as a fierce sense of protection and love overcame her. "I will." She pictured Jensen and Dana as if they stood before her. "I will."

****

Home that afternoon following a fun day at the park, Kellen heard her phone ring. She glanced at the screen to see her publisher was calling. She answered, not knowing what to expect. Her publisher could hate the idea and be annoyed Kellen had taken such a leap to send full illustrations. Not only that, but to state rather boldly that if this book, with those exact illustrations, wasn't published, children's author Kellen Collins would not be sending a book. Something like that could go over very wrong and lead to her never having a contract with her publisher again. "Hi, Stacey."

"Kellen, I received the book you sent. I am holding it now."

Kellen wrung her hands. "And?"

"And...I love it. This is just what we are looking for and what could take your career to a whole new level. Children's books for families created by a real, modern family."

Kellen jittered in place as excitement filled her. "Really?"

"Really," Stacey confirmed.

"That is awesome." Kellen hopped off her stool and danced a jig around the kitchen island. "The twins will be so excited. But two things...Shawn Callaghan has to be listed as the illustrator."

"Of course."

"And Roxon and Weston Collins need to be included on the byline with my name."

"We can do that. I have another bit of good news. We love Shawn's work so much that we want to hire him to do all the illustrations for your future books and other author's books, too, depending on the story. He has a rare talent, and his style will suit many stories we get."

"He'll be thrilled to hear that." Or at least a normal person would be thrilled to hear that, but Shawn had made a commitment to his boss. This news might surprise him, but she doubted he'd accept the role.

"I'll send contracts for all of you to look over. We'll need your document and Shawn's illustrations. We want to get the first proof copy by Thanksgiving. The goal is to have *The Many Colors of Poseidon* published as the first children's book of the New Year."

Usually, she had half a year to prep for release day. "So soon?"

"Absolutely. We're all excited about this."

"We're excited over here, too." She couldn't wait to pass on the good news. "Thank you so much for calling. This is a perfect Halloween gift."

"Enjoy it, Kellen."

"I will. Thanks, Stacey." She pressed the end-call button and did another dance around the room. The urge to tell the twins bubbled inside her like sparkling cider, but she held off so she could tell them at the same time as Shawn, who returned home shortly before dinner.

Since tomorrow was Halloween, Kellen ordered pizza for a stress-free meal that required nothing on her part except asking everyone for their topping choices. Weston wanted pepperoni, Roxon wanted pineapple and chicken, Shawn wanted mushroom, and Kellen wanted onions and green peppers. So, they had two extra-large pizzas with one topping on each half.

Sitting at the kitchen island with the pizza boxes between them, a container of grated parmesan cheese, a bottle of ranch dressing, and cans of soda, Kellen held up her glass. "I have an announcement to make." She smiled around the table but was awarded with raised brows and frowns in return. "I heard from my publisher today. They want the book. The illustrations, too." She peered from Shawn to the twins. "They want to publish the book in January."

The twins high-fived.

Kellen studied Shawn, curious as to what his reaction would be once she told him this next part. "My publisher loved your illustrations so much that they are extending an invitation for you to continue working for them as a full-time illustrator." She peered at her slice of half-eaten pizza. "But that's up to you."

The twins exchanged glances.

She didn't want them to think too much into that, though. "I haven't even told you the best part. All our names will be on the cover. Shawn's will be listed as the illustrator, and your names will be with mine as co-authors."

"Cool. Will our names be above yours? And bigger?" A devilish twinkle sparkled in Weston's eyes.

Kellen laughed. "No. Your names will be beneath mine and probably a little smaller. It'll say *Kellen Collins* then with *Roxon Collins and Weston Collins*, and after that *Illustrations by Shawn Callaghan*."

"But our names will be above Uncle Shawn's?" Weston's grin grew.

Kellen smiled at Shawn. "Yes, your names will be above Uncle Shawn's."

Weston jabbed his fists into the air. "We're going to be famous."

"Yeah. Just imagine…Shawn's company is creating an app inspired by your good deeds, and now my publisher is publishing your idea for a children's book. The two of you are already changing the world, and you're not even in sixth grade yet." Kellen beamed. "I'm proud of you, and I'm glad to call you my niece and nephew."

The twins sprang off their stools and surrounded Kellen. They threw their arms around her middle.

She hugged them back. Over the tops of their heads, she caught Shawn staring. The expression in his eyes had her throat tightening. He appeared as though he wanted to say something, but he didn't. His silence made her curious, but asking him if he wanted to say something when he clearly wasn't ready to voice it wasn't her place.

They finished their pizza.

Then the twins trooped outside with Chip.

Shawn helped her box up the leftovers, which they intended to have for breakfast. Kellen had declared Halloween a no-breakfast cooking morning, since she'd be too busy getting ready for the party.

Kellen waited for Shawn to return from the garage after throwing out the empty pizza boxes. She wanted to tell him something that had been nagging at her all day that he deserved to hear before it was too late, and too late was right around the corner. Telling him this would take almost as much courage as saying those three little words, which she still didn't have the heart to voice, if only to save her heart. But what she was about to say, she owed it to him to voice it out loud. She cleared her throat and wrung her hands. "Shawn."

He was as handsome as ever in a knitted sweater rolled to his elbows, with his hair not as slicked back as on work mornings. The slightly disheveled look was simply adorable.

"I want to thank you for everything you've done, for me and the twins. The book wouldn't have been completed if it weren't for you." Fiddling with her fingers, she paused to collect her thoughts. She wouldn't have many other chances to let him know how he'd made a difference, and she wanted to get her words right. "And I wouldn't have been able to handle this situation"—she waved her hands in an arc to reference everything that had transpired—"without you. You were a constant, sturdy figure for me and the twins when we needed one the most. I know it wasn't an easy decision for you, but thank you for being here for us." She licked her lips. "I hope we did the same for you."

"You did." He stepped closer. His gaze searched hers. "You really did. I—"

The sliding glass door opened then.

Chip breezed through the kitchen, cutting right between them on his way to his bowl of food. He gobbled down a couple of nibbles of kibble then turned, sat on the tile, and gave them the silliest doggy grin.

The twins tramped in after Chip.

Weston skipped over. "Aunt Kellen, can we roast marshmallows in the fireplace for dessert?"

Kellen couldn't help but smile at the sweet request. She opened the pantry and pulled out a bag of large, fluffy marshmallows. "How about s'mores?"

The twins bounced up and down. "Yes!"

"If Uncle Shawn can start the fire, then I'll hunt for the roasting sticks."

Shawn nodded, as if receiving a mission. "I'm on it."

Although Kellen knew tomorrow would be their last day with Shawn, she was determined not to think about it as she roasted marshmallows, laughed, and enjoyed his limited company.

Chapter Twenty-Four

Halloween morning, Shawn woke early. If he saw Kellen's disappointed face, he'd be cut to pieces. Not to mention what Roxon's and Weston's faces would do. They'd shatter those pieces, leaving him as nothing. That was precisely what he felt without them...nothing.

He dressed quietly, skipped breakfast, opting to get coffee on the road, and slipped out the door. The drive to work was unlike any other time he'd commuted. This time, he didn't feel like his future lay ahead. This time, he wasn't going over the many items on his to-do list. All he cared about were the three people he had left behind.

He arrived at work shortly after Mr. Harris did. To calm his nerves, he waited a full thirty minutes before heading to his boss's office. Although, that didn't do a thing to lessen his nerves any. He knocked on the opened door.

Mr. Harris looked up. "Hi, Shawn, what can I do for you?"

"I..." He paused, hoping Mr. Harris didn't take his next words the wrong way. The last thing he wanted to do was cause Mr. Harris to think he was ungrateful. "I have to respectfully decline the promotion to Tokyo."

Mr. Harris straightened. "Are you sure?"

"I'm sure." His heart pounded as he hoped Mr. Harris would take this news well. "This promotion was everything I'd ever wanted, but my life recently changed, and I need to stay." He shook his head. "No…What I'm feeling is more than a need. It's a want. I *want* to stay."

Mr. Harris dipped his chin in a small nod. "Tokyo App will still want Pledge a Gift."

That didn't bother him at all. After all, Tokyo App was a company. "And they can have it. I can work with them from here."

"That can be arranged. The runner-up for the promotion had a great idea for an app, but yours beat it. Your selflessness will give the creator the chance to work in Tokyo now, and also many future opportunities to pitch and design apps that will land in app stores for everyone to purchase." He grinned. "I'll be making a surprise phone call today."

Shawn smiled, knowing how much that news would make someone's day. "Sir, I'd like to continue working for you, but I wonder if there's an opening in the art department."

He raised a brow. "My best computer programmer wants to be transferred to the art department?"

"Yes, sir, I do. I forgot how much I enjoyed designing and was reminded of that recently. I'd like to get back to designing ads, logos, website templates, and app features."

"Your work on Pledge a Gift was magnificent. I'm sure I could find a place for you in the art department. They'd be lucky to have you."

Shawn shifted on his feet. "There's one more thing, sir." He was probably pushing his luck, but if this one condition wasn't met, all of this would've been a waste. "I want to work from home more often so I can complete assignments for you and illustrations for Kellen's publisher."

Mr. Harris blinked. "Illustrations for children's books?"

"Yes, sir." He could be a children's book illustrator and create designs for a tech company. Skills from both went hand-in-hand. He just needed his boss to realize that.

"That's different...you'd be good at that. You have an excellent work ethic. I've never had to worry about you meeting a deadline, and I've never been disappointed by your work. If you want to work from home a few days a week or even full-time and come in for monthly meetings, we can arrange that."

Shawn was lucky to have such an understanding boss. Few people had that. Rarer yet, he had someone at home who believed in him enough to let him go. But he didn't want to leave anymore. He didn't want to leave ever again. "Thank you so much, sir. One more thing, I'd like to have the day off, if that's okay. I have three people at home I need to tell some good news."

Mr. Harris smiled. "Of course. Have a good day with your family."

Shawn left Mr. Harris's office and smiled at the word that tugged on his heart strings—family. That word had taken on a whole new meaning this year. He'd always had a family, of course, but now he had his own family, even if it hadn't started out that way. Going from an uncle to a father figure had been life-changing.

And Kellen... He wondered if the two of them would go beyond being co-siblings-in-law. That would be more than life-changing. It would be everything.

When he arrived home from work, he found Kellen busy in the kitchen. The oven was on, and the smell of pumpkin pie filled the air. She glanced up from the cutting board as she sliced cucumber. "What are you doing home?"

"I wanted to help. Do you need me to do anything?" He removed his jacket and began rolling up his sleeves.

"No, I think our practice run prepared me enough with what to do and not do."

Her answer disappointed him. He had been excited to spend time with her in the kitchen, but he understood why she might be distant today. That was his fault.

"Actually…" She sighed. "Could you cut the four acorn squashes in half? I tried, but…" She pointed at an acorn squash on the counter with a butcher's knife buried in its flesh, as if it was an extra in a slasher film.

"I can do that." He removed his jacket and rolled up his sleeves. In order to cut the acorn squashes in half, he had to give them all good whacks against the counter with the knife and then force the blade the rest of the way through. He placed the halves on a cookie sheet. "Anything else?"

She continued chopping vegetables. "No. I'm juggling balls right now. If you take one, I'll misstep and drop them all."

"I was wondering if we could talk a minute. There's something I want to tell you."

She peered over her shoulder. "Can you talk while I cook? I have a lot to do."

Actually, he wanted her undivided attention. He didn't want her distracted. This news would make her day, but perhaps he should talk to her after dinner when she wasn't as busy or flustered. "Never mind. We'll talk later."

She hopped over to the stove.

"I'll leave you to it." He backed out of the kitchen and snuck upstairs to find the twins in Roxon's room. They were munching on sliced apples with caramel dip while sitting on the floor in front of a small, flat-screen TV, which was playing *Twitches*, staring Tia and Tamara Mowry. He knocked softly.

"Happy Halloween, Uncle Shawn!"

"Happy Halloween. I want to talk to the two of you about something." He sat on the edge of Roxon's bed. "I haven't had a chance to tell your Aunt Kellen yet."

"She's really busy," Weston said.

"She is, so I'm telling you first but only if you can keep a secret. Promise?" He stuck out his pinkies.

"Promise." They locked pinkies, promising not to spill his secret.

"Okay." He lowered his voice. "I called my boss and rejected the job in Tokyo." He waited a beat to explain what that meant. "I'm staying right here." He pointed at the floor.

The twins sprang onto their knees. Their voices lifted. "You're staying?"

"Shh." He laid a finger against his lips. "Not so loud. But, yes, I'm staying."

They flanked his sides and hugged him.

He wrapped an arm around each of them and drew them close. "Nothing will make me leave. Well, just as long as your aunt wants me here."

"She does," Roxon said. "She loves you."

Shawn swallowed. Hearing that filled him with hope. "And I love Aunt Kellen."

Roxon thrust her fists into the air. "I knew it."

"I knew it, too," Weston said.

He wasn't surprised the twins could tell he was in love with Kellen. They were so much like Dana.

"You only knew it after I told you," Roxon accused Weston.

"Did not."

Shawn chuckled. "All right. Points to both of you. You probably knew it before I did."

Weston threw his hands up. "How is that possible?"

"When you're an adult, life can get complicated. Sometimes we can be so focused on our daily lives, our goals, and our careers that we don't let our hearts speak. And we can be blind to what's right under our noses. When you get older, you'll know what I'm talking about. Then again, I hope you don't find out the hard way. Don't be like me."

Roxon slung her arms around his neck. "You're not so bad, Uncle Shawn."

He hugged her back. "Well, thank you."

A clatter of metal pots carried from downstairs.

"I want to ask you two something, and I want you to be completely honest. Can you do that?"

Weston raised a brow. "When have we ever not been honest?"

Shawn's lips twisted into a smirk. "Valid point." He pressed his hands together. "Tonight, at the feast, when all your grandparents are here, I plan to ask Aunt Kellen to marry me.

The *m* word had the twins gasping.

"Do I have your blessings?"

Weston and Roxon conferred with each other

silently, no words necessary; their eyes told each other all they wanted to say. They faced him and gave him identical smiles. "You have our blessing."

Then Roxon gasped. "Do you have a ring? Can we see it?"

"Oh." Shawn cleared his throat as incompetence filled him. "Actually, I don't have a ring yet."

Weston whacked his palm to his forehead. "Isn't the ring the most important part?"

"Yes." Roxon gawked. "You need something to present to her and put on her finger."

Shawn's mouth stretched into an oops-I-messed-up-big-time grimace. "Do you have any suggestions? A plastic spider ring?"

Roxon giggled. "Aunt Kellen would probably like that, but no." Hands on hips, she pondered the problem. After a moment, her eyes lit up. "I know." She picked up a jewelry kit from her desk. "We can make her a ring." She set the kit on the bed beside him. "There's wire we can twist into a ring and beads we can use in the place of diamonds."

Shawn chose a crystal bead. "This is perfect. A ring made by all of us will mean more to Kellen than a ring from a store."

"But you should get her a real ring at some point," Roxon scolded.

"Don't worry. I will."

"What's Aunt Kellen's favorite color?" Roxon swirled her finger through a container of beads. "We could use one of the bigger beads in that color."

Shawn scratched his chin. "I'm not sure."

Roxon arched a brow. "You don't know her favorite color?"

He returned her scrutiny. "Do you?"

She bit her lip. "No."

Weston shrugged.

Shawn inspected the kit. All sorts of beads filled the plastic compartments—heart-shaped beads, rainbow beads, and beads in the shape of stars, large, medium, small, and even tiny beads that Roxon called seed beads. The options were overwhelming. He selected a small, sparkly clear bead. "How about we use one of these in every color?"

Roxon examined the bead. "Like a cluster. Yeah!"

The twins assisted him in making a ring for Kellen, though Roxon did most of the work.

Weston checked in on the progress but was more interested in the movie.

Shawn picked out the beads and handed them one by one to Roxon. When she was done, she presented a handcrafted ring with silver, gold, and cooper wires braided together and a bead in every color knotted together to resemble a blooming flower. "It's wonderful, Roxon. You have a knack for these things."

"Thanks, I want to be a fashion designer when I get older."

"And I want to be an engineer to build planes so I can have a bunch of expensive cars," Weston announced.

"That's a fine thing to look forward to," Shawn said.

Roxon rolled her eyes. "He just wants to be a billionaire."

Weston glared. "So what if I do?"

Their banter entertained him, but if he didn't cut it off at the quick, they'd be at it for a long time. "How should I propose to Aunt Kellen?"

Roxon flattened her palms together and laced her fingers. "On one knee."

"And you should probably say something like 'Will you marry me?' " Weston added, which prompted Shawn and Roxon to erupt with laugher.

"I might have to write that on my hand."

"I have something that'll help." Roxon rummaged through a drawer in her desk and came back with a black suede ring box. "Here. You need a ring box to do it right."

Smiling, Shawn inserted the ring into the box and slipped it into his pocket. "Thank you. Both of you." He pulled them close, grateful to have them on his side and in his life.

"This will be the best Halloween ever." Roxon squealed.

Weston nodded. "I wish Mom and Dad were here."

Shawn tightened his arms around them. "So do I, but they'll be there with us. Right here." He tapped the middle of his chest. "You can count on that."

Chapter Twenty-Five

At the entrance to the kitchen, Kellen paused to survey Shawn unseen. He sat forward in a chair, rubbing his hands together. He appeared nervous. She figured his mood had to do with whatever he wanted to tell her earlier. And she had a sinking feeling that was about him leaving. He probably wanted to apologize again, say he'd still be there for them...on the other side of the world. She shook her head. Not the same. Not the same at all.

The twins occupied the couch. Unlike Shawn, they bounced in place, no doubt waiting for the Halloween festivities to begin.

"Roxy, West, the two of you need to get ready for the party."

They hopped to their feet and hurried up the stairs, casting glances back at Shawn and giggling. In a flash, they were gone.

Kellen lifted a brow. "What was that all about?"

Shawn shrugged. "No idea. They must be excited for the party."

That made sense. "I'm changing, too."

He nodded. "Need me to do anything?"

"No, but thanks."

She was being cold, and she knew it, but she had to be that way to protect herself. This party was like a prolonged goodbye...a slow, self-inflicted wound.

Every minute of the preparations had been excruciating. Heavy with double the load of sadness, Kellen dressed for the party.

Dana would've gotten a kick out of seeing Kellen as a woman of steel after all her not-so-secret attempts at fixing Kellen and Shawn up for this Halloween. Except, this wasn't how Dana would've planned for it to happen. What would she have done if she'd known Shawn was about to leave for Tokyo? Slap him on the back of his head, probably. Tell him he was an idiot, definitely. But Dana would've also known she could do nothing to change his mind.

Sighing, Kellen pulled on her tall, red leather boots. Then she headed back down to the kitchen to check on the food.

Ten minutes before the Cornish hens were due to come out of the oven, the doorbell rang.

The twins' excited shouts floated in the air as they greeted their grandparents.

A moment later, Gina and Stephen, dressed as two ogres in love, entered the kitchen. Gina wore green nail polish, eye shadow, and blush on her cheeks. She carried a red-and-gold canister. "I have gingersnaps. I remembered they're your favorite."

"Thank you." Kellen lifted off the cover and drew in a long whiff of the delicious ginger cookies within. "They look and smell delicious."

"I haven't forgotten about you and Dana sneaking the whole tray of gingersnaps to Dana's room to gobble them up in secret."

"We did love cookies. Especially your cookies, Mrs. Callaghan."

"Oh, please call me Gina or Mom. You used to call

me Mom when you were little. And Dana would call yours Mom, too." Gina's smile doubled. "I loved that."

"And I never minded being called Dad by you, either." Stephen looped an arm around her shoulders and gave her a squeeze.

"You both gave me a second home and were another set of parents. That inclusion made me feel special. And I know my mom and dad did the same for Dana."

Gina patted Kellen's hand. "When you and Dana met, you became an instant package deal. Your friendship together was like a sisterhood. It was beautiful."

Her words struck a chord in Kellen. She turned away so they wouldn't see the mist that covered her eyes. While whisking the gravy, she thought back on her dear, lifelong, blood-bond friendship with Dana.

They had done everything together—ear piercings, trick-or-treating, color guard tryouts, and were usually each other's dates for school dances. They had a real friendship. Not a fake one like most other girls, or one that could be shaken by something silly like jealousy or disliking the other's boyfriend. No, what they had lasted through high school and the years beyond, when many friendships dissolved. Theirs was unbreakable. And then Dana had died. Except, Kellen felt deep in her heart that even death couldn't break their bond. They were still best friends, soul sisters, two peas in a pod. Just like Jensen would forever be her other half. "The holidays will be different without her," Kellen murmured.

"And Jensen," Gina added. "But we'll get through, and it'll be beautiful." She stroked Kellen's arm. "I can already tell. You've done an amazing job. It smells great in here."

"Thank you. Cooking a feast for the first time was an experience. I've already made it clear I'm not doing dinner for Christmas Eve or Christmas Day. That will be the grandparents' jobs." She winked at Gina.

Gina chuckled. "We'd be happy to have all of you on either day." She stirred the pasta salad. "Has Shawn talked to you yet? About anything important?"

Kellen froze. What did Shawn's mother know? "What do you mean?"

"Oh, I don't mean anything specific. Just with his flight tomorrow morning, I've wondered if he's spoken to you or is opening up."

Opening up? She frowned. "No, he hasn't said anything, but…"

Gina perked up. "Yes?"

"He did want to talk to me earlier, but I was so busy I shut him down." She frowned even more. Perhaps she should've let him speak his mind then, when he wanted to. What if he didn't tell her what he wanted to say and boarded the plane tomorrow? She'd never know what was on his mind.

"Don't worry, sweetie, if there's something he has to say, he will."

Funny thing was, that worried her, too. What if his words were the ones she didn't want to hear? Likely, whatever he needed to say would be a long, drawn-out goodbye that would only hurt her more.

The doorbell sounded, alerting them to the arrival of Wanda and Jasper.

"We'll get it," Weston shouted.

"Grandpa. Grandma."

The sound of several pairs of feet coming toward the kitchen had Kellen turning to the entrance to see her parents, the twins, and Shawn. Wanda must've received the superhero memo, because she was dressed as the Queen Mother from the same comic book series as the twins. Jasper, a slacker much like Shawn when it came to dressing up, wore a suit and a red-and-gold mask, clearly a billionaire superhero.

Shawn, though, shocked her. He wore a white shirt, unbuttoned to show the *S* logo T-shirt, a blue suit jacket and pants, and a red tie, pulled loose and draped over his shoulder. His outfit was complete with the faux, black-framed glasses.

The twins must've given him the shirt and glasses earlier. That was probably why they were full of giggles. Shawn wearing a costume was a Halloween surprise.

No, a miracle.

Everyone exchanged hugs and wished each other a happy Halloween.

Kellen checked the timer on the stove. "And you're here just in time."

Five.

Four.

Three.

Two.

One.

The oven beeped.

"The Cornish hens should be done."

"My nose told me when to get here." Jasper tapped a finger to his nose and grinned. "I'll help you get them out."

"Thanks, Dad."

He opened the oven door, freeing the delicious smell of apple cider, honey, and poultry.

Using pot holders and saying a silent prayer, she hoisted the roaster's cover. Underneath sat perfectly golden Cornish hens. Their skin, thanks to the yummy glaze, looked exquisite and gave the birds a rich color.

Everyone let out sighs.

"It's a miracle," Weston whispered.

"Hey, I heard that." Kellen wagged her finger.

"You won." Jasper pulled out a five-dollar bill from his wallet and handed it to Wanda.

Kellen gasped. "Hey." She couldn't believe it. "You were betting I'd burn dinner?"

"After Weston told us your first attempt wound up crispy, I bet your mother five dollars it'd be crispy today, too." He shrugged. "And I lost."

"At least Mom had faith in me."

Shawn stepped forward. "And, to be fair, I was the reason the turkey breast burned. I was on duty and didn't realize the time got away from me until I smelled smoke." He lifted his hands and grimaced in an *oops* gesture. "My fault."

Jasper stared at Weston. "You left that part out."

Weston shrugged. "Oops."

Laughing, Jasper slung an arm around Kellen and kissed her cheek. "I had faith in you, honey. Just a little Halloween fun."

"Then I guess I forgive you. But I hope Mom gets something yummy and chocolatey with that five dollars and doesn't share it."

"Ouch."

"Everyone can go into the living room while I put the crescent rolls in the oven." She pulled out the readied baking sheet from the refrigerator.

"Is that what you call them, dear?" Wanda inspected the mangled strips of dough. "They look more like a mummy ditched its wrappings and left them on the floor."

She grinned. "Who's to say that's not what I was going for? Today is Halloween, after all?"

"You're right."

Everyone trooped out of the kitchen.

Shawn stayed behind, though, standing a few feet away. "Do you need my help setting the table?"

"That would be great. Thank you."

One after the other, he carried out each dish and set them onto the table.

She removed the crescent rolls from the oven and piled them into a napkin-covered basket. "Okay," she told Shawn. "Everything's ready." She took a step.

"I think you're forgetting something."

She lowered her brows. In her mind, she did a mental checklist. She'd remember all the goodies, so what did he mean? "Huh?"

He pointed at her chest. "Apron."

"Right." She stretched out arms to set down the basket of rolls.

Shawn reached toward her. "I've got it." His fingers worked the knot at her middle.

With him so close and his gaze downcast as he untied the knot, she studied him. His jawline didn't bear any stubble, indicating he had shaved this morning. The smell of his cologne, that mouthwatering cinnamon-and-cloves scent circled around her. She drew it in with a long inhale and admired his dark lashes. Her heart called out to him, but she reined it in; he had made his choice. That didn't stop her from taking in the sight of him and memorizing everything before he left.

Around the middle of his face—his cheeks and nose—she caught glimpses of the boy he had been, whom she had first fallen in love with. Now she was in love with the man that boy had become. Just looking at him made emotions swirl inside her—his angular jaw, shapely pink and tan lips, and his green eyes.

He pulled the strings free, loosening the apron. Then he pinched the ribbon around her neck with his fingers and lifted it. Her hair fell onto her shoulders when he pulled it off.

Underneath the apron, she wore her costume.

"You look cute," he said. "I've always loved seeing you dressed as a superhero."

She hoped her blush could pass off as the result of being in a warm kitchen. "Thank you, and you look handsome." And he did. More than handsome—sexy.

"Aunt Kellen." Roxon's voice.

"Uncle Shawn."Weston's voice.

"Come on," they shouted together. "We're hungry."

Part of her didn't want to leave the kitchen. She wanted to stay in this moment forever. Living in this bubble of warmth, delicious aromas, and the intimate stare of Shawn's evergreen eyes would be enough, except she didn't have the power to freeze time. She could only watch it slip away. "We should get in there," she whispered.

"Yeah." He bundled up the apron and deposited it on the counter. "After you."

With her heart thumping the entire way, she led the way.

In the dining room, food covered the table, and everyone sat around it, prepared to feast on the goodies she'd toiled over all day. She laid the basket of rolls onto the table next to the acorn squash. "That's everything."

The places where Jensen and Dana used to sit were open. Kellen hesitated. Should she take the seat Dana used to occupy, the one she referred to as the mother's end, or Jensen's seat, her twin, the one she shared blood with?

"Sit here, Aunt Kellen." Roxon patted Dana's old place.

Kellen made her way to it while Shawn went to the other end of the table, the father's end. Lowering into the chair, she looked toward Shawn. Although an entire table and six individuals sat between them, she felt as though they were the only two in the room, standing face-to-face, a breath apart, nearly touching. The intensity of his lure stunned her. She'd never encountered that before. And she doubted she ever would after Shawn left.

She scooted in her chair. Despite the obvious missing pieces, the table seemed full. All the faces were cheery, and the food appeared appetizing. Even Chip was there, lying next to her chair and drooling onto the carpet.

He gave a soft whine.

"Oh, don't worry. You'll get leftovers when we're done." She smiled at the spread laid out before her. "If there is any food left."

While everyone ate, Kellen peered around the table. Seeing the Collinses and the Callaghans meshing into one big, happy unit swelled Kellen's heart, and

Jensen and Dana had done that with their love in ways Dana and Kellen's friendship hadn't quite done, no matter how lovely and total their bond had been. The love between two individuals had joined their families together in bigger and better ways.

Around the table, Kellen admired the differences in skin tone from her mother's brown to her golden tan to the twins' lighter tan to the medium shades of her father, Shawn, and his parents. Their family was a beautiful mix that breathed life and diversity and love.

A lot really could be achieved with that single emotion. Love could cross boundaries and unify. Her entire family was built upon that, and she was proud to be a part of it.

After everyone had cleaned their plates and were full, Shawn stood. "I know this isn't usual, but I have something to say." He cleared his throat. "This year is different from any other year. We had our losses, which will forever be felt, but we've had our gains, too, and I've had a significant gain."

She looked away when he peered at her.

He paused a moment.

But she couldn't look back.

"Kellen."

Not wanting to be rude, she peered back.

"You've opened my eyes to a whole new life that I never thought possible, or even considered before." He made his way around the table, not once breaking eye contact.

So strong were the beats of her heart, and her breathing so shallow, she feared she'd pass out.

"I have a home because of you, one that I don't want to leave. Not now, not tomorrow, not ever." When he reached her end of the table, he nudged Chip, who occupied the space beside her. "Excuse me, boy."

Chip scurried to Weston's side, letting Shawn take his place.

What he'd said had been exactly what she'd been dreaming about for weeks. Her chest expanded with happiness. Still, beneath it all, a niggling doubt remained she needed to vanquish, and only he had the power to do that. She shifted to meet Shawn's eye. "What about your job and your flight tomorrow?"

"I'm not going."

Those three words meant the world. All the despair she'd felt since finding out about his promotion lifted from her shoulders, making her feel light and weightless.

He knelt beside her chair and held her hand. "I love you, Kellen."

For years, she'd fantasized about this very moment. Foolishly, she'd thought. But here it was. Not a dream. Not a wish. Shawn loved her, and she loved him so much that it felt as though her heart would burst. "I love you, too."

As soon as she shared that, Kellen noticed his shoulders lower.

Then he dipped his other hand into his pocket and pulled out a small, velvet box.

Her breath caught at the sight of it. Tears clouded her vision.

"Will you marry me?" He cracked open the lid, revealing the ring on the inside. The band wasn't silver or gold or platinum. No diamond or sapphire or ruby sparkled in the setting. Not even a cubic zirconia glittered on the cushion. Instead, the ring was made with three different kinds of wire and a bunch of small beads in every color of the rainbow. Such a sweet and simple ring, and she adored it.

"I helped him make the ring," a tiny voice said.

She glanced over his shoulder at Roxon, whose eyes twinkled in the lighting. The fact the twins helped him make it and were in on the secret made her cherish the ring and this moment all the more. She inhaled shakily. "I love it. Thank you." She focused back on Shawn and couldn't hold in her answer anymore. "I will."

Shawn blinked. "You will?"

"Yes, yes, I'll marry you."

He cupped her chin with his fingers and brought his lips to hers.

They shared a kiss that stole Kellen's breath and made her heart feel as though it had sprouted wings.

With just a kiss, he passed his love to her. When he pulled back, he slipped the ring on her finger, sealing their engagement.

As they kissed a second time, the dining room filled with applause and cheers.

Shawn stood and pulled Kellen to her feet.

Once on her feet, she locked her arms around his neck and held him with all her love and happiness. Her heart pounded against her chest. "Thank you for loving me," she whispered.

"No, thank you."

They pulled apart and faced everyone at the table.

Their family's bright faces shone back.

"Another wedding in the family." Gina pressed her hands to her chest. "This is exciting."

"I always knew it would happen," Wanda claimed.

Kellen squinted. "You did?"

Wanda smiled that all-knowing motherly smile. "Of course, I'm a mom."

"I knew it, too." Gina winked at Shawn.

"So did we," the twins chimed in.

Kellen laughed.

Stephen nodded. "I'm proud of you, son. You'll see in time that the choice to stay for your heart was the right one."

Shawn laced his fingers with hers. "I already do."

"You've been a part of the family for years." Jasper inclined his head. "But now I can officially call you *son*."

The smile that formed on Kellen's face radiated from her soul. She had longed for this for so long but hadn't had the guts to go for it.

"I have something else I want to share before trick-or-treating and the party gets underway. I'll be right back." Shawn left and returned to the dining room with a manila envelope, which he held out.

Frowning, she accepted the envelope. "What do you think is inside?" she asked the twins.

"A sports car." Weston mimed turning a steering wheel.

Roxon shook her head. "How could a car fit in that?"

"It could have the papers for one, dummy."

Roxon giggled. "Well, I think it's tickets to a fashion show."

"Let's find out." Kellen lifted the metal prongs.

"Please don't be tickets to a fashion show," Weston whispered.

Roxon elbowed him in the side.

Kellen peeled up the flap and peeked into the envelope. Frowning, she dipped her fingers into the opening. Then she slipped out a packet of papers held together by a paperclip. She read the header on the first page and gasped. She flicked her gaze to him. "You—" Her voice gave out.

"What is it? What is it?" The twins edged closer and peered at the papers.

"Guardianship papers for the two of you." She flipped to the last page and stared. "Uncle Shawn filled them out to be your legal co-guardian."

The twins joined Kellen in gaping.

"For real?" Weston asked.

"So, you really do want us?" Roxon asked.

"Of course, I do. Those are actually copies. I filed them this morning after I left work."

The twins threw their arms around Kellen and Shawn and pulled them into a group hug.

Kellen let herself sink into the moment, with her arms around them—her anchors. She met Shawn's gaze over the tops of the twin's heads. "This is the best Halloween ever."

"Mom and Dad would be really happy that the two of you are getting married." Weston wagged his eyebrows up and down.

Kellen smiled as she thought about Dana cheering and Jensen clapping Shawn on the back. She imagined Dana already planning the details. "They would be thrilled."

Roxon clasped her hands together. "So…when it will be?"

This was everything Kellen had ever wanted and more. Sure, she'd daydreamed about her wedding, with

Shawn as the groom, but reality was different. Reality was infinitely better. The possibilities for what they could do for their wedding were endless. More, the possibilities for their lives together were endless. All of her prayers were being answered. Now, instead of hoping and dreaming and planning, she fully intended to enjoy every moment. A year's engagement to sink into the joy of being engaged was what she wanted now more than anything. "I don't know." She looked to Shawn. "In a year, maybe. How about a small, fun October wedding?"

Shawn nodded. "Our wedding couldn't be anything other than an October wedding."

"Can we wear Halloween costumes?" Weston asked.

Kellen laughed. "A flower girl and ring bearer in Halloween costumes?" She turned to Shawn again. "What do you think?"

He kissed her hand. "I wouldn't want it any other way."

Happiness and love all but burst from her. Today hadn't just been full of Halloween miracles. Today had been beautiful in every way, and she knew every Halloween, and every other day between, would be utterly perfect because the three of them would be together. She squeezed Shawn's hand. "And neither would I."

A word about the author…

Chrys Fey is a disabled, tattooed author of books featuring heroines of steel. Her Disaster Crimes series is a unique blend of romance, disasters, and crimes, influenced by her own experiences with natural disasters.

Fey got the idea for her first book when she was twelve and discovered a rusted screw with a crooked tip buried in grass. That screw was a key to an unknown world with an extraordinary character born in heaven.

She is a fur baby mom of four rescued cats. For fun, she photographs antiques, makes playlists, and creates flip cup paintings of Avrianna's nebula. She loves Halloween, autumn, and gargoyles.

Thank you for purchasing
this publication of The Wild Rose Press, Inc.

For questions or more information
contact us at
info@thewildrosepress.com.

The Wild Rose Press, Inc.
www.thewildrosepress.com